SHERLOCK HOLMES
AND THE MUMMY'S CURSE

PRO SE PRESS

SHERLOCK HOLMES AND THE MUMMY'S CURSE
SHERLOCK HOLMES: GENTLEMAN AEGIS BOOK 1
A Pro Se Press Publication

This story is fictional. All of the characters in this publication are fictitious and any resemblance to actual persons, living or dead is purely coincidental. No part of this publication may be reproduced or transmitted in any form or by any means, graphic, electronic, or mechanical, including photocopying, recording, taping or by any information storage or retrieval system, without the permission in writing of the publisher.

Edited by Dave Brzeski
Editor in Chief, Pro Se Productions—Tommy Hancock
Submissions Editor—Rachel Lampi
Director of Corporate Operations—Kristi King-Morgan
Publisher & Pro Se Productions, LLC-Chief Executive Officer—Fuller Bumpers

Cover Art by Jeff Hayes
Print Production and Book Design by Percival Constantine
E-Book Design by Forrest Bryant
New Pulp Logo Design by Sean E. Ali
New Pulp Seal Design by Cari Reese

Pro Se Productions, LLC
133 1/2 Broad Street
Batesville, AR, 72501
870-834-4022

editorinchief@prose-press.com
www.prose-press.com

SHERLOCK HOLMES AND THE MUMMY'S CURSE © 2015 Stephanie Osborn

SHERLOCK HOLMES AND THE MUMMY'S CURSE

BOOK ONE OF SHERLOCK HOLMES: GENTLEMAN AEGIS

STEPHANIE OSBORN

PRO SE PRESS

CONTENTS

PROLOGUE: MACHINATIONS — 1

CHAPTER 1: PLANNING EXPEDITIONS — 5

CHAPTER 2: INTRODUCTIONS AND REACQUAINTANCES — 25

CHAPTER 3: THE WORK COMMENCES — 43

CHAPTER 4: THE CURSE RISES — 63

CHAPTER 5: SOMETHING OLD, SOMETHING NEW — 85

CHAPTER 6: SHUFFLING THE DECK — 103

CHAPTER 7: HOMING IN ON A MYSTERY — 123

CHAPTER 8: THE MINERALOGICAL ENIGMA — 149

CHAPTER 9: REVELATIONS AND RAMIFICATIONS — 169

CHAPTER 10: THE CURSE WALKS — 189

CHAPTER 11: A ROYAL ALLIANCE — 205

CHAPTER FINAL: CONFEDERATIONS AND COUNCILS — 215

AUTHOR'S NOTES — 229

ABOUT THE AUTHOR — 231

PROLOGUE
MACHINATIONS

Two sinister figures leaned close in the dark room, whispering intently. The small fire in the corner fireplace, intended to take the edge off the wet, raw night, was the only illumination; it threw eerie, flickering shadows across the room, and occasionally cast the pale faces of the conversing men in an almost demonic, hellish red glow.

"Are you certain?" the first man asked in clipped, precise English, taking a sip from his old-fashioned glass.

"Sim, o meu amigo[1], as certain as it is possible to be." The second man, somewhat younger, had an odd, blended accent, indiscernible as belonging to any one particular language, though his Portuguese was flawless. He largely ignored the glass at his elbow, though he had taken a single sip earlier, after shrewdly observing the other man drink first.

"I am not your friend." The first man's voice was as cold as his manner.

"Desculpe-me[2], Professor. I meant no disrespect, I assure you. It is, mm, a turn of phrase. I have been long in another country."

"Then you would do well to, shall we say, re-cultivate your native tongue."

"Your point is well taken." There was a pause before the second man continued. "We cannot let him find the thing. O acordo ainda está em vigor.[3] Ehm, how to say it, ah! She is—"

"Never mind. No, we cannot." The older man leaned back in his armchair. "And yes, the agreement is in effect. Is it possible...mm, yes, that might work. Do you have anything planned for this winter?"

"Não[4]. I have postponed everything, em vista destas novidades.[5] Eh, desculpe-me, I am in England, I must speak English."

---

1   "Yes my friend," in Portuguese.
2   "Pardon me," Portuguese.
3   "The agreement is still in effect," Portuguese.
4   "No," Portuguese.
5   "...in light of this news," lit., "...with sight on this news," Portuguese.

SHERLOCK HOLMES AND THE MUMMY'S CURSE

"Very good. No matter; I can follow you without difficulty. I am also a man of the world. It is rather my plan which would require you to resume your native fluencies. Can you join his party without suspicion?"

"Perhaps. We are known as...rivais[6]. But he has a soft side, which I may be able to exploit to our advantage. But you are right, I must definitely brush up the English if I do."

"Excellent. Do so, then, and see what you can accomplish, thus."

"What CAN I accomplish? What difference can it possibly make, if I join him?"

"Talk him out of the entire thing, if you can," was the dispassionate reply. "The less effort expended, the less likely the effort is to draw attention to...the cause. No one can do that so effectively as you, all other things being equal. Barring that, I am sure you know how to sabotage his operations, and do so...subtly."

"Of course. But...he is a very determined man. Mi curador de yage[7] would call him accursedly stubborn. It may only make him more determined. And he has hired...a detective."

"A detective?! Who?"

"Some former student."

"The name, dolt! What is his name? Do you have it?"

"Holmes. Sherlock Holmes."

"Mm. I have never heard of him." The older man drew over a large note-book which lay on the nearby desk and leafed through it. "No, my records do not show a Holmes at Scotland Yard."

"He does not work at the Yard. He is a private consulting detective."

"Really? Private consulting? How very...unique. I shall have to look into the matter. And why do you think he has hired a detective?"

"Holmes was once his student, and is learnéd in ancient manuscripts, I have it to understand. They wish him to translate for them."

"Ah, well then. This...Holmes...is not along in a professional capacity, but as a mere academic dilettante." He shrugged. "Stop Holmes' arrival. Whatever it takes. You know how. I will back you if you require it. In the Council, and with my...mm, 'machine,' we will call it."

"Muito bem[8]. But if...HE...the master...cannot be dissuaded?"

---

6   "Competitors, rivals," Portuguese.
7   "My curador [or] curandero," a traditional Native healer or medicine man, in this case specifically one who uses a psychoactive plant brew called yage, more commonly known as ayawasca or ayahuasca, rendered in Portuguese.
8   "Very good," Portuguese.

The older man's voice was icily calm as he replied.

"Kill him. Under no circumstances must he be allowed to succeed. Now go."

"Yes, Professor."

As the younger man departed, the older turned back to his desk and lit the small lamp on it. He paused in thought, tapping the side of his index finger lightly to his lips; he nodded to himself, then tugged the bell-pull nearby and waited patiently. When the manservant arrived, he issued an order.

"Charles, find Walker and tell him to see what he can find out about this Sherlock Holmes person. Tell him to activate his group if need arises. I want a complete dossier by the end of the week, sooner if possible. Everything he can find on the man."

"Right away, sir." And the manservant departed.

"This will not do," the professor murmured to himself. "Quite aside from the complexities to my own endeavours, the danger, should they find it and recognise its import, does not bear consideration. It would be disastrous." He drew a deep breath, then shook his head, dismissing the thoughts for the time.

The professor turned back to his desk, where lay some unfinished papers pertaining somewhat to the discussion so recently completed. He pulled them closer and studied them for long moments, then started briefly as an *eureka* moment struck. Reaching for his pen, he dipped it and wrote a title across the first page.

It read, *The Dynamics of an Asteroid*.

Then he leafed through the pages and resumed his calculations.

CHAPTER 1
PLANNING EXPEDITIONS

"Watson, old boy, how would you feel about a trip to Egypt?"

Doctor John H. Watson, M.D., late of the medical department of Her Majesty's Army, looked up from his book in some surprise.

"Egypt? Why on earth would we be going to Egypt? I assume it IS 'we,' is it not? Or are you sending me in your stead for a case?"

"It is 'we,' and it is not a case," Sherlock Holmes averred with a slight smile, in which was a hint of ruefulness. "London crime is slow at the moment, and my reputation is still but budding, in any event. But as you know, I have some small enthusiasm for antiquities, especially in the deciphering of old, or even ancient, texts. And I received a letter to-day[9] from an old professor of mine. Doctor Willingham Adelbert Whitesell holds the Quatermain Chair of Archaeology at Oxbridge; he is returning to Egypt to complete a dig begun last season and wishes me to accompany him. Strictly speaking, the actual dig did not commence last season, I adjudge by his missive; he merely found the general location of what he believes will be the tomb of one of the earliest pharaohs, Ka, or Sekhen, as some make it. Most likely it is a hyphenation of the sort that the ancient Egyptians sometimes did, Ka-Sekhen. He expects to come upon some fascinating inscriptions if the tomb is indeed there, and thought I might be interested, which I am. And I, in turn, thought the climate might be more suited to your healing; the frigid damp of London's colder seasons is hardly conducive to the proper mending from those Jezail bullets, my dear fellow. Why, you were in considerable pain only two days ago."

"How did you know that?! I was at my club all day!"

"My dear Watson, surely by now you know my methods, even if you have not learned to use them yourself to great effect as yet. We have

---

9 "To-day" is an archaic form of the modern "today," in common use in the 1880s and prior; this novel is set in the early 1880s.

worked no less than half a dozen cases, large and small, together at this point."

Watson paused in thought, then looked up.

"It was raining that day, as I recall. I suppose that the sole of one shoe was more scuffed than the other, and one trouser cuff more sodden? Because of my limp?"

"Well done, my friend! Yes, you were undoubtedly dragging that foot a bit, and the walkway outside your club is in dire need of maintenance; it is positively riddled with puddles in foul weather. Also, your shirt was more wrinkled on the side of your sore shoulder, indicating you had stooped over considerably; a not-infrequent habit when it troubles you, I've noticed."

"Aha. I see. Well, yes," Watson admitted. "This accursed cold, wet autumn we are having is certainly not comfortable for one with my particular injuries, and I fear it bodes ill for the winter, as well, especially as it is still more than a fortnight to the equinox. And while said wounds have long since knit closed, it will be at least a year or more before the sensitivity has left them… if it ever does. But are you certain I would be welcome? I do not wish to intrude. After all, the professor invited YOU."

"And he says I am welcome to bring you along, if you are available and so inclined — he read your first few stories, the ones that your colleague Doyle placed for you — and is looking forward to seeing what you make of his dig. Ah, there's no accounting for taste, I suppose." Holmes threw his friend a sharp glance with twinkling grey eyes, just before going off into a gale of the silent laughter with which Watson was, by now, so familiar.

"Hmph. Well," Watson harrumphed, pleased, but raising a peeved eyebrow nonetheless at Holmes' jibing addendum, good-natured though it was. "In that case, yes, I should be delighted to accompany you, Holmes."

"Then do you have the boots fetch our trunks down from the lumber-room and gather your old Afghan campaign equipment, whilst I telegraph Professor Whitesell that we shall join him there as soon as may be!" Holmes studied the letter in hand. "Hm. Perhaps not." He snatched up the envelope and studied it carefully, catching a lens from his desk nearby with which to scrutinise it.

"What's wrong, Holmes?"

"Mm?" Holmes said, glancing up. "Oh, it seems that his letter was delayed in the post. It may well be that our notification and ourselves shall arrive at the same time."

"He has already departed, then?"

"He evidently decamped London as soon as the worst of the heat left the area in Egypt," Holmes said, re-reading the letter with care. "No doubt afraid someone else would find the tomb and rob it before he could get to it, which is a valid concern. And it looks as if he is well to the south of Luxor, though perhaps not quite so far as Assuan. It is not—" He paused, biting his lip in thought, then reached for the large tome of the world atlas on the shelf, flipping through it, studying several pages as he referred to the letter. Finally he continued. "It does not appear to be precisely along the Nile, as so many of the ancient Egyptian sites were. No, it is inland a fair bit, and it does not appear — per the terrain — that this is due to the meanders of the river over the centuries, as it is well out of the reach of such meanders. Most unusual."

"Indeed! It will be quite hot there, then, even in winter! We shall want pith helmets, and cotton and linen clothing, I should think," Watson decided. "I did not make it home with my helmet, and you have none; I will contact my old unit clark[10] and see about the best place for procuring a couple of proper topees for the pair of us. Would you like for me to acquire a couple of sets of Foreign Service togs for your use? I'm quite sure I could lay my hands upon some surplus uniforms which would be entirely suitable..."

"Capital notion, Watson," Holmes murmured absently, still studying the letter and comparing it to his maps. "That, mingled with my own summer wardrobe, should be sufficient. Let me see about the best way of replying. And Watson?"

"Yes, Holmes?" Watson turned, already headed out of the room to see the boots.

"Run down and see if young Wiggins is loitering about in Baker Street, would you? If he is, wave him over and send him up, please."

"But why?"

"Oh," Holmes shot his friend a quick, reassuring smile, "nothing much. Just something I should like him to look into, while we are gone..."

*****

---

10   "Clark" is the British pronunciation of the word "clerk." It is also the source of the surname Clark.

Less than a week later, the pair were on a train heading across France for Marseille, having made the Channel crossing at Folkestone to Boulougne-sur-Mer, following the mail routes. At Marseille they picked up a steamship across the Mediterranean and through the canal to the port of Suez. There, they transferred into a much smaller steamship for the short run down the Red Sea.

The only event which marred the trip occurred when their gear was nearly misrouted to Danzig. Holmes spied their trunks being trundled across the station platform in the wrong direction, however, and quickly accosted the baggage handler, correcting his error.

After that, Holmes was careful to oversee the transfer of their baggage himself, with no further difficulties.

*****

"Well, Watson," an exuberant Holmes said as the tiny steamship sidled alongside the dock at Safaga in Egypt, "I should say we have arrived in the desert, without doubt!"

"Indeed we have, Holmes," Watson agreed, mopping his brow with his kerchief as he patently tried to take it all in. "Look — just here, by the minarets. Why, it's as flat as any skillet."

"Only the coastal plain, Watson. Look farther back, over there, well past all the buildings and date palms, about four or five miles in — see the mountains?" Holmes stretched out an arm, pointing. "Those are known simply as the Eastern Mountains — because they are east of the Nile, I suppose."

"Great Scot, Holmes! I did not realise—! How shall we ever get through all that to Luxor, let alone up the Nile? We should have stopped in Alexandria and taken ship upriver!" Watson's forehead creased in worry.

"No, no, Watson, never fear! This will indeed be swifter, you have my word. When I made our itinerary, I knew what I was about. There is an established road inland from Safaga to Qina, you see, and thence to Luxor; or we can take a barge from Qina up the Nile to the professor's dig, which would be my preferred transport, I think. One should never visit the Nile and not take a barge along it! Or at the least, a river launch, as pharaonic barges are in somewhat short supply these days." An enthusiastic Holmes smiled broadly. "Once we debark here, I must find a telegraph office post-haste and notify the good professor of our imminent arrival; it is likely to take some hours for it to reach his dig site from the telegraph office on his end! Come, Watson, there's the gangplank!"

*****

"Holmes, I am really not at all certain which is worse — the heat, or the ride on these deuced beasts!" Watson complained as their small caravan trudged through the dark, jagged mountains westward, two evenings later. "The ride is rough, they smell to high heaven, and this is positively the meanest-spirited creature I have ever encountered!"

"You are the one who thought riding a camel would be 'romantic,' old chap, not I," Holmes retorted cheerfully, rocking along easily with the gait of his desert mount. "And I told you not to stand there staring in its face, no matter how curious you are — they spit when annoyed! When we make camp, you should at least wet your handkerchief and clean your face a bit better. You still have a brown smudge in front of your right ear."

An irked Watson extracted that same handkerchief from his sleeve, removed his topee, and mopped his brow, drawing the kerchief down his right cheek before glancing briefly at the dark russet smear upon it. Then he reached for his canteen, wet the kerchief, and scrubbed away the offending residue on his cheek before pulling several deep swallows from the canteen. Only then did he reply.

"You cannot tell me that you have expertise riding these nasty-tempered creatures," he grumbled, tucking the moist kerchief back into his sleeve, against his wrist, where it would provide some cooling effect. "Let alone in these damned mountains."

"Nonsense, Watson, the mountains of Afghanistan are much higher! And you have been in those before," Holmes pointed out. "As a matter of fact, I do have some experience on camel-back, from my younger years working under Whitesell at Oxbridge."

"When I was in Afghanistan, I had rather more on my mind," Watson retorted, in high dudgeon. "Like not getting shot, for all the good it did me. Nor was it so hot! And nor so dusty! And NOR was I on a benighted, thrice-damned bloody CAMEL!" Just then, his mount let out an offended-sounding bleat.

"Patience, Watson, patience, my dear fellow. And lower your voice; these animals are highly prized by their owners. It would not do to insult them. I know it cannot be pleasant upon your old wounds, but try to relax as much as possible, and simply roll with the beast's gait; that will be best, I think. This leg of the trip is fortunately short, and we are over halfway through it now. We are, at least, travelling at night, and with plenty of provisions, to include water. Admittedly, it is still very early in the season, so rather warmer than it should be in a few months; nevertheless here we are, and we must deal with it. Be glad we are not travelling in daylight hours, when it would be much, much hotter! In the heat of the day, these mountains can reach upwards of one hundred degrees!"

"I am thankful for that much," Watson admitted. "But...are we certain that there are no highway robbers in these mountains?" He glanced around in unease at the rugged landscape, the sharp edges of the dark mountain scarps illumined a pale silver by the light of a waxing crescent moon, low in the west. The sandy road ahead gleamed a pale gold in that same light. The camels in front of them kicked up a tawny cloud of dust with each plodding footstep, which did not settle until well after the entire caravan had passed; Watson could taste it upon his lips, which felt gritty.

"...Not entirely, no," Holmes conceded then, sparing a surreptitious glance at their surroundings himself — not, Watson suspected, that he had been unobservant before; that would have been totally out of character for Holmes. "One can never be completely sure of such things, in such places as this. But I should think it is unlikely, given so much exploration in and around Luxor — this is one of the most direct routes to maritime shipping, as it happens. And it is an ancient road, having seen its own archaeological digs, as has its terminus on the Nile: Qina was known as Kaine by the ancient Greeks, and Maximianopolis to the Romans, and evidently was, or is, an eastern bank offshoot of the ancient Egyptian city of Ta-ynt-netert[11], or Tantere. So there has been much digging in the region. Traffic through these parts is heavy enough, with sufficient numbers of antiquities passing through, that even if the Egyptian authorities did not provide for such, which they do, I have it to understand that a rather prestigious group of archaeologists, including our host, have banded together to ensure this route is well-guarded. Or at least as much as is possible, in the circumstances." He paused, then placed a casual hand on his hip, before resting its opposite on a rather

---

11   "She of the Divine Pillar," ancient Egyptian; likely a reference to patron goddess Hathor.

thick leather strap, part of the camel's harness; it widened substantially at the end underneath Holmes' hand, and might almost have been a hidden holster for a rifle, or a shotgun. "Nevertheless, things happen. Which is why we are hardly...undefended, ourselves."

Watson brushed his own hip in response, then paused in thought. Finally he glanced around to see who might be nearby, then turned and leaned forward to speak privately to Holmes, whose camel was slightly ahead and to one side. Holmes, in response, twisted a bit in the saddle, the better to face the doctor.

"The choice of our camel-puller was not random happenstance, was it, Holmes?" Watson kept his voice low.

"No indeed, it was not. Omar was known to me, back in the day, as a very trustworthy young camel-puller. Now he is a full-fledged caravaneer, though still young for his status: he owns most of these camels, and is very proud of the fact. Not that he has his own formal caravanserai as yet, though I am uncertain that the terrain is suited to it in any event. More, he remembered me from the time when we were both lads, and promised that both I and my, er, mildly invalided friend — pardon me, Watson, but I played up the nature of your injuries, and for good reason, as I desired you to have the best, most comfortable mount possible, in the circumstances — would arrive safely at Professor Whitesell's dig camp. In fact, he pledged it upon his camel train, which is saying a good bit. Look, up there at the head of the file — he is himself leading us, though he did not have to; as the owner, he could have hired someone, and normally would have done."

Watson was touched by this rare evidence of Holmes' consideration, though he hid it carefully. "But the rest of the handlers?"

"Are hand-picked, known and trusted by Omar. And all are well-armed. We two, our baggage, and some half-dozen crates of imported goods, comprise the whole of his caravan's lading on this trip. We are quite as safe as if we were in the midst of the British Army phalanx. Never fear. By this time to-morrow, we shall be safely at Qina, and may transition back to normal hours, as the trip up the Nile will be during the day, more comfortable, and much cooler on account of the water. I am sorry you are in pain, my friend, but our only other transport option was a dogcart pulled by a donkey, which would have been slower, dustier, and much rougher over mountain roads. Not even the most careless of antiquities experts would trust his treasures to such a conveyance; how much the more my closest friend, whose injuries still cause him pain?"

SHERLOCK HOLMES AND THE MUMMY'S CURSE
Watson never said another word about the discomfort of his mount.

*****

At dawn they camped; as they knew from the previous morning, the heat increased rapidly after sunrise, making it difficult to sleep. So instead, Holmes and Watson sat companionably on camp stools in the shade at the door of their tent, extracted pipes and tobacco, and puffed upon the soothing herb in the congenial silence that befitted a friendship such as theirs.

Half an hour later, a boy — Omar's youngest, as they had discovered the day before — brought them small trays containing their meals: hot shawarma made of stuffed *aish*, a kind of pita or pocket-bread filled with roast mutton and mint, lightly smeared with tahini; and the thick, syrupy-sweet coffee of the region on the side. Sticky pieces of baklava, liberally soaked with honey and carefully wrapped in parchment, baked by Omar's wife before their departure from Safaga, rounded out the meal. It was hardly a feast, but it was flavourful and sustaining, and as Holmes pointed out, it was as good as it was likely to get in that remote part of the world. Hungry, Watson tucked it away with alacrity, Holmes rather less so, as was his wont; and even Watson decided it was tasty. "Though," he admitted, "the mutton could have been a bit younger. It was a tad tough."

"Then it would have been breeding stock, and a source of fleece," Holmes replied, using a piece of the parchment to wipe honey from his lips. "Here, the sheep are only eaten when they are too old and infirm to continue producing. When you are finished, Watson, let us fetch our canteens and go to the water tank and fill them."

"Then what?"

"Sleep if we can; smoke, if we cannot."

"And to-night[12] we reach the Nile?"

"We do."

*****

But they did not. When Holmes woke that evening shortly after sundown, it was with a decided feeling of malaise; at the sound of retching, he turned his head to see Watson kneeling on the tarpaulin floor next to

---
12   "To-night" is an archaic form of the modern "tonight," in common use in the 1880s and prior.

the other folding cot in the twilight, eructing into the bucket intended for his tobacco ash with some violence. The sight sent an unpleasant wave of nausea through Holmes' own gut. The smell, a moment later, only intensified the sensation.

When he could catch his breath for being sick, Watson looked up at Holmes.

"How...how are you faring, Holmes?"

"I...have been better," the detective admitted, sitting up slowly in his camp cot and putting a hand to his belly. "Spoiled food?"

"Most like-likely," Watson panted. "I have already had to rush to what passes for a latrine outside the camp — twice. The diarrhoea is severe, and quick of onset. Forgive my indelicacy, but most of the camp is in the same condition, and it does not do in the circumstances to sugar-coat the matter. Thank God for a pit in the sand, or we should be in foul shape. I'm surprised you have not had similar issues already."

"I did not eat as much for dinner, if you will recall. My appetite, you know, is generally less than yours anyway, as I am thinner; and the heat tends to decrease it further. But that does not mean..." he broke off as a troublesome cramp gripped his belly, "...that I will be unaffected."

"Where?" Watson abruptly bent back over the bucket, gagging, but nothing came up. Most likely, the detective considered, watching, there was nothing left to come up. "Show me. Where?"

"Where what?" Holmes asked, wondering if some part of the statement had been lost in the dry heaves.

"Where in...in your gut? I saw you...wince."

"Ah." Wordlessly, Holmes pointed in the general vicinity of his solar plexus.

"Good, it is still high," Watson declared, waving a hand at his medical bag in the corner. "In there. Go. Find the...the paregoric. And...and a dosing cup."

Holmes immediately moved to the bag and rummaged within, tossing over his shoulder, "Cholera?"

"I...I think n-not," Watson panted, evidently fighting off another wave of nausea. "No m-muscular cramping, no unduly w-watery ex-excreta..."

"Good Lord, Watson," Holmes remarked fervently, coming up with the paregoric. "There is enough in here for an army."

"A-and more in my trunk," he murmured, stammering slightly in his inability to ward off the swells of reverse peristalsis. "I c-came prepared. I've b-been in backwater lands be-before, as y-you so re-recently pointed o-out. It sh-oould d-do for the diarrhoea and nau-nausea, too. Here."

Holmes handed over the bottle and dose cup; Watson measured out a dose and handed it back to Holmes.

"Down the hatch," Watson ordered. Holmes shot the medicine, then grimaced, smacking his mouth in distaste.

"Bleh," the detective muttered. "That was disagreeable."

"Not nearly as much as t-the alternative! Here. My turn. I...ugh. I have to get better, or I-I cannot p-possibly treat t-the entire cara-caravan." He measured his own dose and took it, then hung his head over the bucket as the bitter taste of the paregoric itself, mingled with a sugar syrup to render it more palatable, nauseated him once more.

"The entire caravan team is in this condition?"

His only answer was a nod of the head and another dry retch.

"Perhaps I may be able to help you..." Holmes offered.

"Perhaps I m-may ta-ake you up...up on it," Watson panted.

Holmes sat silently and watched his friend until Watson settled and slumped against the side of his cot, sitting on the tarpaulin floor. Then the detective rose and moved to Watson's side.

"Here, Watson," he murmured, "let me help you lie back down for a few minutes, while the paregoric takes effect."

"I...I'll be fine, Holmes," Watson protested weakly. "YOU need to lie down and let the paregoric take effect, else you'll be in the same shape."

"And I shall...right after I get you back into your bed."

The sleuth would not be dissuaded, and soon Watson was lying quietly in his army cot as relief washed his features. Holmes nodded in satisfaction, then betook himself back to his own cot to lie back down, glad to do so as another gut cramp hit.

But within minutes, Watson was dozing lightly, and Holmes felt his belly relax as the paregoric, so close akin to morphine, took effect. He smiled to himself and drowsed, vaguely aware when Watson roused himself a few minutes later, took the bottle of paregoric and the dosing cup, and left the tent.

*****

After a bit, Holmes was able to gain control of his responses to the drug and rose, finding himself relieved from the previously impending intestinal issues. Having slept in his trousers and vest, he rose, donned his stockings and shoes — after first checking them for scorpions and other such unpleasant creatures — and went to the small washbasin in the corner of the tent. There he freshened himself somewhat before putting on his shirt, shrugging into his braces, and donning his waistcoat. Then he went out in search of Watson.

Holmes found him at Omar's tent; all of the caravaneers, in various stages of disability, lay on pallets nearby, shaded by tarpaulins stretched overhead. Watson sat slumped on a suitably-sized rock close at hand, pale and worn, but functioning. He looked up at Holmes with a wry, weak excuse for a smile.

"I got a dose of paregoric into everyone," he said, "including Omar's son, just in case; the lad was the only one of the lot of us who hadn't got ill, I think because he ate left-overs from the previous night. I scrubbed out the dose cup with sand and water in between each of my patients. It is hardly my preferred cleansing method, but it will have to do in the circumstances. Omar has been extremely apologetic, and swears that he will have his wife clean their kitchen upon his return, upon pain of a beating or some such, though I don't think he's actually serious about THAT. He seems very devoted to his wife. He is quite upset, however."

"Is he in his tent?"

"Yes."

"Awake?"

"The last I checked."

"May I speak to him?"

Watson nodded. "Just don't get him stirred up or he might start vomiting again."

"Of course," Holmes agreed, and stepped inside.

*****

As soon as Holmes entered the tent, he saw Omar lying on a pallet, his son sitting beside him and watching over him. Omar's eyes glittered in the dim light of a tiny lantern, and he fixed his gaze on the sleuth.

"Holmes, my friend," Omar murmured. "I am glad to see you on your feet. My most fervent apologies. I shall have strong words with my wife when we return. I swear to you, by the beards of my fathers, that this has never happened before."

"I believe you, and I think your wife is not to blame, old friend," Holmes told the caravaneer in an understanding tone, utilising that unique way he had about him to soothe. He moved to the side of Omar's pallet, opposite the man's son, and crouched. "Do not treat her unjustly. Save your words for another time, another place, and another person."

"What do you mean? Khalil, your father thirsts. Fetch my water bag."

"Yes, Father."

"I mean, Omar, that I have reason to believe that there is a delaying tactic going on, with its intent being to discourage Watson and myself from proceeding to Professor Whitesell's dig site."

"What? Holmes?" Watson said, coming into the tent to see to his patient. "Why would you think that?"

"Because, my dear Watson, this is not the first attempt."

Khalil brought the water bag to his father, and helped him take several sips. Refreshed, Omar pushed up to one elbow.

"Say on, my friend," he told Holmes, waving a weak hand. "Tell us what is happening."

"I do not know as yet," Holmes said, shaking his head. "But the letter of invitation from Whitesell to myself was delayed by close to a fortnight, and for no reason that I could discern. There were...problems... with our tickets for the Channel crossing; in France, our baggage was nearly shipped off to the Baltic Sea—"

"But that was a simple error," Watson protested.

"No, it was not." Holmes shook his head even more vehemently. "You did not see the orders in the porter's hand."

"Nor did you."

"On the contrary. Though he tried to hide it — a suspicious gesture in itself — I was able to get a very clear reflection in the polished brass railcar plaque behind him. And it very plainly noted that OUR trunks, Watson — yours and mine — were to be redirected to Danzig, while you and I took the mail route. It was no accident. And now this," he pointed out.

"Damnation!" Watson exclaimed. "We're being crabbed[13], as young Wiggins would say."

"Indeed, something like," Holmes agreed.

---

13   To prevent execution of a plan, usually (but not always) by means of diversionary statements. A Victorian slang term.

"*Mish maquul!*"[14] Omar cried.

*****

Holmes helped Watson tend the sick caravaneers the rest of that night and on into the next morning. The men were weak, and in need of some sustenance, but after Holmes' revelation, it was agreed that it was not worth risking consuming more of their potentially-contaminated foodstuffs until they got to their destination in Qina, and could get fresh supplies. Holmes considered this plan with all due diligence, eventually concluding that whoever was attempting to dissuade their further travels was unlikely to know from whence they would purchase fresh food in Qina, and thus untainted food could truly be obtained. Then he unpacked some of his scientific equipment and ascertained that the water they carried was indeed safe to drink, and this provided the refreshing they needed to rest and recover.

"Do you suppose we could try to make Qina to-night?" Watson wondered, as they sat in Omar's tent and discussed the situation with that worthy. "And, once there, should we go on, or go home?"

"Go on, by all means," Holmes declared, firm and not a little angered. "Aside from the fact that no miscreant has ever, nor will ever, make me cow, I will not waste the efforts of Omar and his companions. For this attempt certainly targeted them as well."

"True," Omar agreed, "and we thank you, friend Holmes, friend Watson. Know that the both of you will always have a cup of cool water, and the sanctuary of my tent, when you are in Egypt."

Holmes sketched a half-bow; a weaker Watson simply nodded in appreciation.

"For this, I thank you, old friend," Holmes replied, voice soft. "If ever I may be of service, you have but to ask. Do you think you and your men will be able to depart to-night?"

"Yes, we will see you safely to Qina while the stars are yet out and the moon is high."

*****

They did, though it was well past midnight when they arrived, and the moon not quite so high; their small caravan had not packed and departed camp until sunset was very near, for they were still too weak to

---

14   "Incredible!"

risk departure in the daytime heat. The camels plodded around the edge of the town in the dark, Omar leading them unerringly through the back streets of Qina.

"Where are we going, Holmes?" Watson asked.

"I have it to understand there is a small hostelry awaiting us not too far off the river, Watson. It will have proper beds, though I cannot speak for the coolness of the rooms. Nevertheless, most such about here are composed of thick clay masonry, which resists even the heat of the day, so perhaps it may be comfortable, especially so near the Nile. And there should be food, safe food. Omar will see to that. You may not be able to tell, but I can: he is quite angry at whoever did this. So, too, are his handlers. I think we may safely conclude that the contamination was done by an outside party, back in Safaga. And I pity them, should Omar and his company ever find them out."

A curious Watson twisted and turned to look about him in the moonlight; there were no street lamps, at least in the region of the village where they were. Off to one side could just be seen the minarets of the mosque, black silhouettes against a deep cerulean blue sky, spangled with stars.

"There is considerable stonework. Most of the buildings seem to be stone or stucco. A bit of brickwork, but it seems crude."

"Indeed. That is the, mm, the most convenient, building material here."

"Precious few trees in a desert, I suppose. And what are there, are probably better used for other things than building timbers," Watson decided. The front of the small caravan stopped before a two-storey stucco building. A small sign hung over the front entrance.

"Quite. Ah, here we are, *An Alenwem Alejyed Leylaan*.[15] That sounds promising." Holmes nodded at the sign

"You read — and speak — Arabic?"

"Of course. Do you not?"

"A bit. I'm hardly fluent, but I can get by in an emergency. And you?"

"When I was here before with Professor Whitesell, it was essential. At that time I was his assistant, trusted with probably half the logistics, and a great deal of the linguistics; I could not have got about without at least a fundamental knowledge of the language. I would not claim to be a scholar, but I did well enough. It has been a few years, but it swiftly

---

15   "The Good Night's Sleep," Arabic.

came back to me in Safaga."

"He speaks fluent Arabic, he reads Arabic as well as he speaks it, he rides camels as if born to it," Watson grumbled under his breath. "In addition to being the best damn jack[16] in all of London; London just doesn't know it yet. I shouldn't be surprised, I suppose. His memory is a bloody steel trap. I'm the confounded nickey[17] about these parts." Unseen by him, grey eyes cut to his face, studying it briefly in the dim light, then returned to the sign over the hostelry door.

"I expect we could both use a sound night's sleep, after the last few evenings," Holmes continued, as though he had never heard his companion. "Watson..."

"Yes, Holmes?"

"Our discussion this morning, in Omar's tent..."

"Yes?"

"Would you feel safer going home to Baker Street? If you would prefer, I can make arrangements in the morning to send you down the Nile to a steamer ship in Alexandria. You could be home in a fortnight, if not sooner."

"You intend to go on?"

"I do."

"Then I will most certainly accompany you," Watson said stoutly.

"Are you certain?"

"Absolutely positive."

"Very well, then; it be on your own head," Holmes said, only half-whimsically. "This is likely to be the last sleep in a proper bed that we shall have for some months, Watson; enjoy it."

"I fully intend to, old chap," Watson offered cheerfully, as a handler coaxed their mounts to kneel. Swinging his bad leg awkwardly around the camel's hump, the physician eased himself gingerly to the ground. "Ahh," he murmured, stretching, "much better. Oop!" He staggered briefly, and the alert camel handler grabbed his shoulders, steadying him before he could fall.

"Are you well, Watson?" Holmes murmured with solicitude, dismounting his own camel with his usual grace and coming to his friend's side. "Are your wounds troubling you? The journey hasn't made matters worse, has it?"

"No, no, Holmes, I'm quite all right," Watson brushed off Holmes'

---

16   Detective; Victorian usage.
17   Simple in the head; simpleton; Victorian usage.

concern with a slight smile. "My bad knee is just a trifle stiff, is all, and I'm afraid it failed to entirely straighten out just now. I'll flex it a bit once we alight in our rooms, maybe rub it with liniment, and it will be as right as rain in the morning. It was only that second day I was in pain."

"Ah yes. The first day, one is getting used to it. The second day is the one which hurts!"

"Exactly!"

And, chuckling, the two men entered the hostelry to be led to their beds.

*****

After a substantial, relatively easily-digestible breakfast of *fuul*[18] and hard-boiled egg stuffed in pita, all washed down with that same syrupy-sweet coffee which could be found throughout the country, they departed the quay at Qina, headed up the Nile on the steam launch *Akhenaten*, midmorning of the next day. Their rooms had been comfortably cool, the beds of softest goose down, and even Watson had to admit there were no kinks remaining in his anatomy as he boarded the steam launch.

"I say, Holmes, this is quite pleasant," he noted from his seat at the rail when once they were well under way.

"It is, Watson," Holmes said, standing next to him at the rail and pensively looking out westward. "And it's about time! The breeze is deliciously cool and damp off the water, and the canvas over the launch provides welcome shade against that deucedly hot Egyptian sun! Whenever I am here, I have no doubt why the pharaohs worshipped the sun, for surely the sun controls everything hereabouts!"

"Ha! Excellent point, old man! Listen, do you suppose the captain would mind if I smoked?"

"I shouldn't think so, but perhaps you ought to ask him first."

"Er, I rather ascertained, while we were boarding, that he only spoke Arabic."

Holmes hesitated, then spun and sat on the railing bench beside Watson.

"Old chap, are you requesting of me to ask him FOR you?"

"You're the fluent linguist in this region, not I." Watson shrugged.

"Watson..." Holmes paused, mentally debating his phrasing. "It

---

18 Mashed fava beans; this is a traditional Egyptian breakfast.

has not escaped my attention that you seem to feel...inadequate, in this environment, especially as regards my experience in it. Perhaps this is the way to start...?" Watson let out a soft, rueful chuckle, then leaned toward his friend, dropping his voice.

"Not in this case, Holmes, I fear. Partly for that very reason, I tried to make chit-chat with the captain back at the quay, to no avail. There is a...an accent, a dialect, or the like, which I am simply not grasping, which our good captain seems to have. I might manage to make myself understood, but I swiftly realised I was unlikely to understand HIM. I've no idea if it is a regional dialect, a speech impediment, or what, but despite my best efforts I cannot understand the man for the life of me." He met Holmes' concerned grey gaze. "I hadn't the problem at the hostelry, so it seems to be only the captain. I swear to you, Holmes, I will try — but for now..." He shrugged again, then nodded at the stern, where the captain steered the launch. "It had best come from — and to — you."

"Very well, then. One moment." Holmes turned and called back to the launch's captain. "Aleqbetan, qed sedyeqy aledkhan lh alanabeyb?"[19]

"Webteby'eh alhal, ya sedyeqy,"[20] came the cheerful reply. "'Ela alefhem adenah, bheyth tekwen amenh. Welken aqewl lh an ahedr aletmaseyh! La ted' lh tefqed lh anebweb aletbegh!"[21]

"Neqth memtazh, ya sedyeqy!"[22]

The captain and Holmes both laughed, and Watson frowned, disappointed. Holmes turned to his friend.

"Wipe that scowl from your face, Watson. It's quite all right. Go ahead and smoke, as you like. And I may well join you. But whatever you do, don't lose your pipe overboard. In fact, I recommend a cigarette; I have some already rolled, if you prefer. Or perhaps a cigar from our baggage."

"But why?"

Holmes merely pointed to the riverbank with a long, slim finger. Watson turned to look.

"I see nothing but some deadwood and logs washed up," he noted with a shrug.

---

19   "Captain, may my friend smoke his pipe?" Arabic.
20   "Of course, my friend." Arabic.
21   "The coal is below, so it will be safe. But tell him to beware the crocodiles! Do not let him lose his tobacco pipe!" Arabic.
22   "Excellent point, my friend!" Arabic.

"Look closer. Those are not logs. They are crocodiles. There will also be cobras."

"CROC—! Ah, well then. Of course. Do you have your cigarette case about you?"

*****

The launch travelled swifter, even upstream, than a camel; the terrain changed fairly rapidly from the relatively open desert full of sand dunes and more distant mountains near Qina, to low encroaching sandstone mountains, thence to higher, more rugged cliffs and mountains, closer in, as they neared — and passed — Luxor. Watson happily gazed out at the spectacular temple ruins as they glided past, and Holmes considerately fetched the field glasses from their baggage so that he might get a closer view.

Some two hours before sundown, they arrived at the landing, still well downstream of the First Cataract, though they had yet a considerable traverse west of the Nile to the actual dig site.

"Mr. Holmes?" a young, red-headed man, appearing to be in his very early twenties and with a pronounced Liverpool accent, called to them as they clambered up the gangplank to the quay. "Mr. Sherlock Holmes?"

"Here!" Holmes replied, holding up a hand. "And this is my friend and colleague, Doctor John H. Watson."

"Indeed," the young man smiled, taking their hands and shaking in turn. "My name is Landers Phillips; I'm Professor Whitesell's doctoral student and assistant. We had your telegrams, and he sent me to fetch you back to camp. But you're later than we expected; based on your message from Safaga, we thought you'd be here two days ago, until we got your telegram from Qina this morning."

"A little matter of some…spoiled…food," Watson offered, "and a temporary camp in the desert became an extended stay."

"Oh!" Phillips exclaimed, shocked. "Are you both well?"

"Thanks to Watson, we are now." Holmes shot his friend a smile.

"Good, then. Is Omar here with—? Ah, there he is," Phillips said, as Omar and two of his men unloaded trunks and bags from the rear of the launch. When Phillips put two fingers to his mouth and delivered a sharp whistle, Omar looked up, spotted the younger man, who was now waving, and nodded; he turned to his men and pointed, and they began carrying the baggage up the quay. Phillips continued, "Mind where you walk. Some areas down near the river banks fairly swarm with cobras; I understand they like the water. You'll need to look out by the dig, too. There's a nest of 'em somewhere, because one shows up now and again, but we haven't located where they're coming from. Now, I have a donkey cart over here for all of your things, and a dogcart for us to ride in. The Professor will be waiting dinner on us."

"He still holds communal dinners, then?" Holmes asked, following the young man off the quay and under the shade of a clump of date palms nearby. There, the aforementioned carts awaited.

"He does," Phillips confirmed. "He says it bonds the party better. I'm not entirely sure I agree with him, but there it is. You'll see what I mean, soon enough. And of course prayer tents for our Muslim workers, and such. Climb in, gentlemen. Tariq is driving the baggage cart; he knows the way, and will follow along after with your things. I'll just take care of your travelling expenses and we'll be off."

"No need, my good man," Holmes noted, reaching for his pocketbook. "We budgeted for porters and the like."

"No, no!" Phillips waved him off with a smile. "I have express orders from the Professor, and I dare not contravene them! Else it is apt to be my hide adorning the museum! You are an expert consultant brought in for the purpose of helping us decipher any writings we may discover, so the university will cover your expenses, and glad of it. Dr. Watson, too; it is always good to have a physician on site, in case of injury or the like, as Professor Whitesell said — especially, I suppose, with those blasted snakes in the area, though they've not truly threatened anyone so far. Besides, if we find what we hope to find, it will end up in the British Museum, and we'll all be famous! In with you, now!"

The pair clambered in; Phillips paid Omar and the captain of the *Akhenaten*, then he joined them, took up the reins of the shaggy little pony, and they were off.

CHAPTER 2
INTRODUCTIONS AND REACQUAINTANCES

When they arrived at the dig, there was a large white awning erected off to one side, a big hardwood table standing underneath, set with a pristine white tablecloth and linens, proper silver, crystal, and china; a sideboard sat nearby. Clustered around this awning were several more tables, less elegant, where the local diggers ate. Some of these had canvas shades and others did not. Dirty, dusty Egyptians — obviously the diggers, by the state and style of their clothing — milled around the outer tables, tolerantly awaiting the food. Under the awning a more dapper, if still dusty, group stood. Most of them had skin browned almost as dark as the native Egyptians, proof of their active outdoor profession. One gentleman, somewhat shorter than the others, stocky, and possessed of a white beard and moustache beneath his pith helmet, stood patiently at the entrance to the awning, gazing down the rutted track to the river with bright blue eyes. Upon spying the dogcart, a huge smile spread across his wizened face; he clapped his hands in delight and stepped forward to meet the cart, as Phillips drew the pony to a halt.

"Holmes!" he cried with enthusiasm. "Ah, young Holmes, it is so good to see you!"

Holmes sprang nimbly from the rear of the dogcart, hurrying to the older man, a broad grin on his face. "Professor Whitesell!" he exclaimed. "How delightful to see you again! I'd swear you haven't changed at all!"

He held out his hand to shake, but Whitesell caught him in a fatherly embrace. Holmes stiffened instinctively, but relaxed slightly after a moment, and gently patted the older man on the back. As the embrace eased, he turned to Watson.

"Professor, allow me to present my friend, colleague, and sometime Boswell, Doctor John H. Watson, late of Her Majesty's Army medical department. Watson, this is Professor Willingham Adelbert Whitesell, Quatermain Professor of Archaeology at Oxbridge."

"Pleased," Watson said, beaming beneath his moustache, stepping forward and taking the professor's hand in a firm grip before shaking. "I'm looking forward to picking your brains about what Holmes, here, was like when he was younger."

Holmes' eyebrows shot up, in what Watson mischievously interpreted as surprised dismay, and Whitesell chuckled impishly.

"I think I may just be able to oblige, Doctor. And I'm looking forward to finding out more about the adventures the pair of you have had," Whitesell responded with a grin. "I knew young Holmes was destined for something great, but I'd be damned if I could figure out, at the time, what it was."

"He does hide it well, doesn't he?" an impish Watson tossed back, and watched in amusement as Holmes' eyebrows shifted into a considering, one-raised, one-not configuration. A faint crease of annoyance developed between them. "I swear I could not make out what he was about, when we had only just moved into the flat and were still getting to know each other. The fact that he was pulling my leg half the time, and actually pretended not to know the Earth went around the Sun, only served to throw red herrings across my path." Watson shot a glance at Holmes from the corner of his eye, and noted the detective's cheekbones had grown ruddy.

"Ah! You young scamp, Holmes! I taught you better than that!" Whitesell said, shaking his fist, but with lips twitching, and Watson knew he was trying not to laugh at Holmes' discomfiture.

"A wise man does not always admit to everything he knows," Holmes decreed, giving Watson an austere glance. "Especially when he does not yet fully know the gentleman to whom he speaks."

"You thought enough of me to share a flat," Watson riposted smartly, by way of reminder.

"You had Stamford to vouch for your antecedents," Holmes pointed out. Whitesell laughed.

"Gentlemen, is this a true disagreement, or merely a show put on for my entertainment?" he wondered.

"Neither," Watson offered sheepishly, as a diffident Holmes broke off the conversation. "We are prone to chaffing each other unmercifully when no one else is about, and I fear we forgot we had...an audience."

"Quite," Holmes murmured.

"Then this is a strong friendship! Brothers in all but blood, I should say, by the look of it. Well, well, come along, Doctor, and let me introduce you and Holmes to the others. Holmes, do you remember my daugh—"

A petite, human-sized cannonball with golden hair abruptly launched itself at Holmes, only slowing when it fairly bounced off his chest. He seemed to freeze in place as his arms became unexpectedly full of a very attractive, and very shapely, young woman.

"SHERRY!" she cried, hugging him enthusiastically. "Oh, my dear Sherry! It's been years! Oh, it's so WONDERFUL to see you! You haven't changed a whit!"

With an obvious effort, for the young woman seemed determined to hug him as tightly as possible, Holmes held her at arm's length and stared at her in astonishment. Watson gaped at the scene; not only was the young woman uncommonly lovely, he had never before seen Holmes in such a predicament.

"Leigh?!" Holmes queried, patently shocked. "Is that you?"

"She's grown a wee bit, hasn't she, Holmes?" Whitesell noted proudly. "My little girl is quite the woman now. Dr. Watson, permit me to introduce my daughter, Leighton Quintana Whitesell. Leighton, this is Dr. John Watson."

A beaming Leighton finally moved back from Holmes as Watson stepped forward, taking her hand and bowing briefly over it. "Charmed," he murmured, trying not to get lost in the vivid green gaze.

"Good evening, Doctor, very pleased to meet you," Leighton said with a welcoming smile, then turned back to Holmes, catching his hand and pulling him — unwillingly — behind. Watson was put in mind of a tugboat manoeuvring an ocean liner. "Sherry, you can't imagine how excited I've been over seeing you again! You've already met Landers. Come along and meet the others! You too, Doctor! Are you really Sherry's bosom friend? Da says you are."

"We are dear friends, yes, sometimes in despite of appearances," Watson averred, then cocked an eyebrow at Holmes, who was evidently — as Watson adjudged by his expression —trying not to show his vexation over the situation in front of Professor Whitesell. "'Sherry'? Holmes, what—"

"Oh, that would be her childhood name for Holmes," Whitesell explained, as Leighton towed a red-faced Holmes before them. "She wasn't able to quite manage wrapping her little mouth around the name

'Sherlock,' and so that is how it ended up coming out — with a few intermediate attempts, I suppose, since she had a bit of a lisp, early on. You see, there is some ten or twelve years' difference in their ages, give or take, and she was quite a child when Holmes and I first met, which was actually a couple of years before he began his post-graduate work — she is still some few years from her majority yet, though I might have presented her as an early debutante last season, had either of us wished. But Holmes was at my home a good bit at the time, as you might imagine of a protégé student, and Leighton fairly doted on him. My wife Dulce — Dulce Lucrece Quintana, she was; I met her at a natural philosophy conference at La Universidad de Zaragoza, and we fell head over heels in love — her mother Dulce died, oh, perhaps two years before Holmes became my pupil, and I was busier than I should have been, with a daughter that age; buried my heartbreak in my work, as it were. I was a bad father for a few years, Doctor, though I hate like hell to admit to it, but there it is. Young Leighton was starved for affection, I fear. And while you may not know it, let alone credit it, young Holmes there has quite a way with the children, as it turns out."

"I have seen a little, yes, so I am not totally surprised. At home, he has a positive brigade of street urchins he has marshalled to his cause. You would be amazed at the information they seem able to turn up for him, usually in mere hours."

"I don't doubt a bit of it. I shudder to think of the effect he could have had as the Pied Piper of Hamelin. Not that I can picture him in such a...colourful...wardrobe, mind. But," Whitesell dropped back at the same time as he lowered his voice, nodding at the pair in front of them, "I think Holmes had not exactly considered the passage of time, do you think?"

"Oh, quite," Watson agreed, grinning beneath his moustache as he watched the *H.M.S Sherlock Holmes* being towed to its berth by the tiny tug *Leighton*. "This should prove an interesting evening. Your daughter is...very beautiful."

"Thank you, thank you, Doctor. I agree, but then I am somewhat biased. Come along, then. The meal should be served in a few moments."

They moved on, as Professor Whitesell — and daughter — began the process of introducing the pair to the other members of Whitesell's team.

Behind them, Landers Phillips brought up the rear, hiding a scowl.

The makeshift procession made its way under the awning, stopping before one dapper, if slightly dishevelled, early-middle-aged man. Holmes managed to free himself from Leighton's grip and drew himself up, adjusting his attire as he studied the man only briefly.

"Good evening, Lord Trenthume," he said scant seconds later, proffering his hand.

"Lord Trenthume, may I present Mr. Sherlock Holmes, and Doctor John H. Watson," a startled Whitesell quickly interjected, and the men shook hands. "Mr. Holmes, Dr. Watson, the Right Honourable Michael McMillan Cortland, Earl of Trenthume."

"I have heard a bit about you, Mr. Holmes, and about your nigh-magical abilities," Lord Trenthume remarked offhandedly, "but I put little stock in it. I may be forced to change my mind. How the deuce did you manage to identify me out of the others?"

"There is nothing magical about it, I assure you," Holmes replied with a chuckle. "It is all observation, and then reasoning from what I observe."

"Deduction," Watson supplied.

"Precisely," Holmes agreed. "Observation and deduction. Knowing both proper etiquette, and the Professor, I was quite certain that Watson and I would be introduced to you first. But aside from that, I should have recognised you out of the group, and was already drawing a conclusion as to your identity well before we came to you. For instance, I note that your attire is of the finest linen, in the latest style, and by that style, your suit must be from one of the top tailors in Savile Row. Yet you have a large smudge of red clay across your waistcoat, and have taken no measures to remove it or ensure it does not stain; this argues that you are unconcerned over the possibility of replacing so expensive a garment. You wear a tightly-woven red silk jacquard kerchief, quite costly, about your neck to protect it from the sun, despite a predilection for that colour to fade readily. In addition, you display an intricately-linked gold watch chain, of the type that is sometimes called Byzantine, with a large, filigreed gold fob containing extensive diamond and ruby pavé. Taken all together, these clews[23] say that you have considerable wealth. You carry a brand-new whisk and brush in the rear pockets of your

---

23   "Clew, clews" are the archaic forms of the modern "clue(s)," in common use in the 1880s and prior.

trousers, but there is no sign that they have yet been used; likewise for the hammer slung at your waist. You are younger than the Professor here, yet your physique is that of a mature man, strong and full, and your hair has the slightest tinge of silver beginning at the temples. With this knowledge, as well as the information Professor Whitesell sent me regarding his colleagues, especially the paragraph telling me that the venerable Cortland family continues to finance his expeditions through the beneficent generosity of the most recent Earl, could you be any other than the Earl of Trenthume?"

The others broke into spontaneous applause. Holmes flushed — with pleasure, this time — and sketched a swift bow.

"Well, well, it seems Dr. Watson's little stories are far more accurate than I would have credited," Whitesell chuckled. "No offense, Doctor."

"None taken," Watson waved off the apology with a smile. "It is a common reaction."

"Yes," Holmes agreed, "one of two, diametrically opposed. The other is usually something along the lines of, 'Oh, how absurdly simple!'" and they all laughed.

"Shall we see if Holmes can identify the others?" Whitesell suggested, grinning broadly. "Are you up to the challenge, Holmes?"

"Oh, quite," Holmes replied with nonchalance. "I have already ascertained their identities in any event. We have previously met Mr. Phillips, so I may eliminate him from the equation, though he would have been easy to deduce, merely on the basis of his age. That leaves the other archaeologist, the geologist, and your Egyptian foreman Udail... who is hovering behind you, Professor, awaiting your instruction to have the meal served."

Udail looked startled, and stepped from behind Whitesell. The others laughed again, delighted, and Whitesell instructed, "Yes, go ahead and have the workers served, Udail. We will be ready here ourselves in about five minutes. Feel free to take your own meal with your sons."

"Very good, Professor," Udail said, bowing before departing.

"All right, Sherry," an enchanted Leighton said, clapping her hands, "the other two?"

"Dr. Parker Nichols-Woodall," without hesitation Holmes pointed with one hand, "and Dr. Thomas Brockingthorpe Beaumont." He pointed with the other hand.

"Very good!" Phillips exclaimed, impressed despite himself, as they all applauded again.

"What gave us away?" Beaumont wondered, a hint of French accent lilting his proper English speech.

"The well-used whisk and brush in your back pocket, used for delicately removing dust and dirt from an artefact," Holmes told Beaumont. "I learned their operation well myself under Professor Whitesell, and they still find convenient use in my repertoire, when I am investigating crime scenes that are...mm, older in nature, is perhaps a good way to phrase it. And your accent, obtained from your Occitan father, confirms my deductions...for do you not speak fluent French, Dr. Beaumont?"

"Indeed. I was reared bilingual; my mother was English."

"And per your *curriculum vitae*, have added to those languages. Very good. As for Dr. Nichols-Woodall, he has a specialised hammer, of the type known as a 'rock pick,' hanging from his belt, for chipping off smaller specimens of stone outcrops. More, it shows signs of heavy wear, so I deduce it is likely his favourite hammer."

"You saw all that?!" Nichols-Woodall exclaimed in some startlement. "Why, the thing is half-hidden by the tails of my waistcoat!"

"Excellently done, my boy," Whitesell praised. "And entirely correct in every point. Professor Bell would be quite proud of you, I've no doubt. In fact, I think I shall sit down to-night and compose a letter to him, detailing this little introduction." At this Holmes' lips compressed, and he nodded, pleased; Whitesell continued. "Gentlemen, this is Mr. Sherlock Holmes, normally a private consulting detective, who will, as you already know, be our expert in hieroglyph translation on our little excursion; and with him, his friend and companion — and our physician for this expedition — Dr. John. H. Watson."

*****

On that note, Leighton again towed Holmes, this time to his seat at table, and motioned to Watson to follow, smiling happily. Then she moved around the head of the table to the seat across from Holmes. Phillips pulled out her chair, and her father saw her seated.

Once Leighton was seated, the men took this as their cue to sit as well. Watson noted that Whitesell took the head of the table, as the expedition lead; the financier, Lord Trenthume, took the foot. His daughter sat at Whitesell's right hand, with Phillips next her, and Beaumont sat between Phillips and Lord Trenthume.

Holmes, meanwhile, sat on Whitesell's left hand, a position Watson found subtly significant, especially given the daughter's position. The physician privately wondered if Holmes had realised the social implications, and suspected that the sleuth was being considered — whether willingly or unwillingly; most likely unwillingly, by his earlier behaviour — as a potential family addition. Then again, Watson pondered, it might simply be the position awarded to a favoured former protégé.

Watson sat in his turn next to Holmes, and the geologist, Nichols-Woodall, had the final seat, across from Beaumont. This was, Watson was soon to find, likely highly preferable to having the two men sit beside each other.

The first course was a flavourful, spicy lentil stew, a slightly sweet sauvignon blanc providing a counterpoint, with local Egyptians hired for the duration serving the course. After taking a sip of the wine, a curious Watson glanced at the Professor, knitting his brows.

"Sir, if I might make bold, is this not a European wine?"

"It is," Whitesell smiled, taking a sip and savouring it briefly. "One of my favourites. Is it perhaps not to your taste, Doctor? I can have another fetched, if you would prefer."

"No, no, that won't be necessary. It is very much to my taste; it is an excellent wine. But surely you did not bring sufficient...? The entire dig team?" Watson wondered, suddenly worried for the expedition's finances.

"Ah, I see your concern. No, my boy, the wine is only served in the main tent; you see, the majority of the manual labourers are Muslim, Doctor. They do not drink alcohol, as perhaps you know from your own exploits in the Afghan territories. But my sommelier is Coptic Christian, one Abraam Fouad of Alexandria; he chooses from the selection we brought from a fine London vintner, based on what the cook is preparing for the given meal. He is also the one who serves the wine and any aggregate after-dinner spirits, so that the Muslims among the wait staff do not have to handle it, and thus violate their precepts. Don't worry; I shan't break the bank, I assure you."

"It has always been Professor Whitesell's belief that at least one proper meal a day, complete with the niceties, is a boon to morale during an expedition into the wilds," Holmes elaborated urbanely. "It is why he insists upon a formal — well, I suppose 'semi-formal' is perhaps a better term, given that our tendencies have always been to arrive at table with minimal freshening, in preference to remaining at the dig pits as long as possible — a semi-formal dinner, at the very least. Breakfast and luncheon are somewhat negotiable; dinner is not."

"Except in the event of an emergency," Whitesell added. "Should such a matter arise, Doctor, I assure you that you, your attendants, and anyone you required to assist, would of course be exempt. I suspect that, in a very bad situation, we might well forego it altogether, but fortunately I have never had to do so yet. I do my utmost to maintain as safe conditions as it is possible to do, under such circumstances as we currently find ourselves. Since I often use the same local workers on successive expeditions, and new workers are most usually obtained from the families of my regular workers, it is something of," Whitesell paused to shrug, then added in a slightly gruffer tone, "a family affair, I suppose."

"After all this time, the Professor knows most of the local workers on a first-name basis, Doctor," Phillips informed Watson.

"Oh, of course, of course. Quite understandable. Well, then. Very good. Cheers," Watson offered, holding up his goblet.

"Cheers," came back the chorus, everyone clinking glasses to right and left.

"Tell me, Professor," Holmes queried, tasting his first course, "is old Qusay still working for you?" At this, everyone else also began the meal with alacrity, all sampling both the stew and wine and making pleased sounds.

"No, Holmes, he retired about two or three years after you moved on," Whitesell noted. "Said he was getting too old in the joints for all that work. His youngest son Razin took his place, however."

"Oh, capital. I should like it if you would introduce me to him at some point, Professor; his father was a positive delight, and easily taught me half of my Arabic. Watson, you were noting my fluency on the trip here, and Qusay not only improved my vocabulary, but helped me hone my pronunciation, into the bargain. He quite took me under his wing."

"Really! I should like to meet the son, too, then!" Watson declared. "Perhaps even the father, if he lives nearby. My Arabic could use a little honing," he added sheepishly.

"I'd be delighted, both of you," Whitesell beamed. "Razin is very much a chip off the old block, as it were. I think you'll like him."

Just then, Beaumont looked up and declared, "Ah, this is indeed most delicious, Professor! I had forgotten how much I enjoyed a good lentil stew. The cuisine in the Americas, while excellent, is very different. I have not had a proper lentil stew since...oh! Since that conference,

Parker, when you could not find your trousers, *mon ami*[24]!" he addressed Nichols-Woodall with a smirk, then turned to the others. "He evidently had to borrow a pair from a colleague...who had considerably shorter legs. And they were brown, and he had no brown suit; he wore a grey one...for the keynote paper. It was...quite the sight."

"I should have had my own trousers, thank you, were not SOMEONE at this table less of an atrocious prankster," Nichols-Woodall pointed out with some heat. Beside him, Lord Trenthume blinked in discomfited bemusement. "I should very much like to know how WHOEVER did it managed to break into my rooms at the hotel in the first place."

"Well, *mon ami*, perhaps you should ask Mr. Holmes," Beaumont offered, a mock-innocent smile on his face, but with a disparaging, almost calumnious, look in his eyes. "What a pity there are no longer any clews, after all this time."

"Someone… broke into your room, and stole… your trousers," Lord Trenthume murmured, a perplexed expression on his face. "What an outré thing to happen…"

"You know," Nichols-Woodall remarked, thoughtful, but with a vaguely malicious light in his own eyes, "I recall that colloquium quite clearly, myself. Wasn't that the one where you gave a talk on one of those esoteric theories of yours, and everyone attending the talk was laughing at it? Something about a connexion between alchemy, the Aztecs, and the Amazons, or the like?"

Poor Lord Trenthume began to fidget nervously. He opened his mouth as if to speak again, but seemed to have no idea what to say, and shut it again without having made a remark.

"Ah, yes, I remember," Beaumont agreed placidly. "And it was the Maya, not the Aztecs. Although it is less alliterative, I suppose. Well, radical revolutions in science are often scorned by lesser minds. As I recollect, you attended my talk…"

"Yes."

"…Because no one was there to attend yours."

"Hardly!" Nichols-Woodall bristled. "I had a full—"

"Sherry!" Leighton Whitesell suddenly sang out, in what appeared to Watson to be a desperate effort to either interrupt, or drown out, the caustic conversation at the other end of the table. Lord Trenthume sat up straight in what appeared to be relief at the diversion. "DO you remember the first archaeological outing I ever attended with you? The one just

---

24   "My friend," French.

outside London, where you fell into the pit?"

"Fell into the pit?!" Phillips goggled. "How on earth did THAT happen?"

Holmes flushed, but Watson noted her statements had served the purpose of at least temporarily silencing the rancour between Beaumont and Nichols-Woodall; the attention — and curiosity — of both men, as well as that of Phillips and Lord Trenthume, was now fastened upon the conversation between Holmes and Leighton Whitesell.

"The particular dig Leigh is referencing was in Stonehenge," Holmes said stiffly to the rest of the table, and Watson wondered at the intense expressions which appeared on all the faces at the other end of the table. "Leigh was quite small at the time; the Professor had given her supervision partly over into my hands. I had just finished explaining to her how archaeology 'worked,' as she put it, and showing her how to extract a relic without damaging it, when one of the, ah, unskilled labourers came up with something he had found, wondering if it were anything of import. And while I was studying the object and answering his question, I fear she got quite away from me and lost herself among the standing stones. By the time I caught sight of her again, she was clear on the other side of the structure, headed toward one of the dig fields, and I broke into a run, intent on fetching the young scamp back to her father, lest SHE fall in..."

"But he didn't realise that Da had started another pit on his side!" Leighton giggled. "I saw him run around one of the big — what are they called? The big standing stones with the cross-posts on top?"

"Menhirs?" Phillips suggested. "Trilithons?"

"Yes, those," she agreed, her smile dimpling her cheeks quite adorably, Watson thought. "Trilithons. Sherry ran around one of the trilithons. And then he just...disappeared. One second he was there, and the next, he wasn't!"

"Heavens above," Professor Whitesell murmured, "I remember that! I was at the bottom of the pit Holmes fell in, and I think I broke his fall!"

"Yes!" Leighton giggled again; poor Holmes flushed deeper. "And you both came out simply all over clay mud!"

The table burst into laughter; Watson noticed Holmes shifting uncomfortably, but unobtrusively, in his seat. When the others could catch their breaths, Nichols-Woodall asked, "Did you find anything? At Stonehenge, I mean. Fascinating place."

"Indeed," Beaumont agreed.

"Other than my sacroiliac, no," Holmes grumbled, putting a hand to his back in remembrance.

"Oh, we found what appeared to be a few ancient holes for stones no longer there, long since filled in. Most likely the stones that had been in them had been broken up and used in local construction in later eras. That sort of thing happens quite a lot in archaeology," Whitesell said, dismissing the matter with a wave of his soup spoon. Watson noticed the sidelong glance the Professor had given Holmes, and suspected he was attempting to change the subject to avoid further embarrassing his former student. Meanwhile, the servers removed the remains of the first course, replacing it with the entrée brought straight from the kitchens on the far side of the encampment, a chicken and couscous dish redolent with cinnamon and cardamom. Following close behind, Abraam the sommelier poured a young, spicy sangiovese which proved to pair marvellously with the dish.

"Aha! Not quite as observant as you made us think a bit ago, eh, Holmes?" Phillips jibed the detective, and Watson saw the graduate student throw a quick glance from the corner of his eye at the young woman sitting beside him. *Mm,* Watson decided, *someone is jealous of the lady's attentions.* Holmes' jaw tightened, but before he could reply, Whitesell did.

"No, no!" the professor protested. "Behave yourself, Landers, and mind your manners. Sherlock — that is, Mr. Holmes — deserves our respect, and has more than earned it. It was not his fault, but young Leighton's, for running off! In retrospect, it was probably mine, too; saddling a young, unmarried man such as Holmes was at the time, a man with little experience of children, with a fireball like Leighton, and then still expecting him to fulfil all his other duties? Think of it, Landers. Put yourself in that position! Holmes was, if I recall correctly, some couple of years younger than you are now; Leigh was perhaps all of ten years of age, if that, and a positive mischief just like her mother! How would YOU fare, in the circumstances?" Phillips' eyes went wide, shooting to Holmes, and he winced just before the professor continued. "No, Holmes was already running when he rounded the stone, attempting to protect my recalcitrant young daughter over there from harm. I actually heard his grunt of recognition — just before he landed atop me! No, he saw, but it was too late to stop. I was only thankful that neither he, nor I — nor Leighton — was seriously hurt, in that little incident."

"So someone caught you, then, Leigh?" Phillips asked the young woman.

"Oh yes," Leighton giggled again. "It was one of Da's other colleagues..."

"Professor Gärtner, of Heidelberg University," Whitesell filled in. "He died some three or four years ago, when the tunnel collapsed on him as he tried to excavate that Viking funerary longboat, some fifty kilometres outside Stockholm." The mood at the table quieted at the remark.

"Oh, I remember hearing about that," Lord Trenthume hummed in recollection. "Weymouth told me of the matter. They'd located it and looked inside, and were trying to shore it up while they uncovered all of it, and it all fell in, instead. What a pity. He was a good man."

"And very nice," Leighton agreed. "Even to a silly little girl such as I was." She turned back to Holmes. "Do you recall giving me the pretty stone, Sherry?"

"Oh, you mean the pebble that ended up in my shoe after landing on top of the Professor? I do."

"Well, I took it home and washed off the mud, and put it in the music box Mama gave me before she died," Leighton revealed, sobering. The mood at the table, already serious from the discussion of the dead archaeologist, became positively solemn. "I kept it as a memento for a long time. Then, two years ago, I got it out and had our family jeweller make it into a pretty necklace. See?" She pulled a heretofore-invisible chain around her throat, which brought up the gleaming little blue-green pebble from its hiding place in her décolleté. "I keep it so that, whenever I become melancholy, it helps to remind me of a wonderful day so very close to Mama's death, when my dear friend Sherry showed me how to dig in the dirt to find 'old things.'"

Professor Whitesell looked moved; he harrumphed once or twice, and cleared his throat, but said nothing. Both Beaumont and Nichols-Woodall dropped their gazes to their plates in respect. Holmes nodded, jaw tightening, though whether in stifled emotion or annoyance, Watson could not tell; the detective took a bite of the curried mutton, as did Watson...

...Who looked up to see a white-faced Phillips glaring at Holmes in utter hatred.

*****

As they finally left the dinner table, Watson turned to Professor Whitesell.

"I had it to understand from Holmes that you would like for me to function as a physician for the project," he noted. "And you so introduced me to the others."

"Yes, that's quite correct, Doctor."

"Do you have a regular physician under whom I should work?"

"No. Well, we do, but his wife was expectant and he was unable to come this year," Whitesell explained. "She experienced significant and potentially grave difficulties with their last child, it seems, and he did not wish to leave her. Hence my delight when I found you were available to come with Holmes."

"Aha, I see. Perfectly understandable, then," Watson agreed, nodding sage concurrence. "He was probably wise to remain close to home in the circumstances; I expect I should do the same, were I in his position. Very well then. If you could have someone show me to the surgery, I will commence setting up. I hope there were no medical problems before my advent. We came on as soon as matters could be arranged."

"No, there have not been any medical incidents, not of any import, at any rate," a diffident Whitesell began, "but there is still a problem..."

"What, then?"

"Well, I am loath to say, Doctor, but something seems to have happened to our cargo while en route..."

Holmes and Watson exchanged knowing glances.

"A familiar complaint, I find," Holmes muttered, watching the conversation with perspicacious interest.

"...And, well, the big hospital tent seems to have been...misplaced," an abashed Whitesell continued, not having noticed the exchange. "As well as some of the apparatus."

"Misplaced?!" Watson exclaimed in surprise. "How in the name of all that is holy does a body misplace something as big as a bloody hospital tent? Oh, I beg your pardon, Miss Whitesell!" Watson added, flushing, suddenly remembering the young woman was still with them, and his language had not been the most delicate.

"I assure you, Dr. Watson, I have no idea," Whitesell responded, exasperated. "I am as annoyed about it as you are, I am sure. But the quartermaster is on it, and we hope to have matters resolved within the week."

"Well, that is something, I suppose," Watson considered. "Do forgive my surprise, Professor — I simply had not expected that! What shall we do in the meanwhile?"

"Ah, we had rather thought — hoped may be a better word — that you might treat any patients in the tent you will be sharing with Holmes, here — I presume that is a suitable living arrangement? Yes? Good — and then we would house any invalided patients in their own tents," Whitesell suggested. "It could make for a deal of walking should you have to make rounds, however, and I've to understand from Holmes that your knee is not the best, after your Afghan tour..."

"True," Watson sighed. "It is certainly not an optimal arrangement."

"But if you need help, you have but to ask," Whitesell went on considerately. "I will immediately have someone come by to help. In fact there are a couple of the local workers who normally staff the hospital, in addition to the regular doctor, and you may — and should — call upon them whenever you need help. I will instruct them to report to you after breakfast, lunch, and dinner until further notice, and to remain within reach at all times."

"I will introduce you to them to-morrow[25] morning," Nichols-Woodall offered. "Willingham will likely be onto the quartermaster to see what has been located, and our foreman, Udail, will get the digging started for the day. So I can spare the time to help you get set up."

"As can I, at least for the unpacking of the equipment," Holmes agreed.

"Very well," Watson decided. "I shall take you both up on it."

"I expect this arrangement to be needful only for a few days," Whitesell vouched. "If we simply cannot find the blasted thing, I shall go into Luxor and see about acquiring another."

"What about the medical equipment?" Watson wondered, perturbed. "I did not come prepared to equip an entire surgical hospital with my own instruments; I don't even have enough equipment of my own, back in London, to do so!"

"No, no, everything is fine as far as that is concerned, Doctor," Whitesell soothed. "While it was initially, ah, 'walkabout,' as one of my Australian colleagues is wont to phrase it, most of the equipment did show up only three days ago. But without the hospital tent, we have nowhere to put it."

"Ah, I see," Watson said, nodding. "So the quartermaster has it, and

---

25   "To-morrow" is an archaic form of the modern "tomorrow," in common use in the 1880s and prior.

I will have access to it in an emergency, but it has merely not been put out as yet."

"Precisely."

"Holmes, are you game for living in a makeshift infirmary for a few days, old boy?" Watson asked.

"I shall make do just fine, my dear Watson. However, when I needs must begin unpacking my own scientific apparatuses, let alone spreading hieroglyphic text about the place, we are apt to become chock-full in short order."

"True," Watson considered, while the archaeologists and geologist looked on. "Well, hopefully it will only be for a few days, and if all goes well, I may not even have any patients, or none of significance, at any rate. A splinter here, a blister there, perhaps. A dab of carbolic should do the trick without much trouble."

"Yes, I think we shall do fine, Watson." Holmes turned to Whitesell. "It will do, well enough, sir. We thank you. Now, it has been a long, hard few days of travel; might I trouble you to have someone show us to our tent, Professor?"

"I shall do so myself, my boy," Whitesell said with a smile. "Good night, Nichols-Woodall, Beaumont, Phillips. Cortland, old chap, would you be so kind as to escort Leighton back to her tent? Thank you, sir. Leighton, I shall be back shortly, dear. Now, lads, come with me."

*****

As they walked, Whitesell pointed out various important locales: the foreman's tent, his own tent, Phillips' tent, the location where the hospital tent would be — essentially next to Holmes' and Watson's tent — the artefact tent, where newly-discovered relics were taken to be catalogued, cleaned, and studied, as well as the dig fields beyond.

"...So I know you are a bit away from us," Whitesell explained, "but it has been our experience that the labourers are the ones most likely to need medical attention, because of all the heavy work, you know, and so we put you over here, near the hospital...or rather, where it will be once we have found the deuced thing."

"It is well thought out," Holmes concurred. "That way, should things be going well, and Watson have few patients to attend, he may retreat to our tent to rest, out of the sun, until needed again. But if an emergency should arise in the night, say, he is ready to hand."

"Precisely," Whitesell agreed, nodding vigorously. "If, however, the two of you take issue to being among the, ah, the 'hired help,' I can have your tent moved."

"No, no, it is fine," Watson demurred. "I have no objection."

"And nor do I," Holmes added.

"...As Holmes says," Watson continued, thoughtful, "it is a well thought out plan. I should prefer to be closer to my patients by my natural inclinations, and this will do nicely."

"Excellent. And so here is your tent," Whitesell said, stopping before a large canvas structure. "It is one of the larger ones, as large as my own, actually. I wanted the pair of you to be quite comfortable, and to have the room to spread out your equipment — though I hadn't an idea at the time that it would also be a makeshift hospital, so I suppose it is fortunate. Holmes, while you are 'only' the translator, I fully expected you to be interested in the other matters as well. All of your work on the expedition will be most welcome, regardless of its nature, and I am very glad to hear that you brought some of your equipment."

"Oh, entirely," Holmes vouched, smiling. "Even had the tent been too small for the lot of it — and it may still be, once Watson and I both settle in and spread out — I would have sponged a corner of a tent somewhere, to work with it."

"Excellent, my dear boy," Whitesell said, returning the sleuth's smile. "I have no doubt but that Nichols-Woodall will quickly come to appreciate your skills as a research chemist, and you can assist Beaumont and myself in extracting any relics, into the bargain."

"Precisely what I had hoped, Professor." Holmes' own smile grew wider.

"Oh, my dear boy," Whitesell murmured, sobering, then he grabbed Holmes' arm in gruff affection and clapped his shoulder. "It is so very good to see you again, Holmes."

"And you, Professor."

"Now, your baggage should be inside already, with the camp cots, tables, chairs and the like having been set up previously, and awaiting your arrival," Whitesell continued, stepping back. "Do you both go on in, do what unpacking you feel needful for the night, and perhaps retire a bit early, if you feel like it. You have had a long journey, with one or two...unfortunate impediments...along the way. You have earned it, and that merely by arriving here. Breakfast is at six, which is sunrise; this enables us to reach the dig pits and begin work before the region becomes very hot. Lunch is at noon, and is followed by a siesta, as Beaumont calls it, during the heat of the day. Tea is set out on the sideboard, and is what Leighton calls 'catch as catch can,' and dinner is at sundown, or thereabouts."

"Very good. Thank you, Professor," Watson said. Holmes nodded concurrence, and the two men entered the tent for the evening as Whitesell walked away.

CHAPTER 3
THE WORK COMMENCES

The next morning after breakfast — during which rancour once more erupted between Beaumont and Nichols-Woodall, though this time, it was Nichols-Woodall who provoked it, and both Phillips and Leighton unsuccessfully attempted distractions to interrupt the argument at the far end of the table — Nichols-Woodall took Watson off to introduce him to his nursing assistants. Lord Trenthume nodded at Whitesell before rising and leaving the tent as well. Udail came by to see if Professor Whitesell had any specific instructions, then left to begin the day's dig. Whitesell turned to Holmes, Phillips, and Beaumont.

"Come, gentlemen," he said. "Parker will be along later, and Cortland has volunteered to take on the task of trying to locate that damnably wandering hospital tent."

"I expect that means he'll just be chivvying the poor quartermaster," Phillips opined. "He's a good enough bloke, I suppose, but I don't think the man has ever had a unique thought in his head. He just waits for someone else to come up with an idea, and then pursues it with relentless determination. He makes a nice clothes rack, though."

"Hush, Landers," the Professor rebuked. "It does not do to speak ill of one's patron."

"Even if it is true," Beaumont added. The Professor bit his lip.

"And we?" Holmes wondered, conveniently — and deliberately — offering Whitesell an escape.

"We will go over to the artefact tent, and try to organise what we have discovered thus far," Whitesell explained. "With any luck, someone will discern a pattern in the various relics, and it will lead us to the specific place where the tomb is located."

So they all trooped across the camp to the artefact tent, located on the border between the camp and the dig proper, a curious Leighton tagging along behind.

SHERLOCK HOLMES AND THE MUMMY'S CURSE
*****

Within the artefact tent, a plethora of wooden boxes and trays sitting on rows of tables met Holmes' eyes. Fascinated, the sleuth stepped forward, moving among the tables; as with one mind, the others stood back by the tent opening, letting him explore, and curious regarding his reaction. Even Leighton remained beside her father, watching. A few minutes later, Nichols-Woodall arrived, and joined the group watching Holmes.

*****

Holmes let his hands float through the air over the boxes, studying their contents without touching them. He quickly discovered that many, indeed most, of them were empty as yet, but there were still quite a few relics: small pots and potsherds; a necklace here, a bracelet there, several mismatched earrings; two different bronze mirrors, polish gone, a dull greenish patina encroaching over the entire surface; several plates and cups; the bones of small animals, each showing the classic knife marks of having been butchered. In addition to this collection, there were two stone-carving chisels, one broken, one not; an engraved tablet; two badly damaged tablet fragments; and a mallet.

"Mm," Holmes hummed, thoughtful. "I presume you have a log of the locations where these were all found?"

"We do, Holmes," Whitesell said, moving into the tent. "Over on the table in the far corner. What do you make of it all?"

"That you have obviously found the workers' camp, but not the work site," Holmes decided.

"Why do you think that, Sherry?" a curious Leigh asked, coming to his side and peering into one of the trays; it happened to contain what Holmes adjudged to be charred chicken bones, surrounded by bits and pieces of charcoal. She wrinkled her nose in distaste as she, too, recognised the contents, then looked up at him.

"Because I see much to do with day-to-day living, Leigh, and little in the way of the sorts of tools that would be required to carve out a tomb from solid rock," Holmes replied. "Professor, are these laid out in more or less a representation of where they were found?"

"Good man," Whitesell remarked. "They are, indeed. At least as closely as we could make it, given the tent is not quite the same shape as the dig field. But each tray represents one grid square, so it is reasonably close."

"Capital. Then look here, Leigh: in this tray we have the remains of a fire, into which has been cast the carcase of a chicken. Next to it are a couple of cook-pots, and the remnants of at least one more that has broken. These two squares, and probably several more, would denote the camp kitchen, as it were, likely similar in many respects to our own, saving we have cast-iron stoves versus their open fires, or perhaps some form of rudimentary clay stove," Holmes pointed out, then strode to the next table. "Here we have a small pot of perfumed unguent; can you smell it, Leigh?"

"Yes! Ooo, it still smells good!" Leighton exclaimed, bending over the tray and inhaling. "Um...sandalwood?"

"Most likely," Holmes agreed. "Yes, the ambers, resins, spices and what-not will have helped to preserve the fats into which they were mixed, which is why you can still sometimes recognise the fragrance, even after millennia. And here next to it we have some tiny brushes, a pot of ground charcoal, a bronze mirror, and a comb made of water buffalo horn. What do you suppose was here?"

"Someone's vanity table?" Leighton wondered; the other men stood back with slight smiles, watching silently with pleased approbation as the detective taught the professor's daughter. "They used charcoal and things to line their eyes, didn't they? And so maybe the little pot of charcoal is the liner, and the brushes are for applying it, like actors do. The mirror is to see what they were doing. And of course the comb is for the hair..."

"Very good," Holmes concurred. "Which means that the vanity table was inside what?"

"Well, if it had been a village, it would be someone's home, I suppose," Leighton considered. "But this was a work site, was it not?"

Holmes glanced at Whitesell for confirmation.

"That's correct," the archaeologist averred. "We have not seen any sign of permanent structures. No foundations or the like have been found."

"And there are some broken tent pegs in the corner tray," Beaumont added.

"So it was in someone's tent," Holmes noted. "And in all these adjacent trays, we find various items of jewellery, clothing fasteners, sandal straps, and the like. Which means this all comprised what?"

Leighton gnawed her thumb for a moment, thinking as she looked over the array of items, then finally offered a tentative, "The campsite?"

"Very good!" Whitesell exclaimed, intensely pleased. "You have reasoned through it all very well, Leighton! And Holmes, my boy, that was a lovely example, not just of reasoning, but of teaching!"

"Thank you, sir," Holmes responded, sketching a slight bow, as a delighted Leighton flushed.

"Thank you, Da, Sherry," she murmured.

"So we know where the camp is, and where the kitchens and living quarters were," Holmes determined.

"And the, er, the facilities," Phillips added, flushing in embarrassment.

"The latrines," Nichols-Woodall elaborated bluntly, with a dry grin. "For obvious reasons, we do not have any of, ah, THOSE 'relics' in the tent."

"Eww," Leighton exclaimed, wrinkling her nose in distaste. "Uncle Parker, please!"

"After all this time, surely the ordure does not still...smell?" Holmes asked somewhat delicately. "It has been many millennia!"

"No, no," Whitesell chuckled. "Not in the desert. By now it is all quite desiccated. But we felt it might still be...unsanitary. So we chose not to risk it."

"The workers were not especially happy about finding it, especially those that are Muslims," Phillips noted. "But the Professor explained that it was little more than regular dirt and soil at this point, and it took an expert to even be able to tell…"

"And Udail backed me, Lord bless him," Whitesell added. "So we managed well enough. Everyone understood, and no one was offended."

"Good." Holmes nodded knowingly.

"Yes. So we have the living areas well defined," Beaumont noted, "but the work areas — where the tomb or tombs may be — seem still to be lost to us."

"There are only a few places where tombs can be," Nichols-Woodall pointed out. "The layout of the valley is not unlike that at the Wadi al Muluk[26], or for that matter at Ta-Set-Neferu[27]. There is a large mountain ridge backing the valley, which is what my American colleagues would

---

26   "Valley of the Kings," Arabic.
27   "The Place of the Children of the Pharaoh," Arabic; more commonly known as the Valley of the Queens.

term a box cañon[28], with outlying spurs defining the sides. It is only along these that the tombs could possibly have been built; the sediments in the cañon floor would have been far too thick, even in Ka's time, for a vertical shaft approach."

"Yes, *mon ami*, but that is still a very long base line over which to search," Beaumont observed. "We can reasonably assume that the current surface level is considerably above what it was in Sekhen's day, which means we must dig a trench of unknown depth along the bases of the mountains. And that is a great deal of digging to do, through sand and scree. There is much talus accumulated at the foot of the mountains."

"Granted, but chances are, we only need worry about the vertical faces," Nichols-Woodall argued. "The scarps of the mountains are, traditionally, where the tombs were built, because of the greater stability of the ceilings due to uniform thicknesses."

"That is still a great deal of expanse," Beaumont replied.

"True..." Nichols-Woodall admitted, quirking his mouth in frustration. "We desperately need a way to narrow down the search."

"Professor, I have not thought to ask," Holmes interjected then, "but how exactly did you settle upon this site to begin with, if you had not yet discovered relics here?"

"Oh, well, as you know, I have been searching for Sekhen for a long time," Whitesell explained, and the others paid close attention. "I was re-reading a translation of one of the ancient histories, when I suddenly realised that a particular passage about Ka-Sekhen's funeral seemed more awkward than was warranted. It seemed poorly translated to me. I accessed transcriptions of the original hieroglyphics, compared them to the common translation, and recognised that the translator had missed some complex idioms and metaphors. Once those had been properly inserted, the passage became a kind of riddle, all about 'backbones and ribs,' and 'stones of the sky,' and treaties, and the like. I did a bit of leg work, and found that the little puzzle could only be solved — at least in part — by assuming it described this area. I checked with Parker, and ascertained that the mountains could not possibly have changed to such

---

28   "Cañon" is the original Spanish spelling of the Americanized "canyon." The Americanization was developed in the mid-1800s, but "cañon" remained in usage through the period of this story, after which time (roughly 1890s) the Americanization began to be used more frequently; but it was not fully superseded by "canyon" in English-speaking countries until sometime in the middle of the 20th century, as books from the first half of that century can still be found using the Spanish form. Spanish speakers still use the original "cañon."

an extent in the intervening time as to be unrecognisable. So I filed a request to conduct an archaeological exploration. And here we are."

"Do we have a topological map of the area?" Holmes asked.

"We do," Nichols-Woodall confirmed, going to a stash of large, heavy-weight pasteboard tubes in the corner. "Topographic, geological outcroppings, and more. Some of which I had to make myself; I have been here since the latter part of summer, working." He fetched several tubes and carried them to an empty table, beginning to remove the rolled maps inside. "Perhaps if we all put our heads together over this, we may determine some probable target sites for test pits."

"Capital idea, Parker," Whitesell agreed. Leighton tugged at Holmes' arm.

"Come, Sherry," she murmured. "Let's leave them to their stuffy old maps, and go for a walk."

The men all froze, staring at the pair. Holmes, in his turn, stared at Leighton, who blinked back in confusion.

"My dear Leigh," he informed her, "while I am gratified to see you and your father again after all this time, I am here to work, not to reminisce or to 'catch us up.' I am a part of this expedition team, and I am expected to — and shall — participate in solving the problem of locating Pharaoh Ka-Sekhen's tomb. This is why I came."

"I'll take you for a walk later, Leigh, perhaps during the siesta period, if it isn't too hot," Phillips offered. "But Holmes is right. We need to work for now."

"I want to walk with SHERRY," Leighton demanded. "I see you all the time, Landers. I haven't seen Sherry in years."

"I am busy right now, Leigh," Holmes reiterated. "I need to familiarise myself with the terrain, if I am to be of any use in helping determine where the tomb is."

"But—"

"Go back to your tent, Leighton," a mildly irked Whitesell ordered his daughter, "if you aren't interested in the work. You brought a small trunk of books, needlework, and the like, to include a whole collection of those blasted penny dreadfuls[29] that Phillips got you started on; I'm sure you can find something to keep yourself occupied for the day."

A disconsolate and vexed Leighton wandered out of the artefact tent en route to her own tent, as the men began to pore over the maps.

---

29   A type of cheap novel of sensational, melodramatic style, popular in Victorian Britain. It eventually evolved into the pulp novel of the early 20th century.

Leighton, more than a little impatient, was already waiting in the "mess tent," as Watson tended to term it, when the men arrived from the artefact tent after the luncheon bell was rung. They all took their assigned seats, and Abraam began to pour the wine. A perspiring Watson showed up moments later, having apparently jogged from the tent he shared with Holmes.

"So sorry to be late," he panted, hurrying to his seat. "I've been hauling equipment all over, and tying off tarpaulins, and the like. I'm afraid I lost track of the time. Then, when the gong rang, I had to finish what I was doing before I could come, or it would all have fallen down."

"Well, Doctor, how is the medical department coming along, then?" Whitesell asked, as the meal was served. "It sounds as if you've been quite busy, though I've no idea at what."

"Decently enough, I suppose," Watson replied, digging in hungrily. "Yes, I have been very busy. I have my emergency kit unpacked and more or less deployed, though it is rather crowded in the tent now. I did have the idea to see your quartermaster about matters of a large tarpaulin, cord, and tent pegs, in order to create a kind of lean-to shanty onto the side of the tent in which Holmes and I are staying, where I may place two cots and some tables for equipment," he noted. "At least until the proper hospital is found."

"Capital notion, my dear Watson," Holmes offered. "That should ease the crowding a bit, and allow for a place for any long-term patients to lie close by where you may readily tend them, without our being required to vacate our own beds, or for you to trek over half the camp."

"Precisely, Holmes," Watson said, then downed an entire glass of water at a go.

"I think the good doctor is tired, thirsty, and hungry, after a morning's hot, hard work," Beaumont noted with a friendly smile, as one of the servants came up and refilled Watson's water goblet, only for him to dive back into it. "How far along are you, Dr. Watson?" Watson had to come up for air to reply.

"I have the tarpaulin, the cording, the tent pegs, some folding cots and tables," Watson told him, "and I know where I want everything, and I even have the canvas attached to the side of the tent, but I still need to drive the tent pegs and string it all up properly, then position the tables and such like underneath."

"What about your staff?" Phillips wondered.

"I sent them to help Lord Trenthume and the quartermaster search for the hospital pavilion," Watson explained. "Besides, two of the three are women, one more elderly, and I should think they might not be able to hammer tent pegs into the ground with a heavy mallet. It would hardly be good for my first patients to be my own staff."

"Good point," Whitesell decided. "Cortland, any news on that front?"

"None, Will," the Earl of Trenthume replied. "The thing has simply vanished into thin air, as that American magician is wont to say. I have sent downriver to see about purchasing another one. We cannot go on like this, should something serious happen; Dr. Watson would be overrun, and poor Holmes here would have nowhere to sleep, even with the lean-to arrangement." He shook his head. "And if a *haboob*[30] should come in, it would well and truly be a mess."

"Ooo, good point," Phillips murmured.

"The bloody damn — oh, forgive me, Miss Whitesell — the blasted canopy is likely still lying in the ship's hold, wherever THAT has got to. Off to Timbuktu, I suppose." Cortland rolled his eyes in annoyance.

"How long before the replacement arrives?" Whitesell asked.

"The tentmaker in Luxor indicates we will have it within the week… if nothing else goes wrong."

"Then in the meanwhile," Beaumont offered, "may I suggest that we strapping men go with the doctor after luncheon, and assist him in erecting his, ah, 'adjunct office,' gentlemen?"

"Sounds like a cracking good plan, Beaumont," Nichols-Woodall agreed. "You never know, after all: one of us might wind up needing it! With all of us at it, we can erect the canvas, tie it down well, set up tables and cots, position all the equipment Dr. Watson is willing to leave exposed to the elements under it, and still have plenty of time for a nice cool nap in our own tents."

"Consider it done," Professor Whitesell decreed.

*****

After the meal, they all traipsed off to Holmes' and Watson's tent, where in only a scant quarter-hour, the makeshift medical office was

---

30   "Blasting, drafting," Arabic; usually used in reference to a severe dust or sand storm. It is now the official meteorological name for a sandstorm or dust storm.

erected and its furnishings positioned; even Leighton got into the act, helping determine the best layout for the furnishings, based upon efficiency of movement.

"There," Watson said, hot and tired, but with a satisfied light in his eyes. "Even after the hospital tent is set up and a proper surgery in operation, I think I shall leave this; smaller matters, especially anything that may crop up in off-hours, can be tended here, rather than having to go over to the hospital."

"And you have overflow room, in the event of something...catastrophic," Nichols-Woodall murmured.

"Of course, of course," Watson said. "But let us hope and pray nothing does."

"Quite," Holmes agreed, growing solemn as his eyes became distant with memory. "May Providence watch over us all, in this treacherous desert. I shall never forget the young boy who...became lost in the *haboob*...on my second expedition with the Professor..." He averted his face briefly.

"Oh," Whitesell said, sobering. "I...recollect that..."

"Well, let us all go back to our own tents, relax, and cool down," Beaumont suggested, changing the subject before the conversation became too maudlin. "It has become uncomfortably hot to-day."

"It has, indeed. Absolutely excellent notion, that," Watson declared, mopping his profusely perspiring brow.

The other men dispersed. Watson went straight into the tent; Holmes heard the soft creak of his cot as he stretched out upon it. He turned, intent on going back to the artefact tent to spend more time studying the maps...

...And nearly tripped over Leighton.

"Now for a walk?" she asked with a smile. Holmes subtly took a deep, exasperated breath, let it out; reined in his irritation. *It will not do,* he thought, *to upset Leigh or her father. I should much prefer to remain on good terms with the both of them. I shall have to be gentle, but firm.*

"No, Leigh," he told her quietly. "I have some catching-up to do, relative to the rest of your father's team, as I am so late arriving. I had in mind to return to the artefact tent and continue studying, well, everything that is available to study. Given my background as a consulting detective, the determination of a tomb site is a perfectly reasonable task."

"But..."

"Perhaps, after dinner, you, your father, and I, can repair to his tent and have a nice talk, get properly caught up on one another," Holmes suggested offhandedly. "It would hardly be proper for me to take you on an unchaperoned walk, in any event."

"Well, that's true..." Leighton admitted, considering. "At least until Da says it's all right."

"Exactly." Holmes quickly set his mind onto how to communicate delicately to Professor Whitesell that it was not "all right."

"Then perhaps some tea in the dining tent, at the end of the siesta break?"

"Ah," Holmes said, caught off guard, "perhaps."

"All right," Leighton lilted, happy. "I'll come fetch you for tea, then." She fairly danced off.

And I, Holmes thought, as he headed for the artefact tent, *will make sure to come back and fetch Watson first...*

*****

Holmes spent the rest of the early afternoon poring over the various items in the artefact tent, especially the maps. He located the entry log for the different relics, and tried to compare the locales where they were found to the maps, with some difficulty. There were no grease pencils that he could find — it was his experience that they tended to migrate into the dig fields and become lost, anyway — and he was loath to mark on the precious maps with anything else.

"I believe what I need to do," he mused to himself, "is to create my own map, which will position the various found items on it, as well as pertinent geologic and topographic features, and their relative relations to same. Then I may ruminate on it at my leisure, including in our tent in the evenings, over a pipe. I should fetch my sketch-pad from my trunk." He pulled his watch from his waistcoat pocket and checked it. "Mm. And it is high time I also fetched Watson, as well."

*****

"But Holmes, would she not be ideal for you?" Watson protested, as Holmes dug through his trunk in search of his sketching pad. "Surely you cannot really mean to remain single forever. She is intelligent, beautiful, her father fairly dotes on you..."

"You know my principles, Watson," floated up from the trunk's depths. "That is, in fact, precisely what I do intend. And I doubt the

Professor is looking to marry her off as yet, in any case. It is still some few years to her majority. Young woman she is, to be sure... but the emphasis is still upon *young*."

"Holmes...had you stopped to think about the seating arrangement at meals, and what it possibly implies, in this regard...?"

Holmes' dark head, hidden deep inside the trunk, suddenly popped up, almost cracking against the trunk lid, and he turned to gaze at Watson, grey eyes wide.

"Damnation," he said.

*****

"This will not do, Watson," a concerned Holmes told his friend, sitting on his cot opposite his companion. "I did not come all this way to be married off, like some witless, titled dandy."

"Careful, Holmes," Watson advised, *sotto voce*. "If Trenthume were to overhear, he might take offense."

"None was intended in that direction," Holmes replied. "But we both know the type of which I speak. Historically, there have even been a few in the extended royal family."

"True."

"And we both know I am not that type of man."

"Also true."

"This will take some thought," Holmes considered. "I do not wish to hurt Leigh, nor do I wish to insult the Professor, but..."

"I only wish I had your troubles," Watson grumbled. "I am most like to spend my time extracting splinters and treating bruises, blisters, and scrapes, not fending off the gentle advances of a beautiful woman."

"If you come with me to meet her for tea, I may see what I can arrange!"

"I've no objection, of course, but why do you need me to play gooseberry?"

"I don't NEED you, *per se*," Holmes allowed. "It simply makes matters easier. If there is someone else about, a trusted friend, say, Leigh is less likely to become as demonstrative as she might, otherwise. She was always an affectionate child, and I shudder to think, if we were alone..."

"But is she not a proper lady?" Watson asked, confused.

"Oh, she is a lady, never doubt that," Holmes vouched. "I did not mean to imply differently. But our previous relationship permits for a few more liberties than would otherwise be expected."

"How so?"

A reminiscent smile spread across Holmes' face at that.

"She was an adventurous, precocious youngster, adorable in her own way," he recalled. "And mischievous! The child Leigh delighted in pulling pranks. I had to watch my step around her, and no mistake! A very affectionate child, too — whenever I arrived at their house, I needs must brace myself against the hugs, or I risked being bowled over — you saw how she greeted me when we first arrived? Well, imagine that same greeting, hitting you about the knees! She fairly took the legs from under me once, shortly after I began working for the Professor. I landed on the floor like a thousand of brick, as the Americans say! She was intelligent, curious almost to a fault, and as devoted as any puppy. If she was around, I had a tiny, faithful shadow everywhere I went." He sighed. "But evidently she — and the Professor — expect to pick up the relationship where it left off...and possibly expand upon it. And at her age now, that is...perilous waters."

"Waters you'd rather not plumb."

"Exactly."

Watson sighed irritably and heaved himself to his feet.

"Well, grab your drawing pad and let us go, then," he fussed. "Else she will come looking for you and overhear, and then we WILL have a situation."

Holmes caught up the pad, and they hastened back to the artefact tent, where Holmes managed to complete a rough sketch of the area's topography before Leighton came looking for him for afternoon tea.

*****

Watson considerately buffered Leighton's affectionate nature from Holmes' reserved sensibilities, managing to hide his own disconsolation from the young woman, though he had his serious doubts about whether Holmes was fooled. Others came and went, taking tea before returning to the dig, and soon Whitesell, Beaumont, Phillips, and Nichols-Woodall arrived to escort Holmes back to work. Leighton promptly excused herself, returning to her tent.

Then Watson betook himself back to the tiny infirmary lean-to, alone.

As the group headed in the general direction of the artefact tent, the professor broke the silence.

"I have it to understand you'll be visiting us to-night, Holmes," Whitesell said with a knowing grin. At the back of the group, Phillips blinked, then scowled.

"Ah well, perhaps for a bit after dinner, Professor," Holmes replied, drawing into himself and replacing his normal demeanour with an outward austerity, polite but reserved. Whitesell blinked at the sudden change. "Leighton wanted us all to have a nice long chat to find out what we've been doing in the last few years, so I suggested after-dinner drinks in your tent." It wasn't precisely a falsehood, but it was stretching the truth a bit; still, Holmes never batted an eyelash.

"I...see," Whitesell said, brows drawing together in thought. "Then I shall break out the tantalus[31] and have it at the ready."

"Very good, sir."

"Will," Nichols-Woodall remarked at the door of the artefact tent, "after we perused the maps this morning, I'd like to suggest that perhaps it might behoove us to walk the site, and try to pick up some indications in the doing. In my experience, a bit of field work never hurt anything."

"Capital notion, old bean," Whitesell agreed immediately. "I'm for it. Phillips, you'll be joining us, of course. Make sure to bring a note-pad, and jot down anything we find of importance. Beaumont?"

"Yes, it is a good idea. I will of course attend."

"Holmes? You're the keen-eyed detective here. Will you be joining us in this little constitutional?"

Holmes pondered for a moment.

"No, Professor," he decided, "not this time, I think. I have my methods, and right now I feel I should spend a bit more time familiarising myself with the overall layout — the mountains, foothills, outcrops, stone varieties, the locations of the found relics — before venturing into the site itself. And that means studying the maps a little more. Do not worry; it should not take long. I will likely be able to go out with you all on the morrow."

"Very well, then, young man. You know what you are about," Whitesell said tolerantly. "Come along, Landers, Parker, Thomas. Where

---

31   Victorian liquor cabinet. Most had locks, and some were intended to be portable, as for picnics, camping and such.

did Cortland get to?"

"Oh, he went straight out to the dig pits," Nichols-Woodall remarked as the four departed, his voice diminishing into the distance. "Said something about wanting to find a..."

Holmes waited until they were well gone, then fetched the relic log, pulled out his sketch-pad, and resumed work. He did not stop until the warning gong sounded for the evening meal.

*****

Dinner followed the established pattern; Beaumont and Nichols-Woodall bickered, although it seemed to be less acrimonious than usual, and a nervous, uncomfortable Leighton attempted to divert the conversation from their argument to something more pleasant. Phillips said little, spending most of his time looking down at his food, and only answering if a question or comment was directed at him. He made a few sporadic attempts to converse with Leighton, but she did not encourage him; each time she gently cut him off, he shot a glare at Holmes before returning his attention to his meal. This did not escape Holmes' attention.

Phillips is jealous, he realised, *and not a little. But Leigh has not given me any indication that he has any right to be jealous. Perhaps I can dig into the matter a bit to-night. It will not do to inadvertently create some sort of...what are they called? "Love triangles"?* He sighed to himself. *Bad enough that Nichols-Woodall and Beaumont do not get along. If Leigh's intentions end up causing insult and offense with her, her father, AND her father's assistant, Heaven help us all.* Abruptly, what appetite he had departed him.

Holmes only nibbled at the rest of his meal.

*****

As Holmes, ever the gentleman, escorted Leighton through the darkness to her father's tent after dinner, carrying a small lantern, he broke the affable silence of old friends, but with diplomacy and as much tact as he could muster.

"Leigh," he began with some hesitation, "I noticed..."

"What?"

"Well, young Phillips. He seems rather...possessive...of you."

"Yes, it's a bit annoying," Leighton averred, revealing some pique. "He made some overtures to me, oh, six or eight months ago, and started trying to court me. I wasn't especially interested, and I tried to let him know as delicately as I could. He's Da's assistant, so I didn't want to make him angry or anything. But because he IS Da's assistant, he's over at the house all the time, and...well, he seems to either not take 'No' for an answer, or perhaps he just didn't understand that I wasn't particularly interested. So he kept on courting me."

"Did you know your father planned to invite me on the expedition?"

"He made some noises about it, yes," Leighton admitted. "I was positively thrilled when he told me."

"Did PHILLIPS know?"

"Well, of course he did."

"But did he know of our...previous...friendship?" Holmes pressed, watching her face intently.

"Um, no." Leighton turned a faint pink. "No, I didn't tell him that you and I knew each other...before."

"But why on earth not? Leigh," Holmes broke off the previous inquiry as an idea struck, "are you trying to use me as a shield from Phillips' attentions?"

"Um, well, maybe...maybe a little," she replied in a small voice.

"Are you afraid of him?"

"Not...exactly," Leighton confessed. "I don't think he would hurt me or anything. But...Sherry, you mustn't tell anyone I said this..."

"Of course not."

"...I'm not sure if he's courting me for my own self, or because I'm the Professor's daughter. Do you understand?"

"Mm. Yes, I do. And that is a consideration. Using you to curry favour with your father, possibly to become his heir..."

"Yes," Leighton said with a kind of sad nod. "And Da has done well for himself over the years, and neither he nor Mama came from a poor family to begin with. It... worries me."

"Has he given you reason to think it?"

"No, not exactly," Leighton admitted, shaking her head. "It's more… it's hard to explain. Sometimes… sometimes he seems more to be 'courting' Da than he does me, if you understand me."

"I do. But Leigh, your father is not only his advisor and teacher, he is Phillips' supervisor, as well. So he would naturally desire to curry favour with your father. And he is young; he seems inexperienced and a bit naïve to me, at least in some regards, and he may simply not be subtle enough to realise that the same... mm, methods... are not appropriate for both things."

"Well, maybe I AM misunderstanding him, but it... like I said, it worries me. So it was the only thing I could think of, to stay close to you. And of course I enjoy being around you anyway; you're smart, and fun, and, and I like you, and...Are...are you mad?"

Holmes drew a deep breath, thinking rapidly.

"No," he decided, "no, I am not angry, merely...this complicates things, Leigh," he pointed out. "I am also working for your father, and there is enough bad blood and enmity on the team as it is…"

"Yes. At the opposite end of the table, you mean."

"Precisely. I cannot afford to start some sort of war between Phillips and myself over you. And nor can your father afford it."

"I know, I just...don't know what else to do," Leighton sighed. "Landers may not like it, but he cannot gainsay the fact that you and I are old friends, and so he cannot protest..."

"Does your father know?"

"Yes and no. He knows that Landers asked to keep company with me, and that I was not overmuch inclined...but he does not really know that Landers has continued to pay me attentions. And, like you, I don't want to cause schisms between him and Da, so..."

"I see. Well, let me watch for a while, and try to ascertain which way the winds lie. Perhaps there is something I can do to resolve your problem for you."

"Oh, thank you, Sherry!" And she leaned up and deposited a spontaneous, enthusiastic kiss on his cheek, much as she had been wont to do as a child. He instinctively pulled away a bit from the contact, but despite himself, Holmes smiled slightly at the reminiscence.

At the end of the row of temporary dwellings, hidden in the darkness and well out of earshot, Landers Phillips peered around the end of a tent at the couple, and scowled.

*****

"Well, well, young man, it's good to have you back in my 'house' again, even if the walls and roof are only canvas," Professor Whitesell said after a lively chat among the three old friends had wound down.

"It is good to be back, Professor," Holmes offered. "It has been too long, I suppose. But then, we have both been busy...and Leigh has been busy in her own way, growing up." Leighton smiled.

"How are your parents?" Whitesell asked. Leighton rose casually and fetched a platter of dainty biscuits, surreptitiously watching the exchange, careful to remain silent.

"I...don't know." Holmes leaned forward, catching up the brandy decanter and topping off his drink, by way of averting his face. "Well, I suppose, judging by their last letter."

"Have you been home recently?"

"...No."

"Why not?"

"You know why."

"Still? After all this time?"

Holmes shook his head, sitting back. "Until very Hell itself freezes over."

"You could take him to task now, you know. A sound thrashing comes to mind."

"I could, but what would be the point? It would not make matters any more congenial, nor my welcome any more favourable. And it certainly would not help...them."

"True, I suppose." Whitesell paused, studying the aquiline face half-hidden behind the brandy snifter, as Leighton sat the tray of assorted biscuits in front of them, then resumed her seat. "So, tell me: How much of what your friend Dr. Watson writes, in those stories about your adventures, is true?"

"Ah. Now THAT," Holmes chuckled, setting down his glass and leaning forward again, elbows on his knees, "depends upon to whom you are speaking, I suppose..."

*****

Some hour and a half later, after a relatively congenial evening spent in Professor Whitesell's tent, a tired Holmes — who had had to be alert to project his desired message, while subtly negating Leighton's, the whole time — departed for the tent he shared with Watson. Leighton saw him off at the door of the tent, then tidied away the glassware as her father nursed the last of his brandy, watching her thoughtfully.

"Leighton," he began, "are you and Holmes getting along well?"

"Why, yes, Da, why would you think otherwise?" Leighton wondered, depositing the last of the glassware into the bin to be taken to the kitchens and washed the next morning.

"Oh, I don't know," he pondered, thinking over Holmes' behaviour through the course of the evening, and what Whitesell took to have been unspoken messages the sleuth had telegraphed him. "He just seemed rather...reserved." He paused. "Leigh, my darling girl, I know you have hopes in that direction, but..."

*****

"Well, Da," she said with a smile, carefully avoiding the topic of Phillips lest she cause inadvertent hostilities between her father and his *aide-de-camp*, "Sherry DID ask if I was keeping company with anyone else, when he walked me over here after dinner."

"He did? Well, I stand corrected, then," Whitesell told his daughter. "Perhaps I misunderstood his behaviour. Nothing could please me more, you know; Holmes is a fine young man. Let me know how I may facilitate the relationship. But Leigh..."

"Yes, Da?"

"He was right, to-day: he DOES have work to do, important work. I don't mind you keeping company with him, but under no circumstances will I stand for your distracting him from that work — at least, any more so than the normal vagaries of love are wont to distracting young people the world over. The university AND Lord Trenthume are paying him well for his troubles, and should you cause him to fail to perform up to expectations, the ramifications could be awkward, at the least, and distressing, at worst. It could even cause me to lose all future financing for expeditions."

"Oh! Very well, Da. I understand. I'm sorry."

"Quite all right, dear. Now," he said, rising and placing his empty glass in the bin with the rest, "off to your own tent and to bed with you."

"Okay. Good night, Da." And she kissed him on the cheek before leaving.

He stood at the door of the tent, thoughtfully watching her go.

*****

"...No, Watson, I am quite sure, by the look in his eye, that Professor Whitesell took my meaning, subtle as it was," Holmes asserted. "He and I communicated well back in the day, sometimes able to use little unspoken codes here and there, when in the midst of a delicate negotiation with locals, and I plainly saw the moment when he comprehended."

"But the lady?"

"I am assured that the lady has her reasons," Holmes stated. "I should normally tell you, but I am unwilling to breach her confidence, in the circumstances."

"Perfectly understandable, I suppose," Watson said, hiding a sigh. "But Holmes, if you are desirous of avoiding romantic entanglements..."

"Very much so."

"...Then you should still be careful," Watson recommended. "Miss Whitesell holds you in high regard, and with great affection. Even if she does not mean to, and I am not altogether convinced of that, it would still be entirely too easy for such affection to turn to...something more. I have seen it happen in more than one instance. And that could be..."

"Catastrophic," Holmes finished for him, worried. "I know, my dear fellow. She is...still too young for such matters, in my opinion. But for the sake of the child I knew, I would not hurt her for the world." He sighed. "Damnation, Watson! Why must there always be such deep intrigue surrounding women?!"

"Sometimes, Holmes, I think that it is less the women, and more our culture, which creates the intrigue," a rueful Watson offered. "Were our society as a whole less reticent, there might be less artifice surrounding courtship and the opposite sex."

"Perhaps. But we do not have such a society, so we are forced to plod ahead through the mire," Holmes complained.

"I still say I should love to have your problems, old chap."

"So you are interested in her, then?"

"I...find her very attractive," Watson confessed, as circumspect as he knew how to be, yet still give his friend an honest answer. "But Holmes, if you DO...care for her, in...that fashion, I should never..."

"I do not, nor will not, my friend," Holmes said with certainty, leaning forward and resting his hand on Watson's shoulder. "If I can find a way to divert her attentions to you, it may well be the solution to all our difficulties."

"Then may all our difficulties be less complicated than the favour of a woman," Watson declaimed.

"Amen to that," Holmes replied, fervent.

CHAPTER 4
THE CURSE RISES

"Oh, Holmes, come have a look at this," Phillips called as Holmes entered the artefact tent after breakfast the next morning — alone this time, to his relief. "We found this several days before your arrival, but Professor Whitesell wanted to wait for translation efforts until you arrived. There are a couple more over there, but they aren't in very good shape, and I think we will have to do some work on them before you can translate those...if they ever reach the point where they are translatable. But I was supposed to bring this one to your attention right off, only it slipped my mind in the flurry of your and Dr. Watson's advent."

"Indeed," Beaumont affirmed, as Holmes walked over to Phillips. "It looks to be very interesting, based on what little I could make out; I am not especially adept at the hieroglyphics. But you are quite the ancient script expert, I have it to understand, *mon ami*."

"I have certainly made a thorough study of such matters as ancient scripts and texts," Holmes admitted, "though 'expert' is perhaps overstating the case, at least at this point in my career. Nevertheless, I am confident I should be able to do well by the archaeological team."

"Then sit down and get started, man!" an enthusiastic Phillips recommended, though Holmes detected some challenge in the younger man's tone and demeanour. "We'll work around you. And sing out if you see anything about Ka or Sekhen!"

*****

Holmes spent the rest of the day studying the inscribed stone tablet, producing a small pad and scribbling notes. He never noticed when the others departed at the sound of the luncheon bell, nor when Leighton came — and went, thoroughly discouraged from bothering, or so much as speaking to, Holmes by the other members of the archaeological team — though to her credit, she seemed to realise the need on her own. As the sun sank lower in the west and dinnertime neared, Professor Whitesell, who had arrived at the tent mid-afternoon and worked with the others on organising and cataloguing their finds, started toward Holmes with obvious intent. But Phillips stepped in front of the archaeologist, blocking his way, and both Beaumont and Nichols-Woodall caught his shoulders.

"Leave him be, old chap," Beaumont murmured.

"But dinner," Whitesell began.

"Can wait," Nichols-Woodall said in an undertone. "Look at him, Willingham. He is deep into the translation, and disturbing him now will only impede his train of thought."

"And it might be wise," Beaumont added as an afterthought, "if you keep your daughter from fetching him to dinner, or after dinner. Though I did note that she seemed to understand and approve Holmes' absorption, earlier. Still, it would not do to distract him at this time." Phillips glowered at that.

"Good point," Whitesell rumbled to himself. "All right. We may make the occasional exception to the rule, in the circumstances, I suppose. I'll just have the kitchen take a tray to his tent afterward, perhaps."

"Capital idea," Nichols-Woodall determined. "That way, he may eat at his leisure, when he has come to a stopping-place."

"Come, Professor, let's all slip out and let him work," Phillips suggested in an undertone. "I'll be sure to let Dr. Watson know where he is, so he won't worry. And I'll take charge of keeping Leigh occupied, so she won't interrupt him."

"Good man," Whitesell whispered, clapping him soundlessly on the shoulder, and they all decamped — silently — for the dinner tent.

*****

It was well after dark before Holmes came back to the tent. Watson sat in the corner, reading a book, and looked up when he came in, prepared to point out the covered dish awaiting him, which Professor Whitesell had insisted upon; seeing the preoccupied expression on his friend's face, he chose to say nothing instead, and simply watched. Holmes moved to the rear of the tent and laid a dark grey stone tablet, roughly twice the size of a sheet of telegraph flimsy in area and some inch to inch and a half thick, on the small table in the back of the tent, placing his note-pad next to it. Then the sleuth went to one of his trunks, opened it, and rummaged inside, extracting his microscope from its packing, as well as several items of chemical apparatus. These went on the folding table next to the inscribed stone. Holmes pulled a camp stool up to the table and extracted his jack-knife from a pocket, unfolding it. Watson decided that might be a good sign to interject a cautionary statement at the detective's apparent intent.

"Holmes? Should you risk damaging it?"

"I must," Holmes said, looking up. "There is something not right here. Don't worry, I shall be careful. Such testing as I intend is sometimes done, at any rate, to...verify matters."

Tearing out a sheet of paper from the note-pad, he laid it on the table, then raised the stone. Delicately wielding the razor-sharp jack-knife against the back corner edge of the tablet, he shaved off a small bit of the relatively soft, dark stone onto the paper. Then he extracted a magnifying lens from his waistcoat pocket and studied the cut edge for several moments before turning back to Watson.

"Watson, I need your help. Would you mind...?"

Watson rose without hesitation and moved to Holmes' side. "What do you need, old fellow?"

"This will be a bit awkward. I need you to hold this slate with the cut bit under my microscope's object glass. But let me move it and adjust the positioning. It is obviously far too big for the slide platform, and it would be deucedly cumbersome to try to hold it myself while still using the microscope."

"Oh, yes, quite. Let me see, here."

Watson gingerly took the tablet, located the tiny mar Holmes' knife had produced, and eased it under the microscope's objective lens as Holmes bent to the eyepiece, adjusting the focus. Holmes grunted, and without raising his head, reached out and shifted Watson's hand positioning ever so slightly, before tweaking the focal knobs again. Then Holmes grew silent and still, studying the view through the microscope for long minutes, while Watson held the stone slab as steady as he possibly could. Finally Holmes raised his head.

"Thank you, Watson, you make a fine sample stand." He shot his friend a slight smile of appreciation, and Watson chuckled, setting down the tablet. "Now for the other."

Holmes picked up the paper containing the shavings and upended it over a ceramic mortar, dumping them inside. He ground them down to a fine powder with energetic application of the pestle, then extracted only a couple of drops of some sort of reagent with a pipette, dribbling it into the mortar on top of the powder. He stirred the mixture with the tip of a glass rod, and Watson briefly wondered how he had managed to so pack such delicate equipment that it had arrived all the way in Egypt with no breakage. Another pipette went into another reagent bottle, and the contents dropped into the mortar; the glass rod stirred, and the detective pondered the results again. He extracted a glass microscopic slide, fished out a bit of the solution on the tip of the glass stirring rod, and smeared it across the slide; put on a glass slide cover, and placed it under the microscope, studying the magnified image for long moments. Finally Holmes returned his attention to his friend.

"This is bad, Watson, and I find I am uncertain how to proceed," he admitted. "I intend to smoke for a goodly time to-night while I consider the matter, so be forewarned."

"Well, it should produce a less-thick atmosphere in a tent than in our flat at home!" Watson laughed. "Especially if I tie the tent flaps back. And you can eat that, at some point," he added, pointing at the tray of food. "Would it also help to discuss it?"

"It might. Are you offering your ear?"

"I am."

"Capital. Do you sit down and let me tell you what is afoot, whilst I light my pipe. The food can wait."

"Very well."

Both men fetched pipes and tobacco, packing and lighting those items, as Holmes composed his thoughts. They slouched companionably on their cots facing each other, and Holmes began.

"I was rather enthusiastically asked to examine and translate that," he waved his pipe at the slate on the table, "this morning, it having been evidently discovered perhaps some two or three days before our arrival here. I spent all day studying it, though it did not take so long to actually translate it. For when the others stepped out at luncheon, I checked the log of found relics, and ascertained it had been ostensibly discovered by Dr. Thomas Beaumont on the said date, though the log did not detail the location of the find. This is sometimes an oversight, however, and so I inspected both log and artefact most thoroughly, for it was an... interesting...relic. It appeared to be possibly some stonemason's practise tablet, created before inscribing the actual engraving, for it did not have the usual accuracy of a true inscription, and sometimes such things are in fact found, where the writing was exceptionally complex and the circumstances did not bear mistakes being made in the engraving. Sometimes it even amounts, apparently, to what the engraver WISHES he could write, for not all of them are...ah, shall we say, of a delicate nature. Some are quite crude, to say the least."

"Very well. Go on."

"And so I translated this one, and it reads as follows." He extracted his note-pad again, flipped to a heavily-scribbled page, and read.

> *"'Death shall come on swift wings to him who disturbs the peace of the Pharaoh Sekhen. Curséd be he! They that shall break the seal of this tomb shall meet death by a disease that no physician can diagnose nor cure. I shall cast my fear into him; there will be fierce judgement, and an end shall be made of him. He shall descend in torment to Anubis at a time he does not expect.'"*

"Mm," Watson murmured, in some disquiet. "A pharaoh's curse, to protect his body, his mummy."

"So it would sound, does it not?" Holmes agreed. "But there is a problem. Several, actually."

"What, then?"

"The writing style is wrong, for one."

"What do you mean?"

"I mean, Watson," here Holmes leaned forward, gaze sharp and keen, "that it is the wrong form of hieroglyphics. Just as our modern Roman script is different from that of, say, two or three centuries ago, so too did hieroglyphics change over the course of ancient Egypt's millennia-long history. This," he tapped a long finger on the tablet, "is Middle Kingdom script. But the inscription plainly invokes the pre-dynastic Sekhen, so the script SHOULD be what some are now calling 'proto-hieroglyphics,' not the fully-developed form, let alone the sophistication of the Middle Kingdom. It should be much more crude, Watson. It is not right."

Watson drew deeply on his pipe, then exhaled the smoke through his pursed lips, taking in the information and considering it. Finally he nodded. "Very well. Go ahead. You have something else, it sounds like."

"I do," Holmes conceded. "That is why I had to slightly damage the corner of the tablet. Here." He rose and fetched the slate and his magnifying lens, offering them to Watson. "Do you study the cut I made, and tell me what YOU see." Watson took the proffered items and did as Holmes suggested.

"It is a fresh cut," he observed. "The stone is lighter there."

"Yes, of course; you saw me make it. Look closer."

Watson did.

"Hm. There is a...a rind around the edge," he noted.

"Indeed. That is normal; it would ordinarily denote weathering, both physical and chemical, of the outer layers of stone by the elements," Holmes instructed. "But do you see anything unusual about it?"

"It seems remarkably sharp-edged in its end, within the rock," Watson decided after a few more moments' study.

"Precisely! Very good eye, Watson! You can see it much more clearly under the microscope, of course; there can be no doubt, in that view. Whereas Nature would normally produce a more gradual, less even tapering of the weathered stone, this is uniform, and quite abrupt in its ending."

"But what does it mean?"

"It means the stone has been soaked in something for a limited time, and recently," Holmes explained. "Were it older, the material would have slowly migrated within the stone, and produced more blurring of the boundary. The sharp delineation shows its newness, and marks how far the liquid penetrated. Which is why I then performed a few chemical tests upon the scrapings."

"And?"

"The slate has been washed with acid," Holmes revealed, "most likely acetic acid. This would lightly etch the stone and increase its porosity. And then..."

"Then?"

"Watson," Holmes began, lips twitching, "someone soaked that bloody damned rock in black tea!"

"WHAT?!" Watson exclaimed. "You're joshing!"

"Not in the least," Holmes replied, and both men doubled over in laughter.

*****

"But what was the point, Holmes?" Watson demanded to know, when they managed to sober at last.

"There can only admit to one reason," Holmes declared. "As I said earlier, the acetic acid — easily obtained from vinegar — would lightly etch the surface and make the outer layers of the stone very slightly more porous. Then the tea would be able to soak into the stone and dye it a darker shade."

"But WHY?"

"Think for a moment, Watson. If you had just carved an inscription into a block of stone, what would it look like? The letters, I mean."

"They..." Watson hesitated, and Holmes saw approaching comprehension in his eyes, "would be lighter in colour than the rest of the stone. Just as when you cut the corner of it." He pointed at the tablet to provide antecedent.

"Exactly. And if you wanted to make it appear aged?"

"I would wash it...or soak it...with a dye, to darken the letters," Watson sighed, leaning back. "The thing is a ruddy forgery, from start to finish."

"It is. And the probability is that Beaumont, the ostensible 'discoverer,' is the perpetrator of the forgery. The more so, as he did not record the location of his find."

"But why would he do it? He is part of the expedition!"

"Ah, but only this first time," Holmes pointed out. "It is my understanding that, until he approached Professor Whitesell with something of an olive branch in late summer, they were in fact so competitive as to be unpleasantly acrimonious. You have seen the animosity between him and Dr. Nichols-Woodall, who has long been a respected member of Professor Whitesell's team." Holmes paused, then added, "Moreover, he has spent most of his expeditions in recent years in Western Hemisphere rainforests, not in Egypt. He is not up on his hieroglyphics. And so he erred in his linguistics, by using a much later version of the ancient Egyptian 'letters' than were appropriate for Pharaoh Ka-Sekhen."

"I see. So your dilemma is...?"

Holmes sighed.

"What to do with that knowledge," he admitted.

*****

The pair quietly discussed the situation until late into the night, clear through Holmes' dinner, even after retiring, and finally came up with a reasonable plan. So in the morning after breakfast, Holmes subtly drew Professor Whitesell aside.

"What is it, Holmes?" Whitesell wondered a few moments later, from the sanctuary of his private tent.

"It...is about the stone tablet Dr. Beaumont found," Holmes began.

"Oh, excellent! Did you get it translated?"

"I did. But—"

"Let's hear it, then! What does it say?"

"It is a curse, and translates to, *'Death shall come on swift wings to him who disturbs the peace of the Pharaoh Sekhen. Curséd be he! They that shall break the seal of this tomb shall meet death by a disease that no physician can diagnose nor cure. I shall cast my fear into him; there will be fierce judgement, and an end shall be made of him. He shall descend in torment to Anubis at a time he does not expect.'*" Holmes paused, then added, "But I do not think—"

Just then Udail entered.

"Professor," the foreman began, "I — oh, I am sorry, Mr. Holmes. I heard voices, but I thought it was only Mr. Phillips, and...Forgive me! I will come back." And he began to bow out of the tent.

"No, no, Udail, what is the matter?" Whitesell asked, for the Egyptian was uncommonly pale.

"The carbide lamps have finally arrived, Professor, and the supplies master — ah, the quartermaster, rather, forgive my rusty English — wished to know where you would like them kept."

"Ah, very good. Tell the quartermaster that I shall come by shortly, once Mr. Holmes and I have finished."

"It shall be done, Professor." Udail bowed again. "Mr. Holmes?"

"Yes, Udail?"

"Does it make you fear?"

"What?"

"The curse."

Holmes bit his lip, realising the man had evidently overheard him quote the inscription just before coming in. "No, Udail, it does not," he replied, as calm as he knew how to be. "I can assure you, there is absolutely nothing to fear here."

Udail bowed, a look of scepticism on his sun-bronzed face, and left.

"Well, that was ill-timed," Whitesell grumbled, and Holmes grasped that the archaeologist also understood the significance of Udail's reaction. "Udail is a good man, and an excellent foreman for the archaeological work, very knowledgeable, but inclined to be somewhat superstitious, and a bit of a gossip. The news of the curse will be all over the dig site by sundown, if not sooner. Along with his fear of it."

"Damnation," Holmes expostulated. "And it is totally unnecessary that the workers should fear, for the entire 'artefact' is a fake."

"What?!"

"It is a forgery, without doubt," Holmes reiterated, and proceeded to explain the chain of clews and deductions which proved the matter; having brought the slate with him, he was able to show the professor several of the clews directly. At the end of the tale, Whitesell sat back in his chair with a frown.

"But why would Dr. Beaumont do such a thing?" he wondered.

"It could well be a somewhat puerile prank, I suppose," Holmes offered, "but..."

"But what? Go ahead, Holmes, tell me the worst."

"Very well. It is my understanding that your team and his have been in, mm, some mildly antagonistic competition, for the last several years?" Holmes delicately broached the subject.

"Rather a bit, yes," Whitesell confessed, mildly abashed by the admission. "But I thought the hatchet buried when he approached me about the dig back in the summer. I had sent him something of a peace offering in the spring, so..."

"Do you know if his own team is still working anywhere?" Holmes queried.

"I...don't THINK so," Whitesell responded, uncertain. "I'm fairly sure not...but I cannot say for certain."

"If they are, it may be that he intends to delay your operation in order that his might obtain a 'scoop,' as the American newspapermen say. A sufficiently large discovery might well eclipse yours in the newspapers and scientific journals. It would also," Holmes continued, "explain a few things like the various delays we experienced, and some of your missing equipment."

"Delays? What do you mean?" Whitesell wondered.

So Holmes sat down and sketched out the entire sequence of delaying tactics he and Watson had experienced, from the invitational letter held up in post right down to the contaminated food for the caravan.

"It's just possible, I suppose." Whitesell looked up at Holmes, expression blank. "And you think that the missing hospital tent, medical equipment, carbide lanterns, and the like, are simply more evidence of the same?" the professor confirmed.

"I do," Holmes averred. "Someone does not want this team to find Ka-Sekhen's tomb. For reasons unknown, at least so far. And Beaumont is as likely a suspect as any."

"Well..." Whitesell broke off.

"'Well' what?"

"Nichols-Woodall and I had a spat earlier in the year," the archaeologist admitted. "It was bad enough that he initially signed on with another expedition...until he heard that Beaumont was coming. Then he resigned from that expedition, and made nice with me."

"So Nichols-Woodall is a suspect, as well."

"Yes, but he knows little of hieroglyphics."

"That still does not eliminate him," Holmes pointed out. "It is not an especially skilful job. He may have copied bits out of textbooks on the subject."

"True."

"Are there any other suspects? Is Lord Trenthume focussed on your expedition, for example? Mr. Phillips?"

"Phillips hasn't the contacts to do something like all this," Whitesell averred. "Perhaps the tablet, but not the rest. And he'd have a hard time hiding even that from me."

"I thought as much, but it does not hurt to ask. And Trenthume?"

"Cortland has indeed branched out in recent years," Whitesell admitted. "He is quite wealthy and adores archaeological digs. As between us," Whitesell paused and glanced around. They both listened carefully, and Holmes tiptoed to the tent flap to glance outside.

"We are alone," he murmured, returning to his seat. "You may continue, Professor."

"Um, yes, well, as between us, he is far from the sharpest knife in the drawer — though, knowing you, you have probably already noticed..."

"Indeed."

"Still, he's started financing other expeditions. And takes turn-about attending them," Whitesell informed the detective. "Insofar as I can tell, he seems to think it makes him a dashing figure with the ladies. Leighton tells me it just makes him look silly, but from my experience, not all women agree with her. And as he has yet to marry and produce an heir..."

"Ah. I see. So an important discovery makes him appear more important, hence a more desirable, eligible bachelor..."

"Precisely."

"Of these three, then," Holmes pondered, "which do you think most likely to perpetrate all these things?"

"I shouldn't think it would be Parker," Whitesell protested. "We quite made up our disagreement, I thought. And Cortland surely does not have the wit for such a complex plot...if plot it is."

"True," Holmes murmured. "The circumstantial evidence does seem to point to Beaumont."

"Yes."

"But it is just that — circumstantial."

"True, but still. What should I do? I cannot just throw him off the site! It would hardly be diplomatic."

"My advice would be to say nothing as yet, Professor," Holmes advised after a few seconds to consider. "Give me some time to observe, to look into matters, and try to adjudge what is going on, to the best of my abilities. I will keep you closely apprised of my findings, and perhaps in a few days, we may have somewhat to direct us."

Whitesell gazed at him thoughtfully for a long moment, pondering the matter, then nodded. "All right, Holmes. I'll look to you to tell me what's going on, and what to do about it, once you find out."

"To start, then, do you slip into the village, to the telegraph office, and send a wire to your colleagues back in London. Ask if Beaumont's own team is active elsewhere."

"Well, I will, then."

Holmes left the tent, determined to spend the day surreptitiously observing the entire dig team.

*****

With nothing else on hand to translate, as the other inscription fragments were not in a condition to be read, Holmes spent the day wandering the archaeological site, familiarising himself with the terrain, mentally comparing it with the maps he had memorised, and keeping an eye on the various actors. It was easy to see rumour of the curse spreading amongst the diggers, as Udail made his rounds; easy to see, too, that the workers became uncomfortable with the purported knowledge of said "curse." Holmes began to worry that it could cause more difficulties than merely slowing down the dig.

"It may," he told Watson in their tent after lunch, "end up shutting it down."

"No! Of course not! You cannot think so, old chap," Watson protested. Holmes shook his head.

"But I do. If enough workers become fearful, too fearful to continue, there will not be enough manpower to go on."

"Then we will simply hire more workers."

"And what will happen to these other potential workers, Watson, as soon as the current workers reach their homes and tell all their friends, relatives, and neighbours that the tomb is cursed, and it is a diabolical death merely to work on it?"

"Dear God, Holmes. Surely not."

"I cannot risk it, my dear Watson. For Professor Whitesell's sake, I MUST find out what is going on, and put a stop to it, post-haste."

*****

"I noticed that neither Beaumont nor Phillips came in for lunch to-day," Watson volunteered, after several moments of silence. "You don't suppose..."

"No, Beaumont was in the artefact tent, cataloguing several — legitimate — finds from this morning, and Phillips was in one of the pits where the workers found a large pot. He is endeavouring to extract it entire, without damage. It is heavily decorated, and he and the Professor think it may relate to Ka-Sekhen's tomb, so it is important it should emerge as unscathed as is practicable. And he did not wish to leave it over luncheon, lest its weight, without the support of the surrounding soil, should cause it to fracture. I believe I overheard Udail remarking that Beaumont went to help on that task, when once he was finished cataloguing."

"And Professor Whitesell? Is he upset over this scandalous matter?"

"He is, quite a good bit actually, but is carrying on with the proverbial stiff upper lip," Holmes said, offering a small, fond smile with the statement. "He has been over at least half the site already to-day, I would swear to it. The quartermaster, the artefact tent, the pit where Phillips is working, debating locations with Nichols-Woodall, simply everywhere. And I suspect that it is to distract his mind from worry over this whole affair. And all that after a swift trip to the telegraph office right after I spoke with him."

"Great Scot! He may be our elder by several decades, but it does not seem to have slowed him in the least."

"No, not at all."

"Sheeerry! SHERRY!" came a call from without, and Holmes stifled a groan.

"Oh no! Not now. Not when I have so much on my mind. It will not do. Watson," he murmured, "do you suppose I can slip out through the back tent seam without being seen?"

"No, it's lashed down far too well," Watson hissed, trying hard to refrain from imprudent laughter. "You know, Holmes, most men would give a body part to be in your position with that beautiful girl."

"I am NOT 'most men,' and I find it very annoying," Holmes protested, drawing himself up. "Were she to actually discuss anything of import, it might be less irritating, but I am either forced to reminisce interminably, or to remark on — or endure — seemingly endless 'romantic' vistas, or images, or some concept or other she has taken into her head about Pharaonic Egypt which I then must explain away, or such similar drivel. We have long since 'caught each other up,' as it were, and there seems to be little else to discuss — at least, of anything I find interesting. I have tried to inject some seriousness into the conversations, for I know she has the brains for it, but it seems hopeless; she is at that age where she is uninterested in more austere matters, which she considers dull and boring. No, she is all about sentiment, and flights of fancy, and romance, and such tripe. Ah well. I had hoped to spend the siesta time pondering the clews to this puzzle, but it seems not to be. So I suppose I may as well face the Gorgon."

"Holmes!" Watson remonstrated. "How could you insult that enchanting creature so! And you call yourself her friend!"

"I am her friend," came the counter-argument. "I am simply not her pet toy poodle."

"Um, well...Ah! I have it, then!" Watson said, spinning to the table with his medical equipment. "Quickly! Remove your waistcoat, undo your collar-ends, shuck off your braces, muss your hair, and lie down on your cot!"

"What?"

"Just do it! Hurry! Listen — she's headed this way!"

Without further ado, Holmes obeyed, even daring to unfasten the top few buttons of his shirt for good measure. Watson dragged one of the camp stools to Holmes' bedside, placed his open medical bag on the canvas floor at his feet, and extracted a jar of petroleum jelly. He smeared a thin film of the stuff across Holmes' upper lip and over his forehead, dropped the jar back into his bag, then grabbed a washcloth and the pitcher of water from the washbasin, saturating the cloth, wringing out only a little of the excess before running it across Holmes' face. Then, to Holmes' intense startlement, Watson wrung out most of the water...across the detective's prostrate chest. Holmes gasped in shock and flung his arms out, for the water was cooler than his body temperature... just as Watson completed the ruse by slapping the wet cloth into both of Holmes' armpits, thoroughly soaking his shirt and taking his breath away at the same time.

"Watson! What are you doing?!" Holmes whispered, when he could catch his breath; Leighton's calls were just down the row of tents now. Watson grabbed one of Holmes' feet, dragging it off the cot, to dangle awkwardly a few inches above the canvas floor.

"Hush, close your eyes, and follow my lead! Here she comes!"

"Sherry? Dr. Watson? Are you inside? May I come in?" came the soft hail from without.

"Come in, Miss Whitesell," Watson called in a low voice, "but please, do be quiet."

The tent flap was pushed back, and Leighton entered. She stopped dead, hands flying to her mouth in distress, as she saw the tableau within: an apparently unconscious Holmes, sprawled across his cot, half-undressed, his shirt soaked with what appeared to be perspiration, moisture heavily beaded on his brow and lip, while Watson sat beside him with his medical kit, gently sponging him down with a wet cloth.

"Dr. Watson! What's wrong?! Is Sherry ill?"

"Not too badly, I think," Watson soothed, mopping Holmes' beaded brow with the damp washcloth. "You may have seen him exploring the site this morning, learning his way around a bit better? I think perhaps he may have been trying to learn the grid off by heart...he mentioned something this morning..."

"Yes?"

"Well, I'm afraid he might have got a little overheated," Watson said, only avoiding lying through his teeth by the narrowest of margins and considerable circumlocution. "He appears to have a touch of heat prostration. A cool down, a quart or so of water in him — I TOLD you to take your canteen," he broke off to tell an inert Holmes sternly, "and he'll be fine. If he behaves, I MIGHT let him out again this afternoon, after the siesta — provided he wears his topee, takes at least one canteen full of water and DRINKS from it...and perhaps a moist bandanna, worn about the throat."

"Oh DEAR!" Leighton exclaimed, horrified. "Is he awake?"

"Mmh," Holmes groaned just then, before continuing in a whisper. "Oh, my head. Yes, Leigh, I am awake. Please keep your voice down.

My head..."

"You could be verging on a migraine," Watson scolded. "And no wonder. Am I going to have to follow you around to insist you carry your canteen and use it? You have experience here; I'd have thought you knew better."

"It has...been several years...Watson. One never...forgets how to... ride the bicycle, but...one can get...rusty."

"Oh, you poor thing," Leighton said, in her softest tone. "Don't you worry one whit, Sherry. I'll go tell Da you need to stay in here this afternoon and get well."

"NO!" Holmes cried, lunging upward; Watson immediately splayed his hand across the sleuth's chest and pressed down hard, keeping him prone. Holmes promptly clutched his head and slumped. "No, Leigh, don't do that. I had...rather he...didn't know."

"Ohhhh," Leighton said, in understanding — as she thought. "I see. It would embarrass you in front of Da and the others. Yes, I understand. Um, what shall we tell Da, then, if he notices you're missing?"

"Tell him that, um...that Holmes decided to come back to the tent, to mull over potential clews to, uh, to the tomb's location," Watson suggested, after a moment's thought.

"Yes," Holmes agreed. "Yes, that would do very well, Leigh. Tell him that. But only if he asks. I have no doubt I shall be out and about in an hour or so, with Watson tending me, here. So he may not even miss me."

"All right. Is there anything I can do to help?"

"No, Miss Whitesell," Watson declared. "In fact, I shall have to ask you to leave, and tie the tent flap closed behind you, if you would be so kind. You see, I plan to remove some more of Holmes' garments and apply cool compresses, and it would not do for you to remain."

"Oh!" She blushed furiously. "Of course! I'll just slip out then. Feel better, Sherry! Do take good care of him, Doctor!"

And she was gone, tying the tent flap behind her.

*****

The two men waited until the pattering sound of her footsteps faded into silence, then Holmes sat up, and they both doubled over with laughter, carefully stifled lest she return.

"You...you owe me for that, Holmes!" Watson gasped, before burying his red face in his pillow to muffle his laughter.

"I do, you rascal!" Holmes agreed, practically convulsed with silent laughter. "A prettier improvised plan I could not have devised! The mineral jelly not only appeared to be a film of sweat, it made the water bead up! Where did you get that trick?"

"From you, of course! Where do you think I learned it all? I have paid attention whenever you have disguised yourself, you know!"

"Capital, my dear Watson, positively capital!"

And they doubled over again.

*****

By the time Holmes had stripped off his sodden shirt and vest, dried off, cleansed away the petroleum jelly, and dressed in clean, dry clothing, he and Watson judged that enough time had passed for him to venture forth once more, and he had indeed had occasion to ponder the situation in which the expedition collectively found itself. This time, however, when he left the tent he not only wore his pith helmet, he wrapped one of Watson's bandannas about his throat, and took TWO full canteens — his own and Watson's — slung bandolier-style across his chest.

"Seriously, Holmes, it really isn't going to hurt to take in a bit more water, in this environment," Watson offered, as he handed Holmes his own canteen, back in the tent. "You're entirely too prone to not eating or drinking when you are working, and that simply won't do, here. Professor Whitesell has asked me to maintain 'surgery hours' at certain times of day in the tent, meaning I am stuck here for the rest of the afternoon in any case, so take my canteen too. I'll have one of my nurses fetch a fresh pitcherful from the water butt, so I shall be just fine."

"Fair enough, Watson," Holmes agreed mildly, adjusting the strap across his chest. "I suppose if Leigh starts in again, I can always begin sending her off with alternate canteens to bring me water. I may well float away in that event, however."

"Which will not hurt in the least. Um, does she have any nursing skill?"

"Why, would you like for me to send her here, to help you?"

"It...was a thought."

"She is quite comely, isn't she?"

"Oh, yes, very comely," Watson admitted fervently without thinking, then caught himself. Holmes was grinning at him like a Cheshire cat. "I, uh, I mean..."

"Never mind, Watson. I shall most certainly send her to you as a nursing assistant."

And he was gone, leaving behind a chagrined young physician.

*****

Holmes watched the archaeologists and their workers the rest of the afternoon, but saw nothing of any consequence that he could determine. Phillips and Beaumont finally finished extracting the pottery jar, and Cortland came around to help them fetch it out of the pit, as it was quite large and heavy — and moreover, in one piece, well-decorated over most of its surface, and apparently of the proper age to date to Pharaoh Sekhen's reign. Whitesell and Nichols-Woodall prowled the base of the mountain, where a scarp rose up for more than a hundred feet; from time to time, one or the other would point here or there, so Holmes decided they were discussing possible tomb sites. And despite the detective's fears, Udail kept the local workers going, screening the sand for small items and digging pits in hopes of finding larger items. The slowing of the work, however, was noticeable even to Holmes, who had not been there more than a scant few days. He drew a long, slim finger thoughtfully across his perspiring forehead; the moisture reminded him of Watson's injunction, and he brought up one of the canteens and took a long, cool drink from it.

Leighton did find him, and hovered near for a while, until Holmes expressed mild discomfiture over the possibility that her attentions might give away his earlier "malady" to her father; in reality, he simply did not want to risk offending the older man by being too dismissive of his daughter. Then he suggested she might go to assist Watson in his makeshift infirmary, and reluctantly, she did so.

As the sun moved deep into the clefts in the mountains, casting a long dark shadow over the dig site, the day cooled slowly into evening, and the dinner gong rang the warning. Work ceased for the day, and everyone retired to their tents to freshen up a bit before the evening meal was served.

*****

The gathering around the dinner table, however, seemed electrified.

SHERLOCK HOLMES AND THE MUMMY'S CURSE

Tension fairly crackled under the awning, and Holmes realised that something was very wrong. Watson arrived with Leighton on his arm, but she looked petulant, and he appeared unhappy. Professor Whitesell took his usual seat, but chewed his lower lip and drummed his fingers restlessly on the table top. Phillips glared at Watson, coming over and taking Leighton off the physician's arm before escorting her to her traditional seat between himself and her father. Meanwhile, Nichols-Woodall's expression could most closely be said to resemble a thundercloud. The only people at the main table who appeared unperturbed were Beaumont and Lord Trenthume. *But then,* considered Holmes, *Lord Trenthume rarely looks perturbed, because, if appearances are anything to go by, he seldom has any serious awareness of what is going on around him.* The sleuth idly wondered what went on in the earl's head to render him so completely oblivious so much of the time. *Then again,* he thought, *I am assuming that as much goes on in other men's minds as goes on in mine, which is probably not a reasonable assumption, judging by some.*

Everyone seated themselves, and the first course was served, a spicy mutton stew. Little was said, and the tension did not decrease overmuch as they ate their way through the course. Leighton relaxed a bit, and began to chat casually with her father and Phillips, telling them about how much she'd learned from Watson about treating patients; the news appeared to mollify Phillips, and lighten the Professor's mood. On hearing this, Holmes turned to Watson and raised a querying eyebrow. Watson shrugged, then, under cover of the removal of the first course, leaned over and murmured, "I'm not you."

"Ah." Holmes paused, biting his own lip in vexation. "Sorry about that, old chap."

"Not your fault."

The main course came out, kebabs on a bed of couscous. By this time, everyone seemed relatively jovial...except for Dr. Nichols-Woodall. If anything, Holmes decided, watching him, the thunderstorm was about to break. In the next instant, it did.

"So, Beaumont, did your little device serve your purpose?" With a snide tone, Nichols-Woodall dropped the bombshell into the midst of the table, and everyone stopped, forks halfway to their mouths. Beaumont slowly put down his fork, staring at the other man, eyes narrowed. Holmes surreptitiously took a deep breath, realising the bad blood between the pair was about to come to a head.

"What do you mean by that, sir?"

"I mean," an irate Nichols-Woodall specified, "your little fake 'mummy's curse.'"

"Fake? Curse?"

"Of course," Nichols-Woodall raged. "We should have known you were too dishonourable to truly bury the hatchet, save in our own backs! We know the stone tablet you connived to insert into the artefacts is a forgery! Young Mr. Holmes, there, was too astute for you! He caught all your errors, recognised it for what it was, and came to Professor Whitesell this very morning!"

"So he has translated the inscription?" Beaumont wondered, blasé.

Holmes closed his eyes momentarily, with a silent sigh, at this breakdown of his plans. When he opened them, he cast an admonishing glance at Professor Whitesell, who returned it diffidently, somewhat red-faced. Then Holmes looked down the table at a bristling Nichols-Woodall and Beaumont, facing off against each other across the width of the table, an uncomfortable Lord Trenthume occupying the end seat, more or less between them.

"Yes, Dr. Beaumont, I have translated it," Holmes replied dispassionately, feeling suddenly very tired.

"And you believe it to be a forged item because?" Beaumont pressed.

"Because the particular form of hieroglyphic used is of a much later period than what we are looking for, yet it invoked one of the names of Pharaoh Ka-Sekhen, and because the stone had been treated to give it the superficial appearance of weathered age, despite the very recent carving of the hieroglyphs."

"Well?" Nichols-Woodall demanded, rising partway from his chair. "Even if the log of discoveries was inaccurate, Willingham and I both remember you bringing it in, making so much of it! And no record of where it was found! What are you about, Beaumont?! Did you intend to slip in a fake without our knowledge, then at a convenient time reveal it and discredit us to academia? In the eyes of our friends and colleagues? Or are you trying to frighten the workers, slow down the dig, enable your own team somewhere else to make a discovery first? You and your bloody DAMN FAKE CURSE! I should have shot you as soon as you arrived!" He slammed an angry fist on the table, sending china and cutlery clattering and bouncing, and suddenly a wave of silence washed over the tables of the workers outside the main dining tent.

Beaumont turned away from Nichols-Woodall and gazed at Holmes, as a genial, appreciative smile spread across his face, and he began to applaud slowly.

"Very good," he murmured, his claps accelerating as his voice rose. "Very, very good, Monsieur Holmes, I am sure! Relax, *mes amis*[32]! It is all a joke! Forgive me for the perverse humour, but the good Professor Whitesell made so much of our translator before he had even arrived, that I feared lest his skills fail to live up to his publicity! I would never have allowed the thing to go forward as a true relic, of course not! But I felt it wise to, ah, to play a little prank upon Mr. Holmes, to ensure he was as good as his reputation made him! You have indeed chosen a worthy translator for us, Willingham! But I must ask: why did you yourselves not realise the deception, eh? Why not?"

With a growl, Nichols-Woodall responded, "You KNOW I am a student of geological matters, Beaumont. Give me a stone, I shall identify it, and determine its original locale. I cannot, nor could not ever, read hieroglyphs." He paused, then admitted, "I curse myself that I did not stop to examine the stone of the tablet, for then I might have recognised how it had been treated to resemble an ancient artefact, and uncovered your subterfuge at once."

"And while I did teach Holmes the basics of pictographs, hieroglyphs, and logograms," Whitesell added, annoyed at the not-so-subtle reverse accusation, "he has taken his language skills far beyond anything I taught him, so I did little more than glance at it, trusting him to analyse it swiftly and accurately upon his arrival — which he did. And at any rate I prefer to study the mummies themselves, and to a lesser extent, the architecture. I can translate quite facilely, when the need arises, for that is how I found this site, but I have always used a translator for the expeditions themselves. That way, I have the time and energy to focus upon what I most enjoy. I felt we had obtained a truly first-rate translator in Holmes, and I am now proven correct. Still, I would have been more comfortable with a less...unorthodox...method of testing him, Beaumont. You should have come to me with your concerns."

"I am sure, I am sure, Professor, and I am sorry for the capricious humour, but it does out, sometimes." Beaumont turned to Holmes. "My compliments, Monsieur Holmes. That was quite the feat. Very systematic and logical. You are a very intelligent young man; you will make much of yourself before all is said and done, provided we all make it safely out of this dusty oven of a land with our skins unscathed."

---

32   "My friends," French.

At Beaumont's addendum, so discreetly ominous, Holmes stiffened; he nodded his affronted acknowledgement.

"Um, let's all finish the lovely kebabs now," Leighton offered, just a little too brightly, "and then I'm sure there will be a delicious dessert to follow."

Holmes pushed back his chair and rose.

"Professor, if you will excuse me, I have some work to do in my tent," he said, controlling his insult and exasperation with an effort.

*****

"What?" Whitesell said in some surprise; he had spent the last ten minutes silently reproaching himself for confiding in Nichols-Woodall, against Holmes' recommendation, and it was proving to be a diplomatically difficult meal to get through. He realised suddenly that there were times he regretted insisting upon such communal meals — and this was one of them. "What do you have to do, Holmes?"

"I have sketched out a map of the locations of the relics we have recovered, and had planned to study it," Holmes said, brusque. "Should I deduce from it anything about the location of the tomb, I will of course inform you at once."

Whitesell nodded with a sigh. "Go, then."

Holmes left the table immediately, vanishing into the dark outside the tent.

*****

Back in the tent, Holmes found a folded slip of paper on his pillow, his surname inscribed on the outside. It was a short note in Professor Whitesell's hand, evidently left by that worthy just after Holmes had already departed for dinner, and it read,

> Holmes,
>
> *I just received a wire from my friends at the University. They have confirmed that Dr. Beaumont's team is not active at this time, and that work on his most recent independent dig was completed last spring. I am relieved to say I think we may have no concerns from that quarter, though there are others that come to mind.*
>
> *W. A. W.*

"Hm," Holmes hummed to himself, pondering the information.

"Perhaps it was only a poorly-considered prank, a form of *le bizutage*[33], then."

He pulled out his pipe, packed and lit it, and settled down on his cot in the dim light of the lantern, for a thoughtful smoke.

*****

"Fine job of it there with your deuced 'perverse humour,' Beaumont," Nichols-Woodall jibed again in intense annoyance, after they all watched an offended, irked Holmes depart with ramrod-straight back. "Alienate our translator, while you're about it."

"Once again, I offer my apologies, my friends," Beaumont said, bowing his head in what seemed to be humble obeisance. "It has gotten me into much trouble many times before this, I fear. I will endeavour to make it up to you all in the days to come — especially the talented young Mr. Holmes."

Which was a pretty apology, it had to be admitted.

But Watson thought he was just a trifle too cavalier about it.

---

33   Hazing or initiation ritual, French.

CHAPTER 5
SOMETHING OLD, SOMETHING NEW

The next day, the new tent for the hospital and infirmary arrived shortly before noon. The quartermaster promptly notified Lord Trenthume, Professor Whitesell, Doctor Watson, and Udail the foreman. Udail, recognising the need to erect the tent as soon as possible, showed up at the mess tent just prior to luncheon to obtain permission from Whitesell for appropriating some half-dozen men from the dig, in order to get the task done quickly.

"About time," Whitesell decreed. "By all means, Udail. Take however many men you need for the work, and get the ruddy blasted thing set up! The sooner the better, don't you agree, Dr. Watson?"

"I do indeed, Professor Whitesell!" Watson averred.

"Will you supervise, Doctor?" Whitesell queried.

"If you like," Watson agreed with a shrug. "I doubt I am any more knowledgeable about erecting large tent structures than the good Udail, though admittedly, my military experience taught me a good deal about the subject; but I can certainly direct the placement of cots and equipment to my preference. Udail, I will join you after luncheon, if that is suitable. Sooner, if you require."

"No," Whitesell decided, "we all need to eat. After luncheon is quite soon enough, I think."

"Very good, Professor, Doctor. After luncheon will be fine." Udail bowed and exited the tent post-haste, on his way to organise the matter before the meal should be served.

*****

After the meal, which was for a wonder relatively quiet, they all stood.

"Well, I am off to see about the infirmary tent," Watson declared. "What about the rest of you? Time for an afternoon nap?"

"No, I think not, at least for me," Whitesell noted. "As we get farther into winter, it is cooling off more, and I think I shall begin foregoing a siesta. We are working our way through the grid fairly nicely, too. And it is cool, with a slight, high haze, to-day. So I believe I am for the dig pits, to see what we may find. Phillips, lad, you're with me to-day, if that suits."

"Very well, Professor."

"I think I will join you, as well," Beaumont said. "Perhaps we will find something of actual significance to-day."

"I'm for prowling the rocks," Nichols-Woodall decided; Holmes suspected the geologist felt rather anti-social after the previous evening's dramatics, and frankly did not blame him. "I want to get the best feel I can for the stratigraphy of the region. I think it may help us locate the tomb sites."

"And I shall wander the dig sites, placing an emphasis upon not falling in," Holmes said, carefully hiding his own reclusive sensibilities behind a droll exterior. "In any event, the better I know the layout of the 'crime scene,'" he forced a chuckle at the deliberate pun, "the more likely it becomes that I can figure out the location of the body."

The other men laughed, which was as he had intended.

"Well then," an irritable Leighton declared in annoyance, "if you're all going to be out working in the heat, I'm going back to my tent and reading a book."

"Why, Leighton," Whitesell remonstrated, "I thought you liked the digs."

"...I do," she said, abashed. "I just...hadn't realised..."

"Come along with us, Leigh," Phillips urged. "You know you have fun, out amongst the dig pits."

"Just don't fall in," Nichols-Woodall reminded her with a laugh.

"Well...all right," she decided, mood lightening. "Perhaps for a little while."

"Good," Whitesell said, satisfied. "You can explore for a bit, and we'll be happy to answer your questions, then if you wish, you may go back to your tent a little early, to cool off and freshen up before dinner."

*****

Upon seeing one of the less-experienced diggers uncover what looked like a suspiciously smoothly-curved stone of a particular hue, Holmes cried, "STOP!" before the man could damage it for an ordinary stone. The man froze, and Holmes vaulted nimbly down into the hole and moved to investigate. Pulling a whisk broom from his back pocket, he brushed the sandy soil from the top, then ran his fingers over the surface.

"Mm, yes. I believe you may have found an early amphora," Holmes told the digger. "Most likely from Bronze Age Greece, though it may be Egyptian. Quite probably it was brought over in trade, and contained olive oil."

"But not wine, Mr. Holmes?" the digger asked in a heavy accent.

"Possibly, I suppose," Holmes considered. "There seems to have been a preference for beer in ancient Egypt, but tastes do differ. Let us see about extracting it, and we shall find out."

Holmes removed his cravat, rolled his sleeves higher, and unbuttoned his waistcoat, then reached for a spade and began to help excavate the soil around the vessel.

*****

Soon sweat and dust streaked Holmes' shirt, plastering it to his back as the sun glared down, but the neck and body of the amphora were exposed at last. He handed the spade back to one of the workmen, and wielded his whisk again, using it to uncover the handles on the neck of the pot, lest a spade break them. When he got to the top — it was lying partly on its side, at an angle — the detective got a surprise.

"It is still sealed," he said in astonishment. "That is a rare thing."

"Why, Master Holmes?"

"Because the stoppers are usually of something like cork, which rots over the millennia," he explained. "This one appears to use a clay stopper, sealed with beeswax. Run fetch the Professor; I will keep digging."

One of the workers climbed the ladder and ran to find Professor Whitesell, while the other two assisted Holmes in moving the soil away from the pot, carefully freeing it from its age-old grave.

Within minutes, Whitesell, his daughter, Phillips, and Beaumont stood or crouched at the side of the pit where Holmes worked.

"What have you got there, Holmes, lad?" Whitesell asked.

"A SEALED amphora, Professor," the detective-turned-archaeologist replied, removing his pith helmet and dragging a dusty forearm across his perspiring forehead, leaving a reddish-brown smear behind. "You might want to have Udail fetch the block and tackle; it feels full.

And we have almost got it dug out sufficient to recover it."

Whitesell turned, put his hands to his mouth, and bellowed, "UDAIL! FETCH THE BLOCK AND TACKLE CRANE, PLEASE!"

A rapt Leighton gazed down at Holmes in pride and something like adoration. Holmes, busy determining the best way to free the amphora and hoist it intact once the crane had arrived, did not notice.

Phillips did, and glared down at the sleuth in hatred.

*****

In short order, the heavy amphora was hoisted to ground level, and the group escorted it back to the artefact tent, where Professor Whitesell himself entered it into the records. The digger who had first uncovered part of it, one Ghali by name, tagged along behind. The amphora was carefully positioned upright in a wooden box, and the others stood back to gaze at it in a certain level of awe.

Udail turned to go back to the dig, and nearly fell over Ghali.

"Ghali! What are you doing here?!" he exclaimed. "Lazy dullard! You should be at work!"

"Master Holmes promised we should find out what was in it, once we got it out," Ghali protested.

"So I did," Holmes agreed. "Professor, with your permission?"

"By all means," Whitesell agreed. "Let us find out."

Holmes extracted his jack-knife from his waistcoat pocket, unfolded it, and delicately slid the blade down into the ancient, hardened beeswax, pressing the blade against the inside neck of the amphora, and began a kind of sawing motion, working his way around the seal. When he had completed the circuit, he withdrew the blade, wiping it on his handkerchief before folding it and dropping it back in his pocket. Then he took hold of the knob on top of the amphora lid, and looked at the others.

"It is many thousands of years old," he warned, "and unlikely to be anything but rancid at best. It will not smell good," he directed that last to Leighton, who nodded, backed up a step, and held her own lace-edged handkerchief to her nose. He lifted the cap.

A thick, gelatine-like sludge, a dark olive green, dripped sluggishly from the bottom of the stopper. Swiftly, Beaumont grabbed a nearby teacup, left there the day before by Phillips. He snatched the saucer from beneath and held it under the stopper, catching the torpid, viscous drop as it fell, leaving a string connecting it to the stopper for a brief moment.

Holmes dipped two fingers into the material, studying it briefly before holding it to his nose.

"Olive oil?" Whitesell queried.

"I believe so," Holmes decided, then held his greasy fingers out for the Professor to sniff.

"Yes," Whitesell confirmed, smelling the substance on Holmes' fingers. "A full amphora of olive oil from pre-dynastic Egypt."

"Which in turn proves that they had commerce with early Greece," Beaumont pointed out. "A nice little find. Congratulations, Holmes, Ghali. Very nice indeed."

Ghali looked delighted; Leighton beamed.

"Well, let's get back to it," a sullen Phillips declared.

*****

Mid-afternoon that same day, as Holmes watched from a perch on a large sandstone outcrop, a turbaned head popped up from a dig pit, and a cry went out for Udail. Udail scurried to the location and climbed down the ladder into the pit. Loud, rapid jabbering in Arabic ensued, then Udail climbed halfway up the ladder and looked around.

"Dr. Beaumont!" he called, waving to the nearest member of the expedition's scientific team. "Over here!"

Beaumont hurried over and climbed down, disappearing from sight. Moments later, his excited cry rang out over the dig site.

"C'est beau, ça![34]"

Seconds later, his head reappeared above ground. He cupped his hands and shouted.

"WHITESELL! HOLMES! OVER HERE! COME AT ONCE! WE HAVE FOUND SOMETHING! *C'EST MAGNIFIQUE*![35]"

The others, including Phillips and Nichols-Woodall, neither of whom had been summoned, broke into a run.

*****

As Holmes reached the side of the pit with the others, he gazed down into it, to find an unknown digger, Udail, and Beaumont bend-

---

34 "That's beautiful, that is!" French.
35 "It's magnificent!" French.

ing over a large stone block. It was some two feet wide by one and a half feet high and deep, heavily carved both with illustrations and with hieroglyphs; rather fewer of the latter than the former, and the images still had colouring upon them, various paints and stains bringing them to life.

"Oh, my word," Whitesell whispered. "*C'est magnifique*, indeed..."

"There is a nice piece, and no mistake, Will," Nichols-Woodall murmured to the Professor. "A capstone, maybe, or a foundational stone?"

"I will have to see it in its entirety to tell," Whitesell answered. Leighton, having heard the shouting from her tent in camp, wandered up at that moment.

"Da? Uncle Parker? Is everything all right? I thought I heard shouting."

"You certainly did. Young lady, have a look at this," Nichols-Woodall said, placing a light hand around her shoulders and escorting her closer to the edge of the excavation, as he swept his other hand through the air in presentation. "What do you think of that?"

"Oh my!" Leighton exclaimed, eyes lighting up. "Look at the paintings! How pretty! It fairly brings the old Egyptians to life!"

"*Oui, oui*! Holmes, look, it has writing!" Beaumont exclaimed, Gallic blood coming to the fore in his excitement. "There are hieroglyphs upon it, though they appear to be somewhat fragmentary. Perhaps you can get information from it!"

Udail clambered back up the ladder until he could shout, "Ikhdar rafaah![36]" The order was echoed along the lines, and soon the crane, composed of heavy wooden beams, ropes, and a block and tackle, was wheeled over.

*****

It took over an hour, but eventually the heavy stone block was manoeuvred into position to be hoisted from the pit, and the slow, cautious trundle to the artefact tent began. The scientific team went on ahead and prepared a corner of the tent; it was far too weighty for any of the tables.

When it finally arrived, the three archaeologists, or rather, two plus a student — namely Whitesell, Beaumont, and Phillips — began the delicate task of cleaning the stone without marring the painted illustrations or engravings. Fortunately only three sides of the rectangular stone

---

36   "Fetch the crane!" Arabic.

appeared to be inscribed; there were signs that the other side, as well as the top and bottom, had been originally placed against other stones as part of a structure. Nichols-Woodall used these unmarked faces to ascertain that the stone was indeed of the local rocks, likely taken from the principal mountain at the rear of the box cañon. Holmes, though possessed of sufficient skill to assist in the cleaning, chose to stay back and let the others perform the task, content in the knowledge that his translation job was equally important.

As the dirt was carefully brushed away, Holmes studied the adornments on the stone. His thoughts were interrupted as Whitesell remarked on the same thing.

"Interesting pictographs, wouldn't you say, Phillips?"

"Yes sir," the younger man said. "What do you make of them, Professor?"

"I should say it is part of a victory depiction, wouldn't you, Beaumont?"

"Yes. Or possibly a simple tribute representation," Beaumont replied, considering. "We would need to see the entire mural to tell for certain, I think. But I see no weapons, so I should interpret it as tribute."

"Yes, that is a possibility as well," Whitesell said, running his fingertips through the air scant fractions of an inch above the drawings, as if he itched to touch them, but was afraid of damaging them. "Look. Here are Egyptians in the lead, Ethiopians, Greeks, Phoenicians..."

"It breaks to another block," Phillips said.

"It does. Like Beaumont says, it appears to be part of a mural. Holmes, can you make anything of the hieroglyph inscription? It is likely to be as incomplete as the paintings, but perhaps we can glean something out of it."

Holmes crouched before the stone and studied the glyphs.

"May I touch them, Professor?" he asked. "I should like to ensure that I am not missing any markings which may no longer be visible."

"Yes, I think that will be fine. I see no pigments which might be damaged, in the inscription areas," the chief archaeologist gave permission.

Holmes ran light fingertips over the carvings, searching them out, ensuring that his eyes and his fingers were in agreement regarding what was there. After having slowly traced the entirety of the writing, he returned his right hand to the top of the stone, running his index finger down the text as he translated.

SHERLOCK HOLMES AND THE MUMMY'S CURSE

"It says, '*Here lies Sekhen, never again to...*' then there is a break where the text would be on the lower stone. Then it picks up here with, '*...the great Sekhen, who terrified the world.*'" Holmes glanced up at Whitesell. "There is no doubt. It refers to Ka-Sekhen, and these glyphs are of the appropriate age. I would say this likely came from the lintel of the tomb itself, Professor."

"So it would seem," a delighted Whitesell agreed. "And so it is likely to have fallen from that same lintel, wouldn't you say?"

"I would say so," Nichols-Woodall allowed.

"So would I," Holmes admitted.

"I suppose it makes sense," Beaumont conceded after chewing his lip for a moment, in thought. "But it might still be wise to widen the search a bit, Whitesell. After all, we are in an area which sometimes experiences earthquakes, and periodic flash floods. It may not have ended up so very close to where it started out."

"True, true," Whitesell said. "Parker, you're the geologist. I want you to have a look at the drainage of the valley, and try to get a feel for where this chunk of bowlder[37] might have come from."

"Of course, Will," Nichols-Woodall averred. "I think I'll climb up to that ledge I showed you a few days ago. Would you care to join me? I'll bring the maps, and we can compare the view to them, try to figure this all out."

"Capital plan. Would you object if I brought my daughter along? I think she might like the scenery, and the notion of a puzzle is sure to fascinate her." Leighton, who had stayed carefully in the background, out of the way, beamed at the query.

"And it will get her out of her tent into the fresh air again, right?" the geologist replied, smiling at his informally-adopted niece.

"Precisely." Whitesell laughed. "Thomas, would you supervise the digs? Just in case something else turns up? Have Udail sound the ship's horn if you find anything, and Parker and I will come down straight-away."

"Of course."

"Leighton, Phillips, come with me. Holmes, feel free to add this little 'clew' to your list, and see what you can deduce."

"By all means, Professor."

And they split up.

---

37   "Bowlder" is an archaic form of the modern "boulder," in common use in the 1880s and prior.

Holmes fetched his sketch-book and added the location where the jamb stone was discovered to it. Then he sat for a long time, pondering the entries, trying to see some pattern in them, something that would point the way to Pharaoh Ka-Sekhen's tomb.

Finally he rose and moved to the doorway, to look out over the digging grid at the work going on, lost in thought as he tried to make sense of it all.

He stayed there until the dinner gong sounded the warning.

*****

"Come on, Sherry," Leighton chirped, tugging on Holmes' arm, as they all left the meal tent after dinner. "I want to show you the dig from above."

"Leighton, where are you dragging Holmes off to now?" Whitesell wondered. "It will be full dark soon. It's middling twilight already. Do behave, young lady."

"Da! I'm just going to take him up to the ledge you and Uncle Parker showed me to-day. I want him to see the whole dig at once, like you showed me. I think he'll like the...what did you call it? 'Bird's-eye view'?"

"Oh," Phillips attempted a protest, "you don't want to be climbing a mountain path in the dark, Leigh. It's too dangerous. And Mr. Holmes doesn't know his way around that well as yet. I'll take you, if you insist."

"Silly," she told him. "The moon is rising, and it is nearly full. We shall have plenty of light. Look!" She pointed east, where the great yellow circle of the moon loomed over the dark green oasis that marked the Nile on the near horizon. "Besides, we can always take carbide lamps. And I only want to get caught up with Sherry! It's been so long! We've so much to talk about!"

"Surely you've already had plenty of 'catching up,' Leigh," Phillips protested. "God only knows, you're together all the time, it seems."

"No, Landers! You don't understand!" Leighton exclaimed, frustrated. "Sherry and I...he was my best friend, Landers. Mama had only just died, Da was hurting, I could see that, but I was so lonely, and...and Sherry was always there..."

"But you were only a child, Leigh."

"But I'm not now, Landers. I want to get to know Sherry as an adult, as one adult to another."

"True," Whitesell agreed, considering. "And Holmes will keep you safe, like he always has. Very well. Off with you both."

A frustrated Holmes, who had been unable to get a word in edgewise to protest, cast a weary, jaded glance at Watson, just before he was pulled into the darkness outside the tents.

*****

The path up to the shelf on the mountainside proved surprisingly easy, which was as well, as an enthusiastic Leighton fairly dragged the sleuth up it. Holmes brought along a dark lantern, and Leighton had affixed spare carbide lamps to their pith helmets with leather straps. Soon enough they were on the broad ledge overlooking the archaeological site. The moon, now a paler cast of amber than before, rose high in the east, shedding a soft light over everything before them.

"Look, Sherry," Leighton piped. "Oh, I knew it would look even prettier by moonlight! See? Isn't it lovely?"

"It is," Holmes admitted, studying the terrain below them. "It is also a fascinating perspective of the site. One which may well help me see everything with fresh eyes."

"And the company is divine, too. I do so love being with you, Sherry."

Holmes took that in, and remained silent, feeling her hand still gripping his. After a few minutes, she slid her hand up, into the crook of his elbow, and hugged it possessively. He closed his eyes briefly, drawing a deep, considering breath, and debated how to do what he knew now that he must do. *I have let the matter run on for too long as it is,* he decided. *I wished neither to hurt her, nor to insult her father, but there is no longer any help for it. Watson was right; her natural affections are getting out of hand. I have used every subtle means at my disposal to indicate my predilections, but either she is not so subtle, or she is ignoring them.* He drew another deep breath, and planned his wording carefully.

"Leighton," Holmes began quietly after several more moments, as they surveyed the moonlit dig from the top of the cliff, "this will not do."

"What? What are you talking about, Sherry? What won't do?" Leighton threw him a coquettish smile, leaning into him. "It's a lovely evening, with delightful companionship. Don't you think?"

"I am no fool, Leigh. And while I am flattered, I will not be...seduced." He stood stiffly, refusing to allow her to get comfortable against his side. Leighton's smile faded.

"You...but, but I thought...so you don't really find me...you don't think I'm..."

"It has nothing to do with that," Holmes said, still quiet, but firm. "I did not come here for a...an exotic affair, nor would I permit such a thing."

Leighton cast him a pained glance, then dropped her gaze to the excavation far below, withdrawing her arm from his.

"Then...are you and...and the docto—"

"NO," Holmes said firmly. "We are friends, he and I — and that is not an appellation I ever use lightly. But Watson is quite firmly... attracted...to the ladies, and such matters are illegal in England — and Egypt — in any event, which makes it a thing wholly inappropriate to a consulting detective whose clients include Scotland Yard, even were I inclined to such doings. And that is not what I meant, and I think you know it. My work does not permit of such distractions, Leigh. I will not allow it. Not even for you."

"But...but...we were so close..."

"And you were a child, and I was of age."

"Just barely."

"Still. It is not the same, Leighton."

"Are...are we at least...friends?"

"We are, and ever shall be." Holmes allowed his voice to gentle. "Just as are your father and I. If ever either of you should find yourselves in need, you have but to call, and I will come to your aid, to the best of my abilities. As I said, that is not an appellation I use lightly. But Leigh...nothing more." He shook his head slowly, decisively; then drew a deep breath and pressed his lips together in thought. "If it is a...a holiday romance you are after," he began, still considering, "or more, I believe I know someone who might be willing to oblige. And I can personally vouch for his upstanding character as a gentleman."

"Who? Oh, your friend the doctor?"

"Yes. I have noticed him...watching you, discreetly. And he has admired your beauty to me, several times. Always very delicately, wishing neither to dishonour you, nor to offend me, should it prove that you and I were...involved. If you would like me to...ahem, arrange..."

Leighton sighed.

"He's not you, Sherry."

"No. But I am not the 'Sherry' you remember, either."

"I suppose not. Let...let me think about it."

"Very well."

Leighton turned to him. Concern was writ large in the green eyes.

"Sherry?"

"Mm?"

"Is...is that all of it? The...your profession. I mean," she stumbled over her words, "I remember once, you coming by our home — I hadn't known you long — and you were very sad. So terribly sad; the look in your eyes made me want to cry. I tried to get you to play with me, and you did attempt to, but your heart wasn't in it — even I could tell that, young as I was. After you left, I asked Da what was wrong. I thought I'd done something to make you angry...a-and he said a woman had hurt you, but it wasn't me, it was a grown-up. I..."

Holmes turned away abruptly.

"Yes, there was an incident," he said in a calm, level voice, gazing off east, toward the Nile, hidden in the distant darkness. "And yes, it did influence my decision to forswear all *affaires de coeur*.[38] Because it showed me quite plainly how I might be distracted and misled by such things. And in my business, a man's life may hang on 'such things.' It is a circumstance in which I refuse to place myself."

"I see," Leighton said, in a sad, soft tone, and Holmes wondered if she really did see. "All right, my dear, dear Sherry, I'll leave be. But, but, before we let it all go, you need to know..."

"Know what?" He caught something in her tone and glanced at her over his shoulder, to find her standing in a huddle, her arms wrapped about herself, head bowed, her face inexpressibly mournful.

"You...when I was little, I..." She huffed at herself, then met his eyes for a moment, throwing him a wistful smile, before blurting it out. "You were my first love, Sherry. It was puppy love, without doubt. I wasn't nearly old enough for it to be serious. But I'd hoped perhaps...when I heard Da had invited you...ah, well." She turned toward the downward path, as the sleuth fairly gaped in shock and distress, then reached for her hand to offer comfort.

"Leigh...I had no idea, my dear, I swear. I never meant to wound you."

Another disconsolate smile was tossed to him as she gently with-

---

38   Affairs of the heart, matters of the heart.

drew her hand from his grasp.

"I know. I was a child, and it was silly. Do you remember the crowns of clover blossoms I used to weave for you? From our rear field?"

"Yes." He chuckled at the remembrance. "I forgot to remove one before returning to my dormitory one evening, and I thought my roommate should never let me hear the end of it."

"Watson?"

"No, Summersby. Watson was some years ahead of me, and at another school, at that. We did not meet, Watson and I, until we both found ourselves in search of rooms last year. But I did wonder what precipitated all the odd stares as I walked through the quad that evening."

"Oh. Well, I used to pretend that, that we were getting married, and the garlands were our bridal flowers, and..." She huffed and turned away. "Oh, it all seems so foolish when I say it! I suppose it is better left forgotten, after all. Come, let's go back to the camp."

"Leigh..."

"Are you coming, or not?"

Holmes drew a deep, unsettled breath, both disappointed in how he had handled the matter and concerned for Leighton's pain, and followed her back down to the camp.

*****

Once they reached the base of the mountain, Holmes escorted Leighton straight to her tent, next her father's, then headed thoughtfully for the tent he shared with Watson, across the camp. Neither Holmes nor Leighton had said a word to each other since leaving the ledge high above.

Before he could reach his tent, however, a glaring Landers Phillips intercepted him, blocking his way forward.

"Ah. Good evening, Phillips," Holmes offered, blasé. "Lovely evening for a stroll."

"How dare you?!" Phillips responded in a low, incensed tone. Holmes raised an eyebrow.

"I dare many things. It is the nature of my work. To what, in particular, do you refer?"

"So you ADMIT to it! You filthy, disgusting CAD! Even I could hear Leigh crying when you left her, and my tent is on the other side of the Professor's! You, sir, are no gentleman! You are a rogue, a bounder, and a scoundrel!"

"I am no such thing," Holmes replied, calm, maintaining an even voice. "I cannot help it if she is disappointed in my lack of response."

"Vile, depraved DOG!" Phillips shouted, and shoved the sleuth with considerable force. Had Holmes not anticipated the move and countered it, he would have been knocked to the ground. "YOU TOOK HER UP THE MOUNTAIN! Just the two of you, without escort! KNOWING her father trusted you! You cannot pretend you made no untoward advances against the lady! You have had your eye upon her since your arrival! You should be horse-whipped!"

"I need not pretend, for I did not," Holmes replied, a bit more heatedly than before. He set aside the dark lantern, removed his pith helmet and extinguished the carbide lamp, setting it aside, and eased himself into a slight crouch. Only an expert would have recognised in it the horse stance of Oriental martial arts, and Phillips was no expert. "Had you bothered to ask the Professor, let alone paid attention when you made the journey yourself this afternoon, you would have known, firstly, that the path upward was exposed to ready view from the camp over its entire length, and both he and Leigh knew this, as he showed it to her this afternoon at the same time as you, which is the only reason he permitted the walk to begin with; and secondly, that the Professor watched us with his field glasses, for I could see the glint of the moonlight off the lenses. This was as much for our safety as for propriety, as a stumble off the path in some places could easily have been fatal, especially if rescue was not immediately forthcoming. He simply allowed us the privacy to say what needed to be said in the circumstances. Nor have I 'had my eye upon her,' as you put it, any more than befits two old friends reunited."

"You contemptible, villainous muck-snipe[39]!" Phillips hissed. "What liberties did you take with that poor girl?!"

"None, I assure you."

"LIAR!" Phillips roared. "I'll avenge her honour, for it is obvious you won't do the decent thing! You have had this coming for some time!" And he swung a fist at Holmes, hard, aimed for his face.

It never connected; Holmes threw up a forearm to block the blow, then drove the palm heel of the other hand at Phillips' chest with a punctuated shout of, "HAI," knocking him back several paces, and nearly off his feet. With a loud growl, Phillips stepped back in, aiming a one-two punch at Holmes' belly, followed by a forceful kick directed at his near

---

39   Victorian slang for a person of low morals or a vagrant of an unpleasant sort.

shin.

"Aha! I never knew a proper English gentleman boxer to add kicks to his bouts! A street fighter, however, is another matter!" Holmes, by way of response, dropped deeper into his horse stance, deflecting both punches with his forearms and simply withdrawing his leading foot out of reach of the kick. The kick's lack of connexion nearly threw Phillips over from its sheer momentum.

Then Holmes followed up with a combination of his own, carefully calculated in its intensity: a chambered right punch to Phillips' solar plexus, hard enough to knock the air out of him, succeeded by a left backfist to the face as he stepped past Phillips, throwing the latter badly off balance, leaning backward. This was then closely followed by a rounding calf kick from behind, effectively taking Phillips' legs from under him. Phillips landed hard on his back in the sand with a frustrated cry.

Drawn by the sound of the shouts and fighting, others came rushing up: Watson, who moved quickly to Holmes' side, supportive, and prepared to do battle himself; Professor Whitesell and his daughter, which latter let out a soft scream when she saw Holmes and Phillips fighting; Nichols-Woodall; Lord Trenthume, and several of the Egyptian workers, including the faithful Udail, most of the latter with flaming torches. As Phillips hit the ground, Whitesell bellowed out, "WHAT THE BLOODY HELL IS GOING ON HERE?!"

"It seems, Professor," Holmes began, as Nichols-Woodall offered a hand to help a bloody-nosed Phillips to his feet, "that your assistant completely misconstrued the nature of the stroll I took earlier with your daughter. He waylaid me here, and attempted to assail me."

"Lying mountebank[40]! Libertine! Why don't you stop pretending to be a gentleman?!" Phillips snarled, dragging his sleeve across his face, leaving it rather disgustingly besmeared with blood and mucus. He lunged for Holmes again, but Nichols-Woodall and Udail grabbed him, one by each arm, and restrained him. "Leigh, don't you worry, my dear! I'll publically reveal this damnable blackguard for what he is, and what he did to you!"

"Why, you bloody little bas—!" an incensed Watson began, stepping forward.

"Hush, Watson," Holmes cut him off, but gently. "I appreciate the

---

40   A swindler, a phony, fraud; derived from the French for quacks who sold "patent medicine," of which alcohol was usually the primary ingredient.

vote of confidence, but it is not necessary. Professor, it would appear that Mr. Phillips, here, is completely convinced that I took unconscionable liberties with your daughter to-night. I hope you know that I would never do such a thing."

"I know, Holmes," Whitesell averred, alternating between meeting Holmes' grey gaze forthrightly and glowering at Phillips. "Leighton came straightaway to me and told me all about it. I do hope we haven't breached your confidence in so doing, but I claim a father's privilege and such like, if we might so term it. Given your choice of career, I can't say as I blame you for choosing perennial bachelorhood, though I would have loved to have you for a son-in-law. However, I would have expected Landers to come to us about something of this nature, rather than taking it upon himself to, as he thought, rectify such a situation. Have you anything to say in your behalf, Phillips?"

"I cannot give credence to the notion that you still believe him!" an indignant Phillips exclaimed. "What he—"

*****

"ENOUGH!" A furious, and suddenly very stern, Whitesell cut him off; Phillips gaped in shock. "We shall discuss this further in the morning, Mr. Phillips. Know this for now, young man, that you have seriously, seriously erred. You have thrown massive discord into this team, and severely embarrassed my daughter AND my former student, as well as heaping vile, unfounded accusations upon said former student."

"But, but—"

"Udail?" Whitesell interrupted Phillips' stammerings.

"Yes, Professor?" the chief digger responded immediately, releasing Phillips' arm and stepping forward. "What may I do for you?"

"You are usually up at sunrise, are you not?"

"Yes, Professor. I prefer the morning for prayers and for...thinking. Planning. It is a good way to start the day, I find."

"Excellent. If you would be so kind, in the morning about an hour before the breakfast gong, give or take as is most convenient for you, come by and wake me if I am not already up, then fetch Mr. Phillips and bring him to my tent. He and I shall have a little...chat."

"Yes, Professor Whitesell, as you wish." Udail sketched a slight bow.

"Good. Now." Whitesell turned to his daughter. "Leigh, have you anything to say?"

"Only that Sherry was, is, and remains, a perfect gentleman," Leighton sighed, drawing a weary hand across her eyes.

"But Leigh!" Phillips protested, reaching for her. "I heard you crying, my dearest. He hurt you!"

"Landers Phillips, you insufferable, idiotic boor!" a furious Leighton exclaimed, pulling back and drawing herself up into the very picture of indignant Victorian womanhood. "If you are too impossibly stupid to recognise when a woman has been disappointed in *affaires du coeur*,[41] let alone when she does not want the matter bruited about, then you are absolutely hopeless! Come, Father, let us go back to our tents, put a lid tight upon this miserable day, and retire!"

Without another word, Professor Whitesell took his daughter's hand in his, placing it in the crook of his elbow; they turned in a stately fashion, and with all due dignity, left in the direction they had come. Phillips stood staring after them in astonishment.

"But...but..." he continued stuttering in confusion. "She was CRYING."

"Women do that from time to time," a bland Nichols-Woodall offered dryly.

"Yes," Watson agreed, bleakly amused at the direction events had taken. "Even the best and wisest of them, sometimes; I often think it is part and parcel of the nurturing nature. It does not do to take action until one has ascertained, from their own lips, that action is warranted."

"Which is one reason why," Holmes interjected, "I have taken the standpoint I have with regard to such matters." He turned, catching up the almost-forgotten dark lantern and closing it, before donning his pith helmet once more. "Come, Watson. It has been a very long day."

"It has, indeed," Watson murmured, dropping into step with Holmes as they retreated to their own tent. "Damnation, what a scene," faintly floated back to the others. "I'm sure you could have done without that, old boy."

"Undeniably," came the fainter response, succinct, and the pair vanished into the darkness.

"I...don't understand," Phillips murmured blankly, as the various diggers departed for their beds, and Nichols-Woodall followed. "I was defending her honour. Couldn't they see that? How could she be angry with ME?" He wandered off in disconsolate confusion, leaving Michael

---

41 "Affairs of the heart," French.

Cortland, the Earl of Trenthume, standing alone in the dark.

"I have no idea what the hell just happened here," Cortland complained to the air.

Then he turned and stalked back to his own tent.

CHAPTER 6
SHUFFLING THE DECK

The next morning, some hour or more before breakfast, Watson was awakened by the voices of a male and female raised in argument somewhere across the camp; though precisely what was being said was indecipherable, it sounded more or less like English. He decided, after listening to the tones of the exchange for several minutes, that the woman was winning.

At breakfast proper, he discovered that Leighton had changed her seat, no longer sitting between her father and Phillips, but at the opposite end of the long table, displacing Lord Trenthume, and forcing a slight rearrangement of overall seating. Moreover, she refused to even acknowledge the existence of Phillips, who appeared more than a little downcast, a state emphasised by his two black eyes and very swollen nose. *I suppose I should check to ensure it is not broken, and set it if it is,* Watson thought absently, watching. *Not that he did not deserve it, but Hippocratic oath and such, after all ..*

This new seating pattern also had the effect of placing her some little distance away from Holmes as well, and when he wished her a casual, "Good morning," as he passed by on his way to his seat, she flushed, dropped her gaze into her lap, and barely murmured a response. Holmes gave no outward sign of reaction, but Watson thought his eyes narrowed slightly, and suspected it was in pain.

The physician concluded that the early-morning argument had been an angry Leighton Whitesell — as the only Englishwoman in camp, it had to have been her — dressing down Landers Phillips for his presumption of the night previous. Further, he decided that what was evidently Holmes' refusal to involve himself with the girl beyond their prior relationship, and so publically revealed, had embarrassed her rather decidedly, and this rendered her entirely too flustered to know how to interact with him.

Beaumont, who had been absent from the scene of the fight the night before, appeared to be mildly confused as to the obvious source of strain between the various parties, not to mention the rearrangement of the seating. But Nichols-Woodall leaned over and murmured something in his ear, whereupon Beaumont mouthed the word, "Oh," and nodded his comprehension.

At the end of the communal meal, which was uncommonly silent, Leighton rose without a word and betook herself off to her tent. Phillips watched her go with a hangdog expression, then left the table himself and wandered away in the general direction of the artefact tent — which, apparently by design in the instance, had the opposite compass bearing — presumably to clean and piece together what had been discovered to that point. It not coincidentally, Watson considered, also had the effect of giving him something to take his mind off Leighton Whitesell.

"My," Beaumont observed mildly. "My deepest thanks, Dr. Nichols-Woodall, for giving me the private *mise en garde*[42], as it were. I very nearly put my foot in it most thoroughly with an imprudent question about what the deuce was going on."

"I thought it best," Nichols-Woodall concurred sanguinely. "Your tent is a distance away, and you probably did not even hear last night's little...altercation. Young Leighton can still be a bit...capricious, as well as headstrong, especially at her age; and she appeared decidedly upset by the turn of events, all around, for good reason, I should think. In any case, I saw no purpose in increasing her mortification, so I headed off your questions, Beaumont, with a little word to the wise. She's a bright one, with considerably more audacity, intelligence, and daring than other young women of her age; I must say, Willingham, you brought her up well, and I feel she may eventually prove to be your suffragist successor. But she is not yet even of age, and young ones can be flighty that way. Not that I can blame her. That was quite an unpleasant little tableau Phillips incited last night. And not a tad embarrassing for young Leighton and poor Holmes."

"Indeed," Whitesell rumbled; Holmes chose to remain quiet. "I cannot say Landers behaved as well as Leighton, if we get down to it, and he has several years on her. Holmes, my boy, I offer my sincerest apologies; I had no idea! Landers had made a handful of overtures toward Leighton some few months ago, but nothing seemed to come of it that I could tell; Leighton had indicated her disinterest to both of us, and I had quite forgotten."

42   Warning, caution; French.

"It seems he has not," Holmes offered, with dry wit and a wry smile. "It was neither your fault, nor Leigh's, and you should not apologise for the matter, Professor. Phillips does not come from the more privileged classes, does he?"

"Not entirely," Whitesell acknowledged. "His family is of what is being termed the lower middle class, I suppose. He has seen the streets. But he is a very intelligent lad, so I took him under my wing some while back. And he has not disappointed...until last night. I gave him a VERY stern lecture this morning...after Leigh was through with him. I expect most of the camp could hear it, for she intercepted him with Udail before they made it to my tent; poor Udail promptly fled, and Leighton scarcely let the boy get a word in edgewise. Then she ended her upbraiding by depositing Landers into my care. I suppose his ears are fairly burning by now, because I did not go easily upon him merely because Leighton had already castigated him." He turned to Holmes. "He now knows his error, and has instructions to think upon his behaviour, and then deliver an honest and straightforward apology to you, Holmes. I expect he will be looking for a more private opportunity than the meal table, however."

"Be that as it may, I also gather that, despite my best efforts in the business, Leigh is now more than a little uncomfortable around me," Holmes observed, stifling a sigh.

"A tad, Holmes, a wee tad. But she still cares for your friendship, you know. She told me that much, after the debacle last night: that she was very glad to know you were her friend, no matter what. Seemed to think it was very important — to both of you."

"It is," Holmes admitted, a hint of gruffness to his manner.

"Then give her time, young man, give her time. She will come around."

"Is her emotional state the best, do you think?" Watson wondered, concerned.

"What do you mean?" Whitesell asked, surprised by the question.

"Well, we do not need her falling into a melancholy over the matter," the physician pointed out. "Not out here in the middle of the desert. Were we in London, where she would have friends and wholesome distractions readily available, I should not be as uneasy, but a thing like that could swiftly become quite serious in such a harsh environment as this. Should I pop round and ensure she is quite all right, perhaps?"

Whitesell was silent for a moment, studying Watson, chewing his lower lip in thought. He cut a sidelong glance at Holmes, questioning;

Watson watched as Holmes swiftly manufactured and donned an unassuming, bland expression, and suddenly gathered what was in the wind — or at least, what was in Professor Whitesell's thoughts.

"Oh! No, no," he backpedalled, "I did not mean—"

"Now, now, doctor, I think that may be a capital idea," Whitesell blustered, as Beaumont and Nichols-Woodall looked on in patent amusement. A puzzled Lord Trenthume simply blinked and listened. "Why don't you do that? I think you might be just the man to...cheer her up, don't you know?"

"Well," Watson said, uncertain, "I can try, I suppose. That...wasn't what I had in mind when I suggested...I am a physician, so..."

"Yes, I understand. I'm not trying to put you on the spot, as it were. Look, Doctor," Whitesell said, softening his voice and becoming serious, "I love my daughter. Plain and simple. She is the apple of my eye, as the saying is, and all I really have left of my dear wife. But right now, she is in some considerable pain over this situation, and there is not one damn thing I can do about it. It is, after all, the way the world works. And you ARE a physician, as well as a handsome young male, if you don't mind my opinion. If you could see your way clear to keeping an eye on her, perhaps providing some company if that is not onerous to you, you would at the least have a father's gratitude. There need be nothing beyond your natural inclinations, and I have Holmes' word that you are a perfect gentleman."

"Have no fear on that score, Professor," Holmes averred. Watson felt his cheeks heat from the honour Holmes had just done him as he nodded, still dubious.

"I will see what I may," he finally offered. "Certainly I will attempt to bring her out of her doldrums, and make her comfortable with Holmes once more. Beyond that, I cannot say. It is, at least in part, up to the lady." He paused, then added, "I think I shall see if she will act as nurse again. Is the surgical tent finally set up, with all its equipment and accoutrements?"

"Yes, Udail said that was completed last night — just before the fight broke out," Whitesell said with a sigh. "Good idea; it will be much more proper for a young lady than if the surgery was in your tent."

"Well, and it will not be so crowded," Watson supplied. "Holmes' and my tent was getting a bit cramped, what with my medical equipment, and his scientific apparatus, spread all over."

"Very true. It was always my intention, from the time I knew we would have your help, Doctor. We simply," Whitesell briefly cut his eyes at Holmes, and Watson realised that he must know of Holmes' suspicions, "misplaced some of the supplies in the journey over from England."

"Off with you, then, Watson," Holmes said, flashing him a brief, encouraging smile. Suddenly Watson found himself wondering how much of the previous night's events had been anticipated by Holmes, and played in such fashion as to eliminate all other contenders for Leighton's attention save Watson. It was, he considered, well within Holmes' ability to extrapolate that far in advance, for he had seen him do similar feats; but had the detective actually done so? Watson suspected he would never know, of a certainty. "For we are finished here, and the work I plan to-day is not such that you can help me with, anyway. And Leigh rather needs you, I think."

"What are you going to do, then?" Watson asked, dabbing his napkin to his mouth before laying it aside and starting to stand. Holmes pushed back his chair, as did Whitesell; the others took it as their signal to rise as well.

"I had thought," Holmes began, the corner of his lip quirking in wry humour, "to have another look over the artefacts we have uncovered so far, to see if they might provide any more clews as to where this accursedly elusive tomb might be hidden. However, as Phillips appeared to head off in that direction also, it may be that I should make other plans! It would not do for a fight to break out amongst the antiquities!"

"No, no!" Nichols-Woodall laughed outright. "That would not be good at all! They would be smashed to tiny bits! Willingham, by way of a palliative, may I suggest that we join Holmes, and discuss our findings *en masse*?[43] Certainly our presence should serve as a damper on young Phillips' unbridled passions, and may well prevent disaster befalling our hard-won treasures! What do you say, Thomas?" Nichols-Woodall addressed Beaumont in a friendly fashion. "Do you cast in your lot with my idea?"

"I think it is a good plan, Parker, indeed," Beaumont averred with a smile.

"Yes, yes! A capital notion, Parker!" Whitesell agreed, shaking his head in gratification. "Let us betake ourselves to the artefact tables! Lord Trenthume, would you do us the honour? Dr. Watson, if you should want us, we will be there until at least lunchtime."

---

43   "In a mass," or in a group; Latin or French.

"Very well," Watson confirmed. "Professor, if Phillips is having trouble with that nose of his, tell him to come by the hospital during hours and I'll set it for him, if needs be. I'll make sure your daughter is busy elsewhere so that she need not deal with him."

"I will, young man," Whitesell agreed. "Off with you, now," and Watson headed for the dwelling tents as the rest of the men made their way in the general direction of the dig site and the artefact tent just beside it.

*****

When the men walked into the artefact tent, Phillips was not working. Instead, he was seated on one of the folding stools, leaning forward slightly, holding both hands to his badly swollen nose and grimacing in pain. "Is it broken?" Whitesell asked immediately.

"I'm not sure. I think it may be," Phillips answered nasally, shooting Holmes a dirty look. "It isn't quite the same shape it was before, and it sort of points off to one side now."

"Don't take a swing at a fellow who is more experienced, next time, and it won't get broken," Whitesell replied sharply, addressing more the hostile glance at Holmes than what Phillips had actually said. Phillips muttered something under his breath. "What's that? Speak up, Mr. Phillips."

"I said, you said that already, this morning," Phillips grumbled.

"Or words to that effect, yes. As well as several more. Dr. Watson has offered to treat your nose and set it if necessary—"

"And by the look of it, I'd say it's necessary," Nichols-Woodall interjected.

"—If you will go by the infirmary during surgery hours," Whitesell finished his statement.

"Will that make it feel less like an elephant has trodden on it?" Phillips wondered.

"Eventually," Nichols-Woodall answered, ending the succinct statement with a sound suspiciously like a snort. Holmes assumed by his expression that the geologist was trying not to smirk, and concluded that the other man had had some experience in fights, himself. A quick assessment of Nichols-Woodall's nose reinforced that impression: it was mildly crooked, canting off to the left a smidge, likely placed there by a wicked right cross, the consulting detective adjudged.

"Well, then when do the surgical hours start?" Phillips queried somewhat impatiently. Holmes pulled his pocket-watch and consulted it.

"In a little over an hour," the detective answered. "In the meanwhile, if I might suggest, based on experience," here he cut a sidelong glance at Whitesell, who looked satisfied, "if I were in your position, I should go lie down with an ice bag, assuming we have any ice in camp."

"I'm afraid we do not," Lord Trenthume noted with regret. "I had hoped to arrange it for just such a circumstance...well, for injuries, at any rate...as well as possibly for drinks, but no amount of money can purchase it, at this point. We are simply a little too far from the nearest source, and in too warm a climate, for it to survive shipment. Later in the season we may be able to obtain some, but not as yet."

"Well, but still, Holmes has a point," Beaumont decided. "Even without ice, lying down is certain to help matters. It will definitely reduce the swelling, especially if you use several pillows to elevate your head a little. A cool, moist compress will serve reasonably well in the stead of the ice, also. And this we can provide."

"Very well," Phillips conceded with a sigh. "I fear I am getting little work done in any case, for the deuced thing throbs like blazes, and I cannot concentrate for the life of me. With your leave, Professor?"

"By all means, son, go lie down and try to relax," Whitesell said, gentling his tone, "and then go see Dr. Watson in an hour, and have him fix the thing."

Phillips nodded and left, *en route* to his tent, and the camp cot within.

*****

When Watson arrived at Leighton Whitesell's tent, the door flap was open; Leighton sat at her little table inside, a book open in front of her, but she was not looking at it. Instead she stared into space, an incredibly sad expression on her face.

He cleared his throat loudly as he rapped against the central support pole, and she jumped, startled.

"Oh! Dr. Watson," she said, glancing at the entrance and seeing him waiting. "I'm so sorry; I was wool-gathering. Were you waiting long? What on earth are you doing here?"

"No, I only just arrived. Your father sent me to see about you, Miss Whitesell. May I come in? Or perhaps you might wish to come out?"

"The flap is well open; that should satisfy the proprieties. Come in, whilst I fetch an extra chair from Da's tent."

He stood back briefly while she exited, returning moments later with an additional camp stool. He followed her into the tent then, and saw her seated in her folding chair before taking the stool himself.

"So Da sent you?" Leighton wondered. "Why? Or did he say?"

"Yes. We had some...concerns...about your, ah, emotional state. We did not wish you to fall into a melancholy over this whole very upsetting situation, so at your father's urging, I popped 'round to see about you."

"Well," she answered, and Watson thought the word sounded more like a sigh than anything else, "I suppose that's a reasonable thing, for I am certainly embarrassed and discouraged by all of it."

"Rest assured, anything you wish to confide in me will remain with me, and none other. I take my patients' confidences VERY seriously."

"Oh, I've no doubt," Leighton offered him a meagre, wistful smile. "Sherry has nothing but good to say of you, and he says you are a consummate gentleman."

Surprised, Watson felt himself flush, and tucked his head slightly.

"He does me too much honour," he murmured. "But if I may help, I shall."

"May I ask you a few questions? About Sherry, and, and, things?"

"Certainly. If they do not violate his confidences as a friend, I will endeavour to answer you, if it will help."

"All right. And no, I shan't ask anything too private, I think. He is so intelligent, and he has never been anything but charming to me, even as a child. I can scarce credit it — but I credit even less that he could, or would, tell me a falsehood. So does he really plan to remain single for his whole life, as he said?"

"If he said so, I cannot gainsay it."

"Come now, Doctor," Leighton scolded. "Surely you hold his trust as much as I."

"Well then...he does intend it," Watson confirmed, relenting in light of the girl's prior knowledge, obviously imparted by Holmes himself. "I do not really understand as yet why he feels it necessary, so I do not entirely agree with his decision, but then, it is not my decision to make."

"But you are bosom friends," she pointed out. "How is it that you, of all people, do not understand? Surely you would have discussed such a thing, would you not?"

"We are bosom friends, because we...connected, is perhaps a good word…relatively quickly after meeting," Watson explained. "I hope you grasp my meaning in that. But we have not actually known each other that long, Holmes and I, not really. We met last year when we both went in search of decent, affordable lodgings in London, and decided a particular flat in Baker Street suited very nicely, if we shared the cost. A mutual friend, a medical dresser from St. Bart's named Stamford, introduced us, rather fortuitously, we felt."

"So you have scarcely known each other a year."

"Just a bit over, actually. It was, if I recall correctly, late summer of last year when we were introduced, Holmes and I. The flat he had already found was to our liking; we leased it and moved in, and proved congenial companions. But he only took me into his confidence regarding his cases about six or seven months back. We have but grown closer as friends since then. So yes, I know of his decision, but…well, it is not an easy thing to discuss, as I'm sure you can fathom. Matters and mind-sets have to be just so, for the subject even to come up, let alone be considered in detail. And so I have insufficient understanding, as yet."

"He does not have many friends…"

"No. He does not. Nor does he especially seek for any. But…I think he cherishes those he has, all the more, as a consequence."

"Yes, he said as much."

"And you are one of those friends, Miss Whitesell."

Leighton nodded. "Yes, he said that, too." She sighed. "I didn't mean to offend him, Doctor. I…he was special to me, from the moment I met him as a child, and, and you see, I…" Leighton broke off and sighed again. Suddenly the light broke for Watson.

"You had a case of calf love for him as a child, didn't you?" he asked. She blushed a bright red.

"Well, I did. I…confessed it to him during our walk last night. But… he made it plain that, that it could never be…more than a childhood fantasy…" She raked a distracted hand over her face, tangling her fingers in the hair above her forehead; the action pulled several golden strands loose from her chignon, and they drifted across her cheek. Instinctively Watson reached up to tuck them behind her ear, and she looked up, meeting his eyes, as he did so. He froze for a split-second before withdrawing his hand.

"What shall I do, Dr. Watson?" Leighton asked, her voice soft.

"Are you asking me as a physician, or as a friend?" he wondered.

"You…would still consider being my friend, after what happened with Sherry?"

"It was no one's fault that your respective feelings for each other were not mutual. And you have not parted in antagonism."

"No..."

"Thus, if you are willing, yes, I should like to be your friend."

Leighton nodded slowly.

"Yes, I think I would like that, as well."

"So. Are you asking me as your physician, or as your friend?" he reiterated.

"Both, maybe."

Watson leaned back, considering the situation. He well knew he would prefer more than simple friendship, but that more might not be forthcoming, and it would be unwise to throw away what he did have for what he might not get. Even more, he wanted to be careful to avoid violating her trust in him, her confidences, yet still find a way to help her out of her current doldrums. Finally he decided to ask a few more questions before making a recommendation.

"The other day, at Holmes' suggestion, you came and worked at the hospital for a few hours."

"Yes."

"I...know I was a poor substitute for Holmes, who is the one you would have preferred to be with," he added, "but you seemed to be interested in the work, and at dinner, you were rather enthusiastic..."

"You are no man's 'poor substitute,' Doctor, and I am sorry I gave that impression," Leighton remarked, somewhat shamefaced. "But yes, I had hoped to spend more time with Sherry, and I fear that made me petulant instead of appreciative. Please accept my sincere apologies."

"No matter," Watson waved away the apology. "I was not attempting to reproach you, but rather seeking information. Did you actually enjoy the work itself?"

"I did, yes."

"Well, then. In lieu of sitting here staring into space, as you were when I found you just now, I think it might be better if you were to come to the infirmary and join my staff, at least for the time being. It will give you something to focus on, rather than pining, and I can assure you that the skills you will learn will be useful in future, no matter what comes."

"But..." Leighton began.

"But what?"

"What if Landers, or, or Sherry, God forbid, should be hurt? I..."

"Would not be comfortable tending to them," Watson finished her statement, understanding. "Trust me to take that into account, my dear. I will ensure you are not required to do anything that will make you uncomfortable." He paused, then added, "I cannot speak for Mr. Phillips, of course. But I can readily tell you that Holmes regrets having to hurt you, and still desires your friendship. When you are ready," he amended. She nodded.

"When I am ready," she agreed. "I promise you, Doctor, I will not hold him off forever. Just until…I can forget the embarrassment of, of… oh, Doctor, of that whole dreadful evening."

"Good. Yes, I understand, and so does he, for it was not especially enjoyable for him, either. And since we are friends now, I should like it very much if you would call me John," Watson offered. "You must still call me 'Doctor' in the hospital, of course, but otherwise, if you like, you may use my Christian name."

"I would like that…John," she said with a shy smile. "Do you please call me Leighton, or Leigh, if you would prefer. My closest friends do."

"Thank you, Leighton." He returned her smile. "I think I shall refrain from the more familiar form of your name until we know each other a wee bit better."

"That is fine, John. When do we need to go to the infirmary to begin work?"

"Well," here Watson pulled out his pocket-watch to check the time, "formal hours do not begin for another, oh, half an hour yet. Morning hours are from ten until the noon luncheon bell; afternoon hours from after the siesta, or roughly 2pm, until the dinner warning bell. An emergency is dealt with whenever it comes up, of course, and you would be expected at hospital if and when one is announced. But if you would like, we can go now. There should be no one else there at this hour, as we currently have no overnight patients, and I can give you a little more of a beginning tutorial than you have yet received."

"And maybe we can get to know each other a bit better, my new friend," Leighton said, offering him another smile, her expression lightening.

Watson smiled again and offered his arm. She took it, and they left her tent, headed for the camp hospital.

*****

At the infirmary, the pair started getting to know each other better, around Watson giving Leighton a much more thorough introduction to the medical equipment and techniques. Some fifteen minutes later, the rest of the hospital staff began arriving, and Watson formally introduced them.

"Leighton, this is my staff. You did not get to meet them properly the other day, and I should like to rectify that now. This is Sati, my orderly; Alimah, my emergency triage nurse; and Wahbiyah, my anaesthetist. All, this is Leighton Whitesell, the Professor's daughter. She will be joining us to learn some nursing techniques. If you would all be so kind as to assist her in learning, I would greatly appreciate it."

"It will be our honour," Alimah said with a beatific smile, her white hair framing her dark face beautifully beneath her *hijab*.[44]

"Sati," Watson continued, "I would like for you to begin by showing Leighton where everything is. Leighton, we are all on a given-name basis here; I feel it makes for good morale."

"Except for our greatly respected Doctor," Wahbiyah said with a smile; she seemed not terribly much older than Leighton. "Dr. Watson is a good man, very kind and understanding."

"He is the chief of staff," Sati declared. He was a handsome man, dark-complected as all his fellow Egyptians, tall and slim, yet with a wiry strength which sometimes reminded Watson of Holmes himself. "We owe him our respect, if for no other reason. But he has also earned it, for he is obviously skilled and knowledgeable, and he is also very benevolent and thoughtful. Doctor, if you would be so good as to tell me what Leighton's duties will be, I will keep that in mind when I work with her."

"For now, Leighton will be responsible for stocking supplies, and laying them out on the surgical trays when needed," Watson decreed. "I will add to those duties as she learns her way."

"Very good," Sati sketched a slight bow. "Miss Leighton, would you accompany me, please?"

As the two headed off, Watson put out a staying hand, putting the index finger of his other hand to his lips to indicate quiet, and gestured the two remaining women closer.

"Professor Whitesell has requested I try to keep his daughter's spirits up," he told them in a low tone. "She is interested in the work, and it will

---

44 Head scarf, veil; the cloth that covers a Muslim woman's head and shoulders: Arabic

keep her mind occupied."

"Ah, yes, I heard of the fight of last night," Alimah murmured. "Most distressing for a girl of that age. So you would like us to help you maintain a cheery atmosphere in the infirmary."

"Precisely," Watson said in relief. "And, ah, should Mr. Phillips or Mr. Holmes come in, notify me right away, and if you can, divert Miss Leighton, until such time as I tell you otherwise."

"Very good, sir," Wahbiyah agreed.

"Let us go aid Sati, Wahbiyah," Alimah said to the younger woman. "We can get to know Miss Leighton better in the doing."

Watson watched in satisfaction as the two Muslim women moved to join the other two members of his staff.

*****

The science team had moved one of the tables from the artefact tent to the outside, just in front of the door flaps, and spread out the maps, weighting the corners against vagrant breezes with convenient rocks.

"...So here is the layout of Wadi al Muluk[45]," Whitesell said, running a hand over a map of the Valley of the Kings, "and here is the terrain of our own valley, or cañon, as Thomas here likes to term it." He ran another hand over a topographic map of the area in which they stood.

"I'm not so sure it is Abwab al Muluk[46] we should be comparing it to, Will," Nichols-Woodall suggested. "I'm inclined to think there is more similarity, at least geologically speaking, to Ta-Set-Neferu[47]."

"Possibly, possibly, Parker," Whitesell murmured, studying the map of the Valley of the Queens, putting it alongside the other two. "Yes, I see your point. There is a certain similarity in the layout of the ridges and spurs. Yet, the Valley of the Queens is not so very different, really, from that of the Kings."

"True," Beaumont agreed. "So what are you suggesting, *mes amis*?"

"I think we should mark off the locations of the tombs from the known sites on the map of THIS site," Whitesell proposed. "Then, Parker, you look to see what fits and what doesn't, from a geologic perspective, and that may well tell us where the various pre-dynastic

---

45   "The Valley of Kings," Egyptian.
46   "Valley of the Gates of the Kings," Egyptian; an alternate naming of The Valley of the Kings.
47   "The Place of the Children of the Pharaoh," Egyptian; the formal name of The Valley of the Queens.

tombs are, here."

"It seems a reasonable start," Holmes decided.

"Agreed," Nichols-Woodall assented. "Beaumont?"

"I concur," the other archaeologist said. "It is, as Monsieur Holmes says, a good place to start."

"Well, then, someone fetch the grease pens," Whitesell ordered, "and let us get started."

*****

About half past ten that morning, Landers Phillips walked into the hospital tent, holding his nose and grimacing in pain. He walked right into Leighton Whitesell, who had her back to him, stacking fresh linens, before he knew what he was about. He looked up, startled, to see what he had run into, just as she spun in surprise.

"Leigh!" he exclaimed, and the other staff members spun likewise; Watson cursed under his breath. "What are you doing here?!"

"Helping," she replied tightly. "Which is more than you seem to be doing at the moment."

"Eh," he grunted. "That lout Holmes must have broken my nose last night when I was defending your honour, my dear. I've come to see about getting it set properly."

Leighton drew herself up. Watson swore the temperature in the infirmary dropped twenty degrees in an instant.

"Then you wasted your time and got your nose broken for nothing last night, for there was no stain upon my honour," she told him, her voice ice-cold.

"Perhaps, perhaps not," Phillips replied, face turning red. "But he certainly hurt you, now, didn't he?"

"That is none of your business, MISTER Phillips," she declared, then spun on her heel, gathered the linens she'd dropped, and carted them off to sort through. As she passed Watson, she jerked her head back toward Phillips and muttered, "He's all yours, John."

"I'll take care of it, Leighton," he murmured back, irked at the man himself. "Do you go fold some clean linens, and stay in the back, out of sight. Everything is fine." She nodded, and he walked over to Phillips, as Sati and Wahbiyah eased themselves between Leighton and Watson's patient.

*****

"Broken nose, eh?" Watson noted as he walked up, surveying Phillips' facial bruises, black eyes, and crooked nose. The physician's skilled hands slid lightly over the protuberance, palpating lightly, feeling the bone and cartilage beneath the flesh, as he gazed into the other man's eyes. He did not entirely like what he saw there, and it had nothing to do with Phillips' attitude.

"I think so," a diffident Phillips said, sitting down in the folding chair Watson indicated. "Can you fix it, Doctor?"

"I can," Watson agreed. "Take a deep breath and hold it."

"What? Why?" Phillips asked, as Watson placed one hand firmly behind Phillips' head, and got a good strong grip on his nose with the other. Then he jerked the nose sideways and down. There was a loud, crunching pop, and a trickle of blood surged from Phillips' nostrils.

"EEEYOW!" Phillips screamed. "Hellfire and damnation, Doctor! What the blazes are you doing?!"

"Setting your nose," Watson said calmly. "It was indeed broken."

"Did you have to be so rough?"

"Did you think it would be easy to set?" Watson turned. "Alimah, would you bring me some packing?"

"Right here, Doctor," the older woman said, approaching with the tray she had anticipated and prepared. Lying on it were several rolls of cotton gauze of narrow diameter, and a surgical forceps.

"What's that for?" a surly Phillips demanded, holding his nose tightly with his left hand. Watson smacked his hand away.

"Get away from that," he said, curt, "unless you want me to have to set it again."

"Oh, HELL no," Phillips muttered, dropping his hands to his sides. "What's that for, I asked."

"To stop the bleeding," Watson said, grabbing a roll and shoving it up Phillips' right nostril. "And to help keep everything in place until it can heal."

"OWWW!" Phillips howled. "THAT HURTS!"

"Of course it does," Watson snapped. "You broke the ruddy damned thing by getting into an unnecessary fight last night, with someone far better than you are." He used a pair of forceps to push the roll deeper into the nostril as Phillips yelped and groaned in pain. "It's going to hurt. And I find that injuries that are obtained due to one's own stupidity tend to hurt worse than others." A roll of gauze went into the other nostril, and Phillips let out another roar of pain, which subsided into additional whimpers as Watson used the forceps to ensure that, too, was firmly and deeply seated in the nostril. "Next time, my advice to you, sir, would be to ascertain that a lady actually needs her honour defended, and WANTS YOU to defend it, before taking it upon yourself to do the deed." He took the pad of gauze Alimah handed him, placed it over Phillips' entire nose, then took a full roll of gauze and wrapped it around and around Phillips' head to hold the dressing in place. He finished off by pinning down the gauze, just behind Phillips' left ear, so it could not unwind. "There. We're finished."

"How'b I s'bosed doo breade lig dis?" Phillips demanded to know.

"Through your mouth, until I say otherwise," a terse Watson informed him. "Wahbiyah, please prepare some pain pills for Mr. Phillips. Laudanum, tincture number 23, please. Standard dose. No more than half a dozen to take with him, and one for dosing right now."

"Yes, Doctor." She moved to the medicinal cabinet, unlocked it with a key on her chatelaine[48], and started the work of compounding the medication.

"Mr. Phillips," Watson addressed his patient, "these pills should ease your pain. They will make you very drowsy, however, so I should strongly recommend you return to your bunk for the rest of the day, and remain there until you have finished the course of medication. I will notify Professor Whitesell personally of your indisposition. You are to take the medication every eight hours for two days. By then you should be able to make do with a salicylic acid powder."

"Bud whad ib de paid geds worse?" Phillips asked. "Id does dod feel ady bedder daow."

"You deal with it, and you take a powder in addition to the pills," Watson declared, stern. "Or come back to me. Under no circumstances do you take the laudanum any more frequently, else you may become addicted."

"So?"

"Have you ever seen any of the poor unfortunate frequenters of opium dens, Mr. Phillips?"

"Ub, yes?"

"Laudanum is tincture of opium. Do you want to end up like them?"

"Oh. I see your poidt; do, I doo dod."

"Good. Then do as I say, and everything will be fine. Trust me on

---

48   A chain, usually decorative and hung from a belt, on which women carried keys, household tools, and similar. Common in the Victorian era.

this."

"All righd." Phillips sighed.

"Here you are, Doctor," Wahbiyah said, coming to Watson with a tray on which was a small dark glass bottle; inside were just discernible six tiny pills. Next to it was a small dosing cup containing one additional pill, and a glass of water.

"Excellent, Wahbiyah, thank you," Watson said, picking up the bottle and handing it to Phillips. "Here we are. Tuck this into your pocket, Phillips, then take this pill. It is..." He pulled out his pocket-watch and checked it. "It is nearly eleven o' clock in the morning. Your next dose is due at seven o' clock to-night."

Phillips tucked the bottle into his waistcoat pocket, placed the pill in his mouth, then washed it down with the glass of water.

"Very good," Watson said. "Sati, can you see Mr. Phillips back to his tent? I expect he will be more comfortable there than in a hospital cot, but if he is unused to it, the laudanum may take effect much faster than he expects. Chances are, he is already mildly concussed, and with his nose broken as well, it would not do for him to pass out halfway there."

"I should be happy to do so, Doctor," Sati replied, and escorted Phillips out of the hospital tent.

*****

After Phillips left the infirmary, Leighton returned from the back, where she had put the linens she'd dropped into the dirty hamper to be picked up and washed by the camp launderers. Then she had folded towelling. Now she placed the stack of clean towels into their proper shelf. She turned as Watson came up to her.

"Are you all right?" he asked quietly.

"Yes, I suppose so," she decided with a sigh, leaning lightly against the table. "I could have done without that, however."

"Holmes said much the same thing last night after the fight."

"I'm sure he did," she said, and giggled.

"Well! That sounded good, if unexpected," Watson noted.

"I suppose," she considered. "John, tell me something."

"If I can, of course I shall."

"Were, um, weren't you just a, a little hard on poor Landers' nose?" she wondered. "They might have heard him scream in Cairo!"

"No, my dear, I did not take out my feelings on Phillips, I assure you," Watson chuckled. "No matter what I may have thought, what I may have said — and I freely admit to dressing him down. But I have too much respect for my chosen profession for such as that. No, setting a nose is not fun in any event, either for physician or patient, though it is rather harder on the patient! Every nose I have ever set — and there have been a few — and every nose I have ever seen set — and those have been even more — the patient has reacted in the same fashion. Though if it makes Phillips think before leaping in next time, I am glad of it!"

Leighton fairly doubled up in giggles, and Watson grinned.

"I take it, you approve of him using his head for something more than a hat rack, next time?" Watson asked.

"Oh, John! Indeed I do!" she agreed. "Oh, do understand — he is a nice enough man, and quite smart in his own way. But...he was reared in a bit, um, less refined an environment than you and I," she explained. "I just..."

"No, it's all right, I see," Watson cut her off. "Is he trying to court you without your permission, then?"

"Didn't Sherry tell you?"

"Oh no, not unless you told him to, or gave him permission to do so," Watson said. "That would not be respecting your privacy."

"Well then, yes, he is," Leighton confessed. "That was part of the reason for staying so close to Sherry, you see, to ward off Landers' attentions. And Sherry knew, and, and agreed. Now, with everything that has happened — I just don't know. I don't mind being friends with Landers, but—" She broke off abruptly with a sharp inhalation.

"What is it? What's wrong?" Watson asked, concerned. Leighton gave him a rueful grin.

"Let us just say I suddenly understand Sherry's point of view a lot better," she offered, wry. "While I'm not of a lower, um, class than Sherry, I know he's very, very smart, and so learnéd. Me? Well, not so much, I suppose. I...guess I can understand why he wouldn't be interested, even if he was 'so inclined,' as I think he put it."

"Do not denigrate yourself, Leighton," Watson advised. "You are a lovely woman, with intelligence, wit, and fire. Just because you were not able to catch Holmes' eye — and I have yet to see any woman who could do so — does not make you incapable of catching another's." At that remark, Leighton scrutinised him intently, and he suddenly realised the way his statement might be taken. "Oh, I, um, that is, I didn't mean..."

"Hush, John," she told him with a gentle smile. "Sherry already told me you found me attractive, and I'm flattered. I just wondered if you realised beforehand how you had phrased that statement."

"I...did not," he said, sheepish. "In light of that, I am no longer certain I should make the offer I was about to..."

"What was it?"

"Well, since Holmes is no longer available for the purpose, I was going to offer to keep you company, so as to help you avoid Phillips. But perhaps you had rather I didn't."

"Really? You were going to do that? Just to help me avoid Landers?"

"I swear," Watson averred, putting his hand to his chest. "I had no ulterior motives behind it."

"Hm." She pretended to consider, then smiled. "I think I should like that, John."

CHAPTER 7
HOMING IN ON A MYSTERY

"It has to be," Nichols-Woodall decided, tapping the maps with his index finger. "These right here. These would be the best strata for excavating with the tools that they would have had to hand."

"Do you think so?" Beaumont asked, considering the idea. "Why?"

"Because they are soft enough for the brass and bronze chisels the workers would have used to cut the stone, but strong enough to stand up to the intervening time without collapse."

"I think I agree with him, Thomas," Whitesell said. "What say you, Holmes?"

"It makes sense to me," Holmes agreed. "Especially based on the incised rock I translated the other day, which discovery site seems to me to point to that general area, though I think based on that alone, I should move a smidgen farther to the south. I defer to Dr. Nichols-Woodall's superior knowledge of the strata, however."

"But if I understand correctly," Lord Trenthume interjected, "the stone we found the other day is a different kind from the stones you are proposing they excavated, Parker."

"It is," Nichols-Woodall admitted. "But that is not a difficulty, milord. They may well have dressed harder stones, not only to help support the doorway arch, but to face the façade, and thus make it stronger, more resistant to weathering. They desired their tombs to last for the ages, but needed the rock in which they situated them to be soft enough to carve out such a large space."

"Aha, I see," Lord Trenthume replied, and subsided.

"It does, as you say, make sense, Parker," Beaumont noted. "Where is the softest point, do you think? Is that not where we should begin digging the exploration trench?"

"Right here." Nichols-Woodall pointed to a spot on the topographic map. "I think we should start digging trenches here..." he pulled the map over, "and here."

"Where is Phillips?" Lord Trenthume wondered. "We should have him fetch Udail, to start the trench digging."

"Oh, he is indisposed and lying down, Cortland," Whitesell said. "I had a note from Dr. Watson a bit ago. His nose was indeed broken, with possible concussion into the bargain, and Dr. Watson set the nose, then sent him off to bed with some laudanum for the pain, to sleep it off. I suspect he will be invalided for some few days."

"Which will teach him to pick a fight with Mr. Holmes, here, next time," Nichols-Woodall chuckled. "That was a nice combination you used, Holmes, if I may say so. Never mind, milord; it isn't that important. In fact, I think I shall go find Udail myself; that way, I can tell him exactly where I want him to begin digging."

"Very good, then," Lord Trenthume said. "It is almost time for luncheon, so the rest of us may as well repair to our tents to freshen up a bit, while you and Udail get the logistics laid for the work this afternoon."

*****

Unsurprisingly, Landers Phillips was not at luncheon that day; Leighton Whitesell, much to her father's delight and Holmes' secret pleasure, came to lunch on Watson's arm, the two of them laughing at some unheard joke.

"Dr. Nichols-Woodall will be a bit late," Whitesell announced to the wait staff. "He went to the dig pits to fetch Udail and tell him where to dig exploratory trenches this afternoon. You may begin service when you are ready, and he will join us as soon as he may."

"Da!" Leighton clapped her hands happily. "You have figured out where it is?"

"Where it most likely is," Whitesell corrected. "Yes, we believe so. It will take some digging to verify it, however. So. Have you had a... pleasant morning, my dear girl?"

"I have, Da," she said, offering a shy smile to both her father and her companion. "John, here, has taken just as good care of me as Sherry has."

"'John,' is it, eh?" Holmes murmured to Watson, under cover of the first course service.

"It is now," Watson replied in kind. "I am still not sure where this is going, though."

"Time enough for that, old chap."

"True."

*****

The entire team, including the diggers, were excited over the possibility of finally finding the tomb, and the season was now late enough to work throughout the afternoon, with some slight considerations of health and safety, to include water-bearers moving through the dig field to ensure that those in the pits, working with spades and picks, remained well-hydrated. So Udail asked for volunteers to work through the siesta, and had them aplenty; in fact, there were none left who wanted a siesta, so the break was promptly curtailed. The work commenced enthusiastically right after lunch on the two sites selected by Dr. Nichols-Woodall, and continued until the dinner warning gong. By that time, both trenches butted up solidly against the bluffs in question, and were fully twenty yards long, four to five feet wide, and nearly six feet deep...

...And contained absolutely nothing.

*****

Dinner proved as disconsolate as luncheon had been exuberant. Once again Leighton was walked in by Watson, with a groggy Phillips wandering in moments later, and the three were informed of the lack of discovery.

"Aw," Leighton murmured, disappointed.

"Yeah," Phillips agreed, wistful — or as much so as a man thoroughly stupefied on narcotics, with a huge dressing over his nose, could be. "It, ub, would be dice...to, uh, fide it, already."

The others blinked in surprise, distracted from the previous conversation by Phillips' obvious intoxication. Watson scrutinised Phillips briefly with a professional eye, then threw Professor Whitesell a glance that managed to be simultaneously warning, sympathetic, and sheepish, just before he shrugged with the faintest hint of a wry grin, and the Professor nodded his understanding of the unspoken message: *It will be best to ignore the majority of what Phillips says, for now — it is apt to be the laudanum talking, but it is a necessary evil, so please bear with it.*

"Landers, my lad," Whitesell murmured, loud enough for everyone at the table to hear, but gentle enough to convey his compassion, "are you sure you should be at table? You appear to be a bit... groggy."

"Ub, probably nod, Professor," Phillips admitted slowly, swaying slightly in his chair. "I'b sdill tagig de laudadub. Bud I god hugry, ad I figured id would be bedder if I ade sobedig."

The others took this in, translating the man's speech with varying degrees of facility. Finally Lord Trenthume queried, "Did he say laudanum?"

"Yesh, I did," came the response from Phillips. "For by dose." He pointed in the general vicinity of that appendage; given the large bandage on it, it was hard to miss.

"Aha. That explains much. One of us will see him safely back to his tent after dinner, Will," Beaumont addressed Whitesell in a quiet, unassuming voice. "Dr. Watson, *mon ami*, surely he does not need to be wandering about like this, by himself? While taking the laudanum?"

"No, he really shouldn't," Watson admitted. "But as I saw Sati, my orderly, leave the infirmary as soon as the warning gong rang for dinner, then spotted him crossing between mess tents as I was escorting Leighton to dinner, I think Phillips, here, was likely in safe hands. Sati has been popping over two or three times daily to see about him in any event."

"Yesh," Phillips slurred, nodding. "Sati. He'ped be ged doo didder. Cobig bag doo ged be afder. Good bad, he is."

"'Good bad'?" Lord Trenthume puzzled.

"I think he means, 'good man,'" Holmes suggested.

"Yesh. Good bad." Phillips nodded again.

"Ah. Capital," Whitesell decided, then seemed to have a thought. "Abraam? No wine for Mr. Phillips to-night. I think the laudanum is quite enough as is."

"Yes sir," the sommelier replied discreetly from the corner of the tent. "I had already rather anticipated it."

"Very good, then."

The table fell silent as they all began the first course.

"I am so sorry, Professor, about the lack of findings to-day," a sincere Watson took the opportunity to say, after several moments. "I thought surely you had it. Where will you try next?"

"Parker has several more ideas," Whitesell said, confident, nibbling absently at his food while keeping a concerned eye on Phillips. "We shall try each in turn, and if there is anything here to find, sooner or later, we shall find it."

*****

But they didn't. Trench after trench was cut, with no luck, and no tomb. His frustration rising, Professor Whitesell even began to doubt himself.

"Maybe we are not finding it because it is just not here," he said over dinner one evening fully a week later. "Perhaps I was wrong about this location. Perhaps I was wrong about the entire thing."

"No, Da!" Leighton exclaimed. "Surely not!"

"I do not believe you were wrong about the translation, Professor," Holmes said. "Once you told me about the particular passage, I found it in my texts, and studied it myself. And I firmly believe that your translation was more nearly accurate than the original translation was. It may be," he suggested, considering, "that this is simply not the site the text describes, after all, in despite of the apparent resemblance, and we shall have to find another."

"I think Holmes is correct," Beaumont offered. "We are merely digging in the wrong cañon. When once we find the right one, we shall find the tomb quickly, I think."

"Well, then. What do you recommend, gentlemen?" Whitesell asked, spreading his hands.

"I recommend we keep looking a little longer, Will," Nichols-Woodall declared, staunch. "We haven't exhausted all my options quite yet."

"I say we return to Cairo and research the text further," Beaumont said in an assured manner. "Perhaps we can locate the true area, so."

"I can't — no, I REFUSE to believe that the Professor could be wrong," Phillips said, steadfast. By this time he had finished the laudanum pills and Watson had removed the majority of the packing, though he was still taking powders for pain relief. There was still a fair amount of swelling and bruising, enough so that his speech continued mildly nasal, but he had returned to work...and consequently had noticed that Watson was now keeping company with a very cheerful Leighton Whitesell. The glares that had been reserved exclusively for Holmes were therefore now being transferred to the physician, and the student assistant was doing everything in his power to curry favour with the Professor, whether subtle or, more often, not so much so. Consequently, at this somewhat bombastic declamatory statement, most of the eyes at the table rolled in bored distaste, then ignored him altogether.

"Cortland?" Whitesell polled.

"I think I should split the difference, Will," Lord Trenthume offered.

"Try for a few more days; then, if we still have found nothing, repair to Cairo and ponder the matter. I see no point in wasting monies by digging pointless holes in the earth."

"And finally, Holmes," Whitesell said.

Holmes did not answer right away, but sat with his brows knit in thought.

"What is it, Holmes? Is something wrong?" Whitesell wondered, concerned.

"No, nothing, Professor — and everything," Holmes replied thoughtfully. "Because everything indicates, to my mind, that the tomb should be here, somewhere. And my gut is in agreement. Which latter virtually always means that my subconscious has deduced something of which my conscious mind has yet to become aware." He looked up and met the Professor's vivid blue eyes with his own grey gaze. "I think we should continue the search, Professor — right here."

"But Holmes, where else can we dig? The only sites left to try are composed of hard stone," Whitesell protested.

"Then you try the hard stone," Holmes announced.

"But the ancient Egyptians could not possibly have cut it with their bronze tools," Beaumont protested.

"Unless the strata change with depth," Holmes pointed out. "Just because what is on the surface in the modern day is too hard for bronze chisels, does not mean what is below, what was on THEIR surface level, was so hard as well. Professor, I would like to strongly urge you to at least finish out the calendrical week."

"Where do you suggest we try next, Holmes?" Nichols-Woodall asked. "My geological extrapolations have proven fruitless; what does your detection indicate, based upon the clews we have?"

"Over in the corner of the valley formed by the highest spur and the main range," Holmes said. "That is where I would try, for it is a strong area of the mountains, and the spur would act as a buttress, stabilising the entire structure — and surely, with their construction skills, the Egyptians would have known this. Moreover, everything I have seen — all the clews I have to hand — point to that area, at least in my mind. Meanwhile, I shall go to the artefact tent first thing in the morning and pore over the clews again to see what else I may find."

"The infirmary has been slow of late, and I don't have to be there until mid-morning," Watson noted. "If I may be of help, Holmes, you have only to ask. They can always send word if an emergency arises."

"Thank you, old chap; I shall take you up on that."

"I'll see word is sent to Sati, Doctor," Whitesell said. "That way, you may stay with Holmes all morning, and be fetched if needed."

"Very good," Watson agreed.

"So, gentlemen, what say you all?" Whitesell addressed the others.

"It's as good a plan as any, Will," Lord Trenthume said. "Sounds good to me."

"And me," Nichols-Woodall said.

"I suppose I shall go along with it, then," Beaumont agreed.

"Then to-morrow we dig in the corner of the spur," Whitesell decreed.

*****

The next morning after breakfast, the group split up. Holmes and Watson, accompanied by Lord Trenthume, removed to the artefact tent. Holmes produced his handmade map, and Watson and Lord Trenthume helped him verify the entries he had made upon it, fetching the artefact log as well as the artefacts themselves as confirmation. It was well past Watson's normal infirmary hours when they finished, but it all graphed to the appropriate spots on Holmes' chart. The detective studied his map, then sighed.

"I see nothing here that points me elsewhere than I recommended last night," he said. "Lord Trenthume, would you mind fetching that small clay tablet which Dr. Beaumont and Mr. Phillips found a day or two ago? I want to review the inscription again."

"Certainly, Holmes, it is just right over here," Lord Trenthume said, going to fetch it from its tray.

"Watson, would you care to learn a thing or two about hieroglyphs, while I work?" Holmes asked, reaching for the tablet. "Sometimes I find it is true that explaining a thing to another person may clarify it in one's own mind. So if you have any curiosity on the matter, it may kill two birds, as the saying is."

"I have been quite curious, actually, Holmes," Watson replied, pulling up a stool to sit at the detective's elbow.

"Very good. Let us start with some basics..."

*****

"Get Holmes!" Whitesell called from somewhere near the cliff's base, voice echoing among the rocks. "Tell him we've found the entrance to the tomb! There are inscriptions!"

Holmes, who had been seated at the artefact table for the last hour, studying the clay tablet discovered the day before and using it as a lesson in translation for Watson, glanced up at that worthy, who now stood beside him. Two sets of jaws dropped. Instantly Holmes rose and shoved the tablet back into Cortland's grasp, and the pair scrambled out of the tent, sprinting for the base of the bluff. Behind them, Lord Trenthume scurried to put the fragile clay tablet someplace safe before running after them.

Professor Whitesell, so excited as to be nearly hopping up and down, stood there awaiting them, several diggers clustered around. Behind him, its top some two feet below ground level, its threshold at the bottom of a large pit, was a stone lintel and door, cut directly from the bedrock. The lintel was inscribed all around with ancient hieroglyphics, and Holmes crouched low to glance over them, as Udail studied how best to open the door without causing damage. Significantly, one block near the top of the left-hand side of the door frame was missing; the stone which they had found a few weeks prior, and which fragmentary inscription Holmes had translated, appeared to be a perfect fit for the gap.

"Well?" Whitesell demanded of Holmes, delighted. "I knew it! I told you we'd find it! Very well, so I had a bit of hesitation; it was still here, right where you said! Pharaoh Ka-Sekhen's tomb, right here, in the bloody hardest stone in the entire area!" He danced a few jig steps before turning to several workers. "Start cutting a ramp into the side of the pit. There are certain to be several large antiquities inside, sarcophagi and such, and it will be far easier to bring them out if we do not have to contend with ladders and block and tackle rigs." The men nodded and moved to one side, commencing to murmur among themselves about the most likely place to construct such a ramp, the gradient required, and the length it needed to be.

"Professor," Holmes began slowly, still considering the writing on the lintel, "I see nothing here about any pharaoh, let alone the names Ka or Sekhen. But I DO see quite a few warnings, of the, 'Abandon all hope, ye who enter here'[49] variety."

"Nonsense," Whitesell declared, eager. "Nothing new. Just more evidence of the so-called 'Mummy's Curse.' I put no stock in it. There

---

49   Dante Alighieri, The Divine Comedy, Part 1: The Inferno, most commonly paraphrased.

are precious few such real inscriptions as it is, which makes it a discovery, as well. They were likely all done for show — a baseless threat to strike fear into the hearts of the ignorant. Besides, look! Right there is where that lintel-stone came from, the one you translated a week or so back! And that certainly DID invoke Sekhen! Come, let's get down into the pit and see what we may find!" He promptly began scaling nimbly down the wooden ladder near the corner.

"Do you anticipate that one of, if not the, earliest pharaohs would have already established the need?" Holmes pointed out, climbing down, as did the others in their turn. "Surely Ka-Sekhen's tomb would have been created too early for grave-robbers to be desecrating the pharaonic tombs regularly. It was the pharaohs of the ninth and tenth dynasties that were most prone to inscribing curses, were they not? And we are presumably excavating the very first pharaoh. I put it to you that he would have had no reason for such a thing."

"Well, you do have a point..." Whitesell's moustache seemed to wilt slightly. He turned to study the oversized doorway which now loomed over them.

"All Holmes is saying is to be careful," Watson offered gently. "It may be the tomb of this Ka-Sekhen, or perhaps one of his near successors, or it may not. Don't some of these tombs have so-called booby traps? Or even faked entrances?"

"They do, and you are both right," Whitesell said with a sigh. "I really must learn not to get so heated over a discovery."

"It is a splendid discovery, whether or no, Professor," Phillips pointed out, shooting an annoyed glance at Holmes. It registered on the sleuth at that moment that the student assistant never had apologised as per Whitesell's orders; undoubtedly he was still resentful, and the hostile glance served to prove as much. "It is obviously a newly discovered tomb for SOME important Egyptian, which is wonderful. And if it is Ka-Sekhen's, so much the better."

"True, lad, true," Whitesell agreed, "but Holmes and the good doctor are perfectly correct, as well. It is far better to go inside cautiously... assuming there IS an 'inside,' I suppose...and emerge whole with our discovery, than to rush in where angels fear to tread and end up joining Ka-Sekhen in the realm of Anubis, as it were."

"Professor, come and see," the digger beside Udail remarked in heavily accented English. "Is not this the latch?"

Whitesell knelt beside the Egyptian and studied the small device the man had found, inset into the doorframe. He put out a hand to examine it more closely.

"Careful, Professor," Holmes murmured, watching, studying the entire doorway for possible traps.

*****

"I am, my boy, I am," Whitesell muttered absently. "I think that this is indeed the lock. It is a small latch set into a recess of the right lintel." He glanced up, to see Holmes' grey eyes intently scrutinising the framework, and recalled Holmes' principal occupation, deciding that caution likely dictated obtaining the detective's go-forth, as well. "Do you see anything, young Holmes?"

"May I?" Holmes asked permission, stepping forward.

"By all means." Whitesell backed up several paces to provide room, as did the digger and Udail, thus allowing Holmes to come in and run light hands gingerly over the entire structure, as high up as he could reach. Phillips scowled and folded his arms in impatience as he watched. "Anything there?" Whitesell followed up.

"Nothing that I can discern," Holmes admitted, moving back. "But there could easily be a deadfall on the other side of the door, so I do not recommend rushing through as soon as it is opened."

"No, no, I'm an old campaigner in that regard." Whitesell threw him a smile. "Even if there is no trap against grave robbers, the structure can still be unsound. And there is always the matter of determining if the air is bad." He nodded to his foreman. "Udail?"

"Yes, Professor?"

"Use the end of your spade, and stand as far back as you can, then press the latch." Whitesell waved to one of the other diggers standing by. "You over there, get a candle ready."

"No need, Professor. I have matches for my pipe." Holmes rummaged in his pockets before producing his waterproof match container.

"Very good, Holmes." He turned back to the other worker. "Go get torches, lanterns, and carbide lamps. Udail, go ahead with opening the tomb."

Udail nodded his understanding, then backed up, obeying the professor, as the other digger ran off to find the lighting equipment.

*****

When the spade handle depressed the latch, there was a single soft click. Udail glanced at Whitesell, who nodded and made a pushing gesture. So Udail used the spade handle as a probe, gently pressing against the door until the leverage point was found. As the airtight seal broke on the chamber within, there was a soft sough of air; dust swirled from the edges of the door, and it abruptly yawned into a pitch-black maw. A gust of warm, musty, stale air met their faces; Lord Trenthume wrinkled his nose. Udail, somewhat unnerved, backed up.

When no indication of deadfall or imminent roof collapse was forthcoming, a fearless Holmes strode forward, striking a match. He stepped onto the threshold and thrust his hand, holding the match, into the opening. It flickered from the breeze borne of motion, but burned brightly. Holmes whipped the match back and forth through the air, extinguishing it before it could burn his fingers, and turned.

Scanning the assembled group, he realised that no one was wearing a carbide lamp, and the worker had not yet returned with any. *Mm. Not even Whitesell expected this so soon,* he thought.

"Bring torches," was all he said.

*****

Professor Whitesell led the way. Within was a large anteroom, covered on all four walls with the most archaic form of hieroglyphics known, which Watson himself could tell matched the style of writing upon the doorposts outside, especially after Holmes' tutorial. The floor was inlaid with an intricate, patterned mosaic which seemed to represent a map of ancient Egypt and her occupied territories, with small tiles of what looked to be pure gold marking the ancient cities, and a trail of lapis lazuli forming the Nile; a large, bright golden star, the featured item in the mosaic, apparently represented the tomb's location, a matter which even Watson thought odd. The high ceiling was painted to represent, as closely as possible, the night sky; the stars appeared gilded in some fashion. *If the floor has gold in it, chances are, the ceiling does, too, I suppose,* the physician considered.

*****

On the far side of the chamber was another door, in similar style to the one through which they had already passed. Whitesell, Phillips, Beaumont, Lord Trenthume, Nichols-Woodall, and faithful Udail promptly made a bee-line for this door. Several diggers followed somewhat reluctantly, muttering in discontent, their faces blanched in fear, with downcast countenances. Holmes snatched a torch from one of these latter as he passed; the startled digger flinched badly, then stared at him for a moment as though he were possessed, before shrugging and moving on. Holmes turned to study the inscriptions upon the walls, holding the torch high.

"Anything interesting?" Watson wondered, wandering over to Holmes' side.

"Rather," Holmes muttered, lost in his musings.

"Did you note the floor mosaic?" Watson asked.

"Indeed. Quite intricate."

"I never heard of a Pharaoh's tomb marking its position on a map, did you?"

"No. Most unusual."

"Am I bothering you?"

"Not particularly. You point out matters that I had myself noted, and which, I believe, factor into this—" He waved his free hand at the carved wall.

*****

A feminine squeak at the outer door interrupted his train of thought before he could say more, and they looked up to see Leighton Whitesell dancing happily through the opening.

"We found it! We found it! Sherry pointed the way, and Da found it!" she sang, and clapped her hands in delight. "John, Sherry, isn't it WONDERFUL?"

"Indeed it is," Watson smiled, coming to her side and taking her hand into the crook of his arm. "Shall we go into the next room when the door opens?"

"Watson, don't let her go rushing off to the front," Holmes warned, pausing in his mental translation of the walls to turn and look at them. "Just because the vestibule, as it were, appears danger-free does not argue that there will not be more dangers deeper in."

"Oh, bosh, Sherry!" Leighton exclaimed. "Don't be such a spoil-sport!"

"Tut, my dear! A young lady of your breeding, and using such language!" Watson laughed, teasing her gently.

"Sorry to be a 'spoilsport,' as you put it, Leigh," Holmes replied, his tone a bit sharp and brooking no denial, "but some pharaohs were known for protecting their tombs in every possible way — including setting traps for the unwary. Your father has experience with these; you do not. Nor does Watson. I should not wish either of you to be hurt. So you will follow your father and his colleagues, well back in the group, or I shall ensure you remain here. And believe me, I CAN ensure it."

"But—"

"No, no, Holmes is quite right, my dear," Watson agreed, "we must be cautious and allow those with more acquaintance with these matters to take the lead. And never fear, my dear Holmes, I'll not let this lovely woman walk headlong into danger."

"Very good, Dr. Watson," Whitesell's voice floated back to them, and they realised he had been listening to the conversation. "Most appreciated. Thank you, Holmes, as well. Leighton — behave yourself, my dear little girl. You are entirely too impetuous and headstrong for your own good sometimes. Stay with our obliging doctor, and the both of you, do what Holmes tells you — he knows what he's about. I need to concentrate on this, and I cannot spare the thought processes to worry about keeping my daughter out of danger. So if you will not obey Holmes' instruction, go back to your tent."

"Yes, sir," Leighton said with a defeated sigh. "I'll listen to Sherry, and stay with him and John."

"I'll take care of the matter, with Holmes' advice, sir," Watson offered. "Never fear."

"Very good then. Thomas, where was I…?"

Just then, Phillips glanced back and glared at the trio in something very like hatred; Holmes raised an eyebrow at the other man's scowling expression. Realising he had been caught staring, Phillips wiped his expression and quickly returned his attention to the work on the inner door, just in time for it to slide open. Everyone jumped back for a moment, and even Holmes paused to ensure all was well: should a mass exodus become necessary, he intended to be ready and available to help everyone get out safely.

Professor Whitesell studied the doorway for long moments before thrusting his torch through. It sputtered briefly in the musty, ages-old air, then blazed strongly as circulation established itself from the outside, through the antechamber, and into the interior room. He nodded.

"Come along, then," he told the others, "but slowly and carefully.

Don't touch anything. Watch your step. And keep an eye out! We don't want to trigger anything nasty."

The group moved forward and through the door, Holmes bringing up the rear.

*****

"Oh, my dear Lord in heaven," Whitesell gasped in delight, staring at the only object in the inner chamber. Said inner chamber was rather plain, save for the starry sky pattern continued from the ceiling of the previous room, and some extensive, though basic and unadorned, hieroglyphic inscriptions on the walls. The floor was of simple, close-set native flagstones, smooth and polished. The featured object, however, was not ordinary at all. "I have never seen the like. What a lovely material for a sarcophagus!"

"Great Scot," Dr. Nichols-Woodall remarked in astonishment, staring at the large bowlder. "I don't think I've ever seen stone like that anywhere in Egypt, have you, Cortland?"

"No, not in all my extensive travels in this land," Cortland, Lord Trenthume replied, eyes wide. "Though...it looks familiar, somehow..."

"Yes, it does," a dreamy Leighton whispered; no one seemed to notice her comment, however. Holmes merely stood and studied the large thing in the centre of the inner chamber.

The entire group gazed as though mesmerised at the gleaming, dark blue stone shot through with white specks like stars. The block was some six feet long, three feet across at its widest point, and three feet deep. However, it was not quite rectangular, Holmes decided, but rather more sub-hexagonal, and irregular. There was no carving at all on it, nor was it shaped in any fashion other than the original rough shape of the stone, all of a single piece, which had then been highly polished.

"It's beautiful," Leighton murmured, and this time the acoustics of the room carried the sound to everyone in it. "It looks like the night sky."

"You are right, my dear, it does," Watson agreed, spellbound. "No wonder the ceiling is so decorated. It is indeed splendid. Quite a fitting resting place for a king."

"Except it isn't," Phillips declared bluntly, tone verging on insolent rudeness. Holmes observed he spoke more AT Watson than TO him.

He cannot get over his fixation on Leighton, the sleuth decided. *He simply transferred the bulk of his hostility from me to Watson, following Leigh's transfer of affections. Watson, you had best watch your back, old chap. Though Phillips IS rather slow on the uptake. He is only now noticing what I observed from the moment I entered the room.*

"What?" Professor Whitesell exclaimed in shock. "What do you mean, Landers?"

"Mr. Phillips is correct," Holmes agreed, moving to the fore to prevent Phillips from gaining control of the conversation; he did not wish for some sort of verbal joust to erupt. "I saw it, from the first moment I laid eyes on the stone. Professor, study this object more carefully. See, there is no lid, nor even an incised line for one. This is no sarcophagus. It is a solid block of stone, carefully interred."

"By Jove," Whitesell said in surprised realisation, running his hand along the smooth, polished stone. "So it is. Why on earth did they do that?"

*****

Holmes had spent the rest of the afternoon copying down the hieroglyphics on the lintel of the tomb entrance while the others detailed the tomb findings — or lack thereof; and all evening he sat on a stool with the lantern on the tiny table inside their tent, translating painstakingly, while Watson read a book. Finally he sat back and put his hand to his aching back with a slight groan. Watson looked up.

"What is wrong, Holmes?"

"Oh, nothing in particular, Watson. Too many hours spent hunched over this text, and too little proper back support, I suspect."

"Is there anything I can do to help ease your back? How much longer do you have to go, do you think?"

"Oh, I am finished." He stood and stretched.

"You have it, Holmes? The translation?"

"I do. At least the entryway text. It will take a good deal longer to copy down and translate the extensive inscriptions of the anteroom."

"What does it say, then?"

"It appears to be a variant on the ancient Book of the Dead, which is believed to have been collected and come into common use in ancient Egypt during the so-called New Kingdom, though many parts of it are far, far older. Much, I suppose, as we would use a modern hymnal, which is a collection of works of varying ages. This could be one of the original sources for the text. And as I said when it was discovered, it consists of numerous curses to the effect of, 'Abandon all hope, ye who enter here,'" Holmes noted. "Here is one example." He picked up his note-book and read,

"Get back, you crocodile of the North! The haje-snake[50] is in my belly, and I have not given myself to you, but you to me! So your flame shall never be upon me! Enter here and die, oh you crocodile of the North!"

"What is an haje-snake?" Watson wondered.

"I cannot be completely certain, but it is most likely an Egyptian cobra; it is not an asp that I can tell, judging from the context of some of the other inscriptions, for there are symbolic references that seem to point to the hood of a cobra in a few," Holmes noted, somewhat abstracted as he studied his rendering of the lintel inscription. "It is not an uncommon term in the Book of the Dead, but scholars have not decided upon its exact meaning there, as yet, either. Here is another curse, even more ominous.

"Thou art a flame, the son of a flame, first bit by the haje-snake, to whom was given your head after it had been cut off. Even so shall you be if you breach what lies within. But the head of Osiris shall not be taken from him, and my head shall not be taken from me."

"Good Lord, Holmes!"

"Indeed, Watson. But not Osiris."

"Wh-what? Osiris? What—"

"Oh, that was intended to be a joke," Holmes said, glancing up with a rueful grin. "The expression 'Good Lord' standardly references the Judeo-Christian God Jehovah, not Osiris...never mind. Listen to this:

"Go back! Retreat! Get back, you dangerous one! Do not come against me, do not live by your magic; may I never have to tell this deed of yours to the Great God! The crocodile speaks: 'The sky encloses the stars, magic encloses their settlements, and my mouth encloses the magic which is within it. My teeth are a knife, my tusks are the Cobra Mountain. Woe to all who enter here!'"

Watson blanched.

"Is...is that the name of the mountain the tomb was in?" he asked.

---

50   "Venomous-snake-snake," from the Egyptian/Arabic word haje. Used to refer to either the Egyptian cobra or asp, though in this case it is the cobra, Naja haje, that is referenced, a relative of the cobras of India. It may then be literally translated as "cobra-snake."

"It would appear that is how the ancient Egyptians knew it, yes."

"And we marched right in, every last blessed one of us," he whispered. "What does it mean, Holmes?"

"It means, my dear fellow," Holmes said in wry whimsy, the corner of his lips quirked, "that whoever put that stone slab inside didn't want anyone bothering it."

*****

"I am afraid I simply don't recognise it, Will," Nichols-Woodall told Whitesell the next morning after breakfast, as they all sat talking over the remnants of that meal. Watson had already long since headed for the hospital, earlier than regular surgical hours; there were a few minor patients to care for, though nothing serious, he had assured Whitesell. Leighton opted to go with him to help out, and she left on his arm, as Phillips glared daggers at their retreating backs. "I've never seen a stone like that before in my life, though from the crystalline structure I might take it as being perhaps a granite or a gabbro, depending upon its chemistry."

"But you're the geological expert here, Parker," Whitesell protested. "Surely you know what it is, and where it came from. As large as it is, it cannot possibly have been transported far."

Nichols-Woodall spread his hands in frustration.

"Any ideas, Thomas?" Whitesell tried.

"I am the archaeologist, like you, *mon ami*," came the reply. "I am no expert with the stones, as is our friend Parker, here. If he does not recognise it, who am I to say otherwise?"

"Holmes?" Whitesell queried then. "You're not a geologist, *per se*[51], but Dr. Watson's stories indicate you have a wealth of knowledge on the subject, nonetheless..."

Holmes bit his lip, thinking; finally he shook his head.

"I recognise it," Lord Trenthume remarked. "I just wish I could recall where I've seen it before."

"No offense, Cortland, old fellow," Nichols-Woodall pointed out, "but that isn't much help."

"I know," Cortland complained. "I've racked my brains, trying to remember. But I just can't bring it to the front."

"Perhaps," Holmes suggested, "a divertissement is in order, milord."

---

51   Greek via Latin. Lit. "by itself," can be rendered loosely, "as such."

"What did you have in mind?" Cortland wondered, raising an intrigued eyebrow.

"Whenever there is 'something sitting right under my nose,' as Watson likes to put it, and I know it is there but cannot pull it to the fore, I do something — anything — to take my mind OFF it," Holmes explained. "I play my violin. We decamp for a concert or an opera. Read a book. Go for a walk. Do whatever suits your fancy and your resources out here in the desert; but make sure it will take your conscious mind completely off the subject at hand. This allows for the subconscious to do its work and identify the pertinent fact for you. For that matter, we might as well all do. It is almost time for luncheon as it is, and I note that the wait staff are becoming anxious to clear the table and prepare it for that meal in any event, so we should probably all escape for a bit of recreation, or work, of some sort."

"But if any of you go for a stroll, and especially the Earl," Phillips interjected, "in the name of all that is holy, milord, take your revolver with you. I never saw the lot of cobras in the area! They seem to have fairly come out of the woodwork in the last two days. I saw three this morning, just while I was, ah, well, emptying the jordan[52] into the trench in the brake[53]." He flushed.

"There is likely an underground stream flowing down from the mountains around which they have nested, and our dig has disturbed their dens," Whitesell said, serene. "Cobras are, for the most part, placid creatures, else the Hindi would not be able to so easily tame them. Pay attention to your surroundings, take your revolvers as Landers recommends, and you will be fine."

"But it is a recommendation that we would all do well to heed," Nichols-Woodall pointed out.

"True, true," Beaumont agreed. "Whitesell, you are more the expert of Egyptology: is it not so that the cobras may be using nearby tombs as dens and nests? Might not they lead us to the tombs?"

"Well, it is certainly possible, I suppose," Whitesell decided. "They may have found small natural crevices in the stone, even down into the rooms. I have heard of it happening. But even if they have not, their lairs will certainly be in amongst the rocks and stones, and the vibrations produced by our picks and spades will have agitated them."

"Then Phillips is indeed correct, and we should all take heed,"

---

52 Chamber pot.
53 Shrubbery or brush; an area overgrown with brambles, brush, or cane.

Holmes averred. "Lord Trenthume, do you betake yourself off for whatever diversion best suits you — but be sure to carry a loaded revolver. I think my time may best serve by transcribing the engraving within the antechamber, for later translation."

"Well done, Holmes," Whitesell said, pleased. "Now let us all return to our tents and load our pistols."

"And I shall contact some of my colleagues and see if I cannot identify this blasted blue stone," Nichols-Woodall declared. "Will, would you object if I took a small sample of the slab, for identification purposes?"

"You want to whack it with that bloody damn hammer of yours?!" Whitesell said in horror. "Knock a chunk off it? Certainly not, Parker! We don't know what this thing is, or what kind of importance it had, or may have. And there are aesthetics to consider!"

"But, Will, if I am to identify it..."

"No, Parker. I'll not hear of it. There's an end of the matter."

"All right, Will, but you do make it damnably hard to do my blasted job," Nichols-Woodall complained. "Phillips, would you have someone bring the dog-cart around? I need to run into town and send some telegraphs..."

"Certainly, sir," Phillips agreed.

*****

Watson was, with the assistance of the assigned nursing staff, attempting to teach a willing Leighton Whitesell some of the finer points of nursing, specifically the proper administration of hypodermic syringe injections, when a loud male scream rent the air from somewhere across the camp, though it sounded to be relatively nearby to Watson's experienced ear. The entire hospital staff froze in shock, and within moments, a babel of voices outside rushed toward the infirmary. Over the babel, he heard Udail calling his name.

"Dr. Watson! DR. WATSON! Help us!"

Watson dropped what he was doing and rushed to the door of the hospital tent, just in time to meet Udail at the head of a yammering, agitated procession of men. In their midst, one of the diggers, pale even through the sweat and dirt that coated his face, lay on a cobbled-together stretcher made of several spade handles lashed together with sashes and scarves, being carried by the others. His expression was contorted in pain; his knee was drawn up, and he clutched his calf, rocking back and forth and groaning.

"What happened?" Watson demanded of Udail.

"Snake," Udail said simply. "Cobra."

"It bit him?!" Watson cried, motioning the jabbering, upset gaggle of men to put his newest patient on the nearest empty bed.

"Yes, Doctor, there on the leg, where he is holding. He was, ah, relieving himself, and did not see it in time."

"What is his name, and can he speak English?" Watson directed the question at Udail, while turning to his staff and firing off orders. "Leigh, fetch the alcohol and some clean cloths. Sati, I need the tourniquets and some gauze bandaging. Alimah, do you find the scalpels and the cups. Wahbiyah, the topical cocaine. Hurry."

"His name is Salah, Sayyid[54] Doctor, and yes, he speaks English," Udail responded, as Watson's medical staff broke into a coordinated flurry of activity — except for Leighton, who responded quickly, but was a little more flustered than the others. The workers sat the makeshift stretcher holding the injured man down atop the nearest cot, sliding out the spades, then stepped back. "Out with you!" Udail told them. "Sayyid Doctor Watson will tend Salah, and he needs room to work! He cannot work well with you leaning over him at his elbows!" The men cleared out, and Udail crouched beside the stricken man. "All will be well, Salah, do not fear. Dr. Watson is a good man, a good doctor. He will take the best care of you. Sayyid Doctor," Udail said, "this man is my cousin. I know a bit of medicine, so I understand..."

"Was that him screaming a few moments ago?" Watson asked, as Leighton set up a table for the instruments beside the patient, and the others placed the sterile implements he had requested upon it. Leighton then returned with a tray containing a basin, pitcher of water, clean towel, and soap, and Watson thoroughly washed his hands before she took it away again.

"It was," Udail averred. "He was just outside the camp."

"Good," Watson declared, seating himself on the stool Sati placed for him by the bedside. "The quicker he gets medical attention after being bitten, the better the prognosis." He nodded at Udail. "I will do my best, my friend. Was it a deep, hard bite?"

"It was deep enough," Udail decided. "I cannot say how hard."

"Hard," Salah affirmed, the first coherent word he had spoken.

---

54   "Master," Arabic. In this case it is intended to indicate the chief physician.

"Salah, khalil[55], try to relax. The good Dr. Watson knows what he is doing. I will wait just outside, and you have only to call to me."

Salah nodded, grunting in pain, and Udail bowed and left the tent, but Watson could see him hovering just outside the opening. The cacophony of voices outside quieted immediately, however.

"Salah," he said to his patient, "I do not wish to offend, but I need to see the limb where you were bitten."

With little hesitation, Salah hitched up his garment to just below his knee. The leg had already started to swell and discolour rather badly, and the two puncture wounds were obvious on the outside of the lower calf, oozing blood. Leighton emitted a gasping sound that Watson absently suspected was a stifled scream, then was silent. *Good girl,* he thought in abstraction, focussing most of his attention on his patient. *It isn't pretty, but such things never are. If you can stomach this, you will indeed make a fine nurse.*

"Mm," Watson hummed, studying the wound with swift precision. "Sati, my friend, can you remove the sandal on this foot without showing his sole?"

"I can, Doctor."

"Do so. I'm worried of the foot losing circulation from the sandal straps if it swells much more. Let me see the tourniquet..." he said as Sati began work on the sandal straps. Within moments the tourniquet was skilfully tied just below Salah's knee, its tightness carefully checked, and Watson looked up. "Leigh, let me see the soap and water again. I need to remove some of the dust and dirt from the area of the bite, before I proceed further."

With Leighton's help, Watson quickly cleaned the worst of the sweaty dirt from several square inches of the skin around Salah's injury, then swabbed it with alcohol to sterilise it. Salah hissed loudly, then let out a stream of curses in Arabic. By this time Sati had the sandal off, and Salah's feet draped with a sheet to avoid unintentional insult to the other Muslims in the room.

"I am sorry, Salah," Watson murmured, examining the wound with care. "Alcohol does burn like fury, I know. My friend Holmes has told me so, often enough! Let me do something about that, because what I have to do next will hurt a lot worse, otherwise." He picked up a swab and the bottle containing the topical cocaine solution, dipping the swab into the liquid before slathering the area of the bite with the drug-

---

55   "Good friend," Arabic.

saturated swab, making sure that the solution also dribbled into the two fang marks. Within seconds, Salah eased, relaxing into the bed. Watson nodded to himself, disposing of the swab with care, then reached for the scalpel. Seconds later, two cross-shaped incisions had been made, one in each fang mark, and Watson turned to Alimah, who had the small glass cups waiting, a little tuft of absorbent cotton wool in the bottom of each one. Watson took the first; Alimah picked up one of the long medical swabs and struck a match, lighting the cotton wool on the tip of the swab, then shaking it through the air to extinguish it. She held it still for Watson to hold the cup upside-down over it, then Watson quickly placed the warm cup over one of the incised bite marks. Seconds later, he and Alimah had repeated the process, placing the second cup over the other fang wound.

"What are you doing?" Leighton asked softly, watching from the end of the bed.

"Alimah heated the air inside the cups," Watson explained, his gaze never leaving the two cups, "which caused the air to expand so that, as they cool, a slight vacuum will be produced inside them. Do you see what is happening?"

"The flesh is bulging up into the cups," Leighton said, fascinated, "and the two wounds are bleeding more."

"It is pulling out the poisoned blood, Mistress," Alimah said, her gentle voice lilting. "It is safer than sucking with the mouth, though I have done so in an emergency. It does not do to swallow, or to have ulcers in the tongue, lips, or gums, however."

"I...can see why," Leighton murmured, still observing. "And...the cotton wool is..."

"Helping to soak up the contaminated blood," Watson finished for her, glancing up with a smile. "There are, as Alimah suggests, several ways to do this, including using rubber squeeze bulbs on special cups similar to these, but this is what we have to hand, and it is probably the best way, in my professional opinion, as these kinds of cups are much easier to clean afterward. Alimah, as badly as he was bitten, I think I want to run a second set of cups on him, possibly a third."

"Very good, Doctor. I will prepare two more sets." And the Egyptian woman, older than any of them, smiled beneficently and moved to prepare more of the glass cups, which sat on another table nearby, where she had placed them earlier for convenience's sake, anticipating the need.

"Salah, how are you feeling?" Watson asked.

"It does not hurt so much anymore," Salah informed him. "And I am not so dizzy, I think."

"Excellent," Watson declared. "You are very fortunate, Salah: the cobra did not hit any major blood vessels, but injected its venom into the muscular tissue. I will swab the area with anaesthetic again when I take off the cups, and that should make it feel even better. You will undoubtedly have some bruising, old fellow, but you would have that anyway. Better a few bruises on a live body than the alternative, however, wouldn't you say?"

"Yes," Salah said decidedly.

After a few more moments, Watson gently broke the seal on the cups, careful to catch up the soiled cotton wool inside without touching it, as he lifted them away; Alimah took them from him and set them aside to dispose of the cotton wool and cleanse the cups later. Then Watson dabbed a bit more of the cocaine solution directly on the incised wounds, and he and Alimah placed fresh cups over them, repeating their earlier procedure.

"Is he going to be all right, John?" Leighton asked the physician.

"I think so," Watson concluded. "It was only one bite, and the venom of the Egyptian cobra is some six times less toxic than the king cobra of the Indian subcontinent. And the snake did not hit any major blood vessels, as I said; that would have been very bad, and he might not even have lived long enough for them to bring him here. The prognosis is good. He is not convulsing, his pulse is strong and steady, and his eyes are tracking well. We shall have to watch him for a few days; cobra bites have a nasty tendency toward necrosis—"

"Necrosis?" Leighton asked.

"Tissue death," Watson explained. "The tissue around the bite can become gangrenous. But there are ways to treat that, now, that will prevent calamities such as the loss of his leg." Salah's eyes grew wide, and his forehead puckered in worry. "Not to worry, Salah, you're in good hands. Carbolic generally sets matters right, and I have that aplenty, and more beside. If it should become necessary," he added, "I can grow a bread mould that would have amazing results when placed upon such wounds."

"Bread mould?" Leighton wondered.

"Yes," Watson said with a smile. "Strange to say, isn't it? Makes me sound rather like a quack! But no, I have been keeping up with the research being done on the *Penicillium* family of moulds. It is most fascinating. They have not isolated the important extracts yet, but I have hopes."

"Doctor," Alimah asked, "will you wish another round of cups?"

Watson studied the wounds, noting that some of the swelling was starting to diminish in the leg. "No, I don't think so, Alimah," he determined. "It looks quite good. We may be able to elevate it soon, and I don't want to over-do the blood-letting, in any event."

"Shall I remove the cups and bandage the limb for you, then?" Alimah asked with a smile. "I am very experienced, I assure you."

"Very good, Alimah. Remove the tourniquet at the same time, I think. You might dab the area with some carbolic before you bandage it, too."

"I shall. And perhaps your lady friend may wish to observe. I can teach her about the techniques while I am about it."

"Leigh, what say you?" Watson looked up at the younger woman.

"I'm game," Leighton averred staunchly. "I want to learn how to help someone like Salah, here."

"I think you may make an excellent nurse, with a bit of training, Leigh," Watson said, rising from his seat and moving aside to let Alimah have it. "I have known some to faint at a sight like this."

"I agree, Doctor," Alimah lilted. "She has the head, and she has the heart."

Leighton and Watson exchanged happy smiles, and Watson went to wash up.

*****

After a few inquiries, Watson discovered that Holmes had disappeared into the ancient vault with a large sketch-pad after lunch, there to copy all of the hieroglyphics upon the walls for later translation.

Watson himself had finally finished his duties in the hospital infirmary, ascertained that poor Saleh was doing as well as could be expected, then taken Leighton and gone for a walk, careful both to carry his revolver and to watch for snakes. The others were out and about as well, engaged in various tasks.

"Let's climb the mountain, John," Leighton suggested, cheerful. "It's later in the evening now, and it will be cooler up there."

"No, Leigh, I should much rather remain close to the camp."

"But why?"

"It is still too hot, for one! But mostly because the local cobras seem to have got their tails in a knot," Watson explained with some fanciful humour, "and not only will it not do for ourselves to run across them, as the dig's physician, I must stay close in case of medical emergency. You saw the mess earlier to-day. Among others, Lord Trenthume has gone for a stroll, as well. Holmes sent me word a bit ago that the Earl is trying to clear his mind and recollect something that may be important to the study of the crypt. It will not do for me to be too far away to help, should he become careless and be bitten."

"Ooh," Leighton groaned, "the nasty snakes. Yes, this morning was positively dreadful. I shouldn't want to experience it, or have to watch you experience it, either, John. And Lord Trenthume does seem to be rather absent-minded, doesn't he? Well, I shan't argue, because I don't want to anger one, either! That and the hot sun are the only things about this adventure that I simply don't like."

"What about the dust and dirt?"

"What about it?"

"Most women of your age and breeding would find it distasteful, at the least."

"But you can't dig for archaeological finds and not get a bit dirty and dusty, John! That's part of the fun and the excitement of it all!" She glanced about and saw no one else. "Do you want to know a secret?"

"What?"

"Da has forbidden me to go into the dig pits! He says it isn't lady-like. Otherwise, I should be right down in there with the rest of them, digging in the dirt and finding some glorious old, perfectly unique specimen!"

"You are quite a unique specimen yourself, Leigh," he replied, chuckling. Leighton returned his smile, pleased and happy.

"Do you suppose it would be safe to walk around the perimeter, then?"

"I think so," Watson considered. "I have my service revolver, and it is loaded. Here." He offered his arm, and they set off on their perambulation, chatting happily as young lovers are wont to do.

CHAPTER 8
THE MINERALOGICAL ENIGMA

Two hours later, the pair returned to the camp proper, in time for dinner. Cortland was also back, safe and sound...but without any more notion of where he had seen the strange night-sky-like stone than he had before. Nichols-Woodall was still absent, evidently communing with his colleagues from the vantage of the telegraph office in town; whether said communion would be fruitful or not remained for his return.

Holmes was also back, but withdrawn, quiet and thoughtful. He sat just outside the flap of the tent he shared with Watson, studying his transcription and occasionally scribbling notes in the margins.

"What are you doing, Sherry?" Leighton wondered as she walked up on Watson's arm.

"Mm? Oh, beginning a preliminary translation of all those hieroglyphics inside the crypt, Leigh," he responded a bit absently. "It looks to be quite unusual..."

"Well, it can wait," Professor Whitesell declared, coming around the corner of the tent. "I've been looking for you lot. The servants are only holding dinner until I could find you."

"Professor, I should really prefer—" Holmes began.

"No buts, young man," Whitesell blustered. "You know my rules, well enough." Holmes sighed.

"What about Nichols-Woodall?" Watson asked. "He hasn't got back yet."

"Had a note from him, carried back by the dog-cart driver," Whitesell said. "The responses to his telegrams indicated that two of his mates were not so far away. So he took boat downriver to Luxor, to consult with a couple of his colleagues. He'll likely spend the night and be back to-morrow, hopefully with information." He gave Holmes a stern mock-glare. "All the more reason not to let those of us left here escape a nice, communal meal."

"I really think this is more important," Holmes declared.

"But Sherry, you haven't had anything to eat since breakfast," Leighton protested. "You spent luncheon in the crypt, and didn't even come out for tea! Did you at least carry your canteen?"

"I did," Holmes said succinctly. "And used it."

"Well, that's better than nothing," Watson remarked drily.

"But you didn't eat! That can't be good for you, can it, Da? John? Tell him it isn't good for him."

"I've done so many and many's the time, Leigh," Watson said with a wry grin, shaking his head. "When he gets that mind of his focussed on something, little else matters."

"Well, I matter!" Whitesell boomed cheerfully. "And last I checked, I was in charge of this dig. And I say: COME TO DINNER!" He laughed, then added, "I expect all THREE of you at table in five minutes!" He headed off in the direction of the mess tent, whistling jauntily.

"If we must, we must," Holmes huffed.

He put away the sketch-pad within the tent, then joined Watson and Leighton.

*****

Dinner was mildly more congenial without Nichols-Woodall to snipe with Beaumont, though Phillips maintained a towering silence and sent many a glare at Watson, who sat beside an effervescent Leighton, who was in turn occupying Nichols-Woodall's vacant seat. It seemed their afternoon stroll had not escaped his attention, even ensconced in the artefact tent as he had been, and he resented it vehemently. It had long since become patently obvious to Holmes that Phillips had intentions toward Leighton, intentions which had been thwarted by first Holmes and now Watson, and in despite of Leighton's wishes, as she had told him. So Holmes had kept a wary watch on matters, but there was no indication, to the detective's practised eye, that Phillips intended to do anything this time...other than glower and sulk. *After all*, the detective considered, *Watson's personal history in the Army is well-known, and that is unlikely to be something with which Phillips wants to tangle, even with Watson's mild disability.* After a couple of futile attempts by Whitesell to draw Phillips into the conversation, the professor forbore, and confined himself to a discussion with Holmes, Cortland and Beaumont for the rest of the meal.

The professor maintained an enthused chatter over the discovery of the crypt, and what could possibly be the point of interring a mere stone slab within it. This chatter was bantered back and forth by both Beaumont and Lord Trenthume, with a thoughtful Holmes occasionally offering a bland observation. The sleuth also noted that Beaumont seemed to be intent upon drawing Whitesell out on what he believed the crypt to represent; but the younger archaeologist certainly did not volunteer any information himself. Cortland was nearly as enthusiastic as Whitesell, however, and the pair babbled back and forth for over an hour, through all three dinner courses.

Just then, Watson leaned over and tapped Holmes' arm beneath the level of the table.

"Holmes, do you need me for anything after dinner?" he murmured.

"No, not particularly. Why?"

"Leighton has invited me...I had thought to visit with the professor and herself in his tent."

"Ah," Holmes grinned. "Go right ahead with your courting, old fellow. I have plenty to do as it is, and I am likely to still be up when you return."

"Not on my account, I hope. It will all be very proper and aboveboard."

"No doubt, my dear Watson. But the inscriptions were copious, and will take some little time to translate. And they are the oldest Egyptian script I have ever seen, so they will not be easy. I only hope my translation skills are up to it."

"Do you have reason to think you may have difficulty?" Beaumont interjected the question. "Forgive me, *mon ami*, I did not mean to eavesdrop, but I overheard you mention the inscriptions, and I am curious."

"It will certainly not be elementary," Holmes admitted. "While I have considerable skill with the Middle Kingdom inscriptions from my prior work with the Professor, and some experience with what are called by some, 'proto-hieroglyphs,' I had not thought there was a form of the writing that was older still, but this does appear to be."

"You translated the lintel writing readily enough the other day, old chap," Watson pointed out.

"Yes, but as I told you at the time, Watson, the curses seemed to be based on...or perhaps, part of the original source for...the Book of the Dead. So after getting the first bits, I had some expectation of what came next, within reason. The outer room is another matter altogether, and does not seem to relate to anything I have ever seen before."

"Then you have your work cut out for you, son," Whitesell said. "But you have a talent for it, and I am convinced I could not have put the matter into better hands. If anyone can do it, you can."

"Thank you, sir."

"Very good," Beaumont said. "Let us hope so."

But Holmes noticed that Beaumont watched him surreptitiously through the rest of the meal.

All told, though the meal had been delicious and it was entirely true that Holmes had skipped lunch, he was more than glad to see the meal behind him, and betake himself back to the tent, there to resume perusing the hieroglyphs from within the crypt.

But this time, when he finished, he scanned the area around the tent with every sense he possessed. Thus satisfied that there was no one else about, he opened his trunk, dug down to the bottom, and triggered the door of a hidden compartment. In this, he safed the sketch-pad, out of sight, before locking the trunk and tucking the key away on a chain hidden around his neck.

Then he dimmed the lamp for Watson's convenience when he should return, and went to bed.

*****

Nichols-Woodall returned late the next morning, somewhat downcast.

"They did not recognise it, either," he admitted to the others at lunch. "Neither Gottlieb nor Åkerman. There is not a stone in Egypt, they said, that matched my description, nor yet even my detailed sketches. They wanted to see samples, but I told them I could not take samples due to the possible value of the object — if we can ever identify it! Then they suggested I take photographs of it and send them, but I told them it would not help, for a photograph would not depict the rich, nuanced shades of blue and teal to be found in the stone. So they threw up their hands in vexation."

"Surely it is not a huge nugget of...what is the stone? Lapis lazuli?" a naïve Phillips wondered.

"No, no," Nichols-Woodall demurred. "It is not the right shade of blue, for one thing. You see, Phillips, lapis lazuli was used extensively in ancient Egypt, and is a not-uncommon find. I would have recognised that instantly. But this stone has more green in it, and high quality lapis lazuli is a pure, rich caerulean blue, indeed sometimes what is called cobalt blue. Even the lower grades are more of a faded indigo than this stone. And as valuable as it was, and is, I doubt that so huge a nugget would have warranted interment instead of use — in cosmetics, in jewellery, in decorative inlay..."

"Well, it was just a thought," Phillips said, with a rueful grin and a shrug.

"A good thought, nonetheless," Whitesell commended. "Sometimes the things that are the most obvious are the things we miss, after all."

"True," Nichols-Woodall admitted. He offered the young man a friendly smile. "Have you yet studied the petrology of Egypt, Landers?"

"The stones of the area? No sir, not yet. I have the various dynasties down, and can identify pottery with the best of 'em, but I haven't got to the rocks quite yet. I know that the relics of certain dynasties are most often found in certain strata, but I fear I could not recognise those strata in the field if my life depended on it. I was hoping to begin working on that during this expedition, but so far, well..." He shrugged.

"What are your plans for the afternoon, then? If you are free, perhaps you might enjoy accompanying me; I plan to hike the mountains in the area and see if I can find a match for our big blue stone."

Phillips' eyes lit up, and he gave a querying glance at Whitesell, who nodded his permission.

"Sounds first-rate, Dr. Nichols-Woodall," he replied. "I should like that, very much."

"Good. Go fetch your topee, a full canteen, a revolver in case of snakes, and a kerchief for your neck," Nichols-Woodall instructed. "It will be hot."

*****

Holmes slipped into the inner chamber while no one else was there: Phillips and Dr. Nichols-Woodall were off hiking the area, studying the stones; Professor Whitesell was in his tent, reviewing his textual translation for clews about the mysterious stone slab; and Udail had come to fetch Dr. Beaumont to look at another pot, possibly a second amphora, that had been found in one of the pits, though this one appeared broken, or at least cracked. So a solitary Holmes now stood and stared thoughtfully at the large blue-green bowlder in the light of the modern oil lanterns hung from the ancient torch sconces.

After a few moments, he removed one of the lanterns and walked over to the side of the stone, running his hand lightly along its smooth surface as he moved to the rear of the chamber. Once or twice he bent over, examining rough places near the base of the polished stone. Then he crouched down low so that he would be hidden from the entryway by the stone itself, and produced several items from his pockets, arranging them on the floor.

The first thing he did was to set the lantern on the floor and pick up a small velvet pouch. From this he produced a jeweller's loupe; he placed it to his eye and leaned close to the side of the slab, studying the surface and the crystalline structures thus revealed.

"Mm," he grunted, leaning back. He returned the loupe into its protective pouch and set it aside, then picked up a small note-pad and pencil stub, and scribbled several short notes. Putting it down, he studied the remaining tools he had brought before selecting another.

This new tool proved to be an unglazed piece of ceramic tile. This he held to the corner of the slab. He pressed into the slab with it, exerting some force, though careful not to break the tile, before dragging it along the edge of the slab. A soft scraping noise made itself apparent, and he withdrew the tile, studying the surface. A powdery streak ran along it, a light bluish-green in most places, but a nearly-invisible white in a few spots.

Just then, faint voices filtered through from the outer door, the light in the outer chamber flickered, and Holmes froze, hands hovering over the tools he had laid out. The voices moved on, fading into the distance; the light filtering through from outside steadied, and he relaxed, letting out a breath he had not realised he'd held.

That would have been...unpleasant, he thought. *Professor Whitesell would likely throw me off both the expedition and the site, were I caught at what I intend. It would be well within his rights, I suppose, but unwise, nevertheless. It's quite a pity that he refused to let Nichols-Woodall properly study the slab, for there would almost certainly have been an identification by now, if he had. Especially after consulting the other geologists. And given the condition of the base of the stone, it would hardly harm it unduly. I shall have to adjudge later whether I may take the geologist into my confidence in helping me identify it, for he certainly has the greater knowledge and experience.*

He bent back to work, scribbling more notes before reaching for a small dropper bottle and a rag. Extracting a full dropper, he rose, stooping low, until he could reach the top of the slab without presenting too large a form above it, and scanned the surface. Locating several of the larger whitish crystals, he placed several drops of liquid on each one, and watched closely. Nothing happened, and he used the rag to wipe off the residue before ducking behind the hulk of the rock once more.

Several more scribbles went into the note-book, and he reached for his jack-knife. Unfolding it, he brought the blade to bear on that same corner of the slab on which he had wielded the ceramic tile. But instead of shaving off bits, as it had done with the inscribed slate, his knife slid off without so much as leaving a mark on the stone. When he examined the blade, however, he was dismayed: a long scratch had been left in it, and the section of the blade's edge that had contacted the slab was now dull.

"Damnation," he murmured to himself in chagrin. "The stone is quite hard, then. I shall have to sharpen this blade, and try to polish out the scratch. That puts paid to the notion of trying to take an inconspicuous sample, and I dare not use the knife as a chisel lest I break the blade outright."

He picked up the note-pad and pencil, scribbling a few more notes, before he gathered up his utensils, replaced them in his pockets, and slipped out, unnoticed.

*****

Back in the tent he shared with Watson — who was still in the infirmary with Leighton — Holmes took the opportunity to study his notes in private.

Colour: blue to blue-green, some areas cream to white
Lustre: non-metallic, dull, slightly waxy
Streak: also blue-green, some areas white
Carbonic acid test: no result. Therefore the white crystals are not calcite or similar.
Hardness: >steel; therefore >4 on the Mohs' scale

"Hm," he said. Then he pocketed the small note-book, rummaged in his trunk and extracted a whetstone. He pulled his treasured jack-knife, a childhood Christmas gift from his parents, from his waistcoat pocket and commenced sharpening it, deep in thought.

*****

SHERLOCK HOLMES AND THE MUMMY'S CURSE

Since it was still early in the afternoon, Holmes wandered over to the dig pits and looked across the valley, debating what to do next. Professor Whitesell could be seen in the near distance, papers in hand, wandering about somewhat absently, and consequently in constant danger of falling into one of the pits; Holmes realised he was likely attempting to correlate locations with his translation. Beaumont was still working with Udail to extract the pot, which evidently was intact, after all — Holmes knew if a pot were found intact, it was likely filled with something, dirt at the least, which had prevented its being crushed, and this tended to render it very heavy and awkward to move.

Just then, Nichols-Woodall walked across the far end of the valley, Phillips tagging eagerly behind like a puppy. The pair disappeared around the far spur; ten minutes later, Nichols-Woodall appeared on top of the spur, headed higher, onto the ridge proper. It took Phillips fully five more minutes to reach the top of the spur, and he paused and leaned his hands on his knees once he had reached that level; he appeared to be panting. Holmes took the behaviour to indicate that Phillips was not in nearly as fit a physical condition as Nichols-Woodall.

Well, perhaps he will be too tired to give anyone the Evil Eye tonight at dinner, for a change, the detective considered with amusement. Then it dawned upon him that that meant the geologist would likely not be back to the camp UNTIL dinner.

Holmes turned casually and headed back into the camp.

*****

The dwelling area was largely deserted at that time of the afternoon; everyone was out at the dig field, working in the kitchens, or staffing the infirmary. Holmes made his stealthy way toward Nichols-Woodall's tent, glanced about to verify no one was in sight, then slipped inside.

On the table in the corner of the tent lay the various field tools of a geologist, most in duplicate. This included several rock hammers. Some had chisel heads, others had pick heads for harder stone. Holmes hefted one of the pick-headed hammers and examined it for a moment before he slid the handle under the waistband of his trousers, adjusting his waistcoat to cover the hammer's head, then slipped back out of the tent and headed for the crypt, stopping by his tent for his sketch-pad on the way.

*****

Once at the top of the ramp leading to the entrance, he paused and opened his sketch-book, flipping several pages over and extracting his pencil from an inside pocket. Studying the sketch-book intently, he wandered absently down the ramp and into the antechamber.

A quick glance around ascertained that both it, and the inner chamber, were still empty, and he immediately made his way into the inner room. There, he resumed his position behind the slab, where he knelt, discarded his sketch-pad, and studied the side of the stone presenting to him. He ran his fingers consideringly over a slight knob along the base of the stone. He pulled out his handkerchief and spread it on the floor beneath the bulge. Then he hesitated, thinking.

Well, after all, Professor Whitesell did not forbid ME, he mulled. *And someone has to do it, or it shall never be done.*

Finally he withdrew the rock hammer from his trousers waist. Flipping it so that the pick's point was down, he placed the point gingerly near the base of the stone protuberance. Then he averted his face, closed his eyes, raised the pick head, and brought the point down with appreciable force on the bulge of rock.

There was a sharp *crack!* and a slight crumbling sound. When Holmes looked back down, the lump of rock lay on the handkerchief, with a few chips and crumbles lying next it. A small rough area near the floor was the only thing that marred the polish of the slab.

He wiped off the rock dust from the tip of the pick and replaced it in its camouflaged position at his waist, partly underneath his waistcoat. Then he carefully folded up the handkerchief, stone chips and all, and put it in a pocket. Retrieving his sketch-book, he returned to the anteroom, recorded a few more hieroglyphs, then strolled out of the vault.

*****

Moments later, he was back in Nichols-Woodall's deserted tent, replacing the borrowed rock hammer precisely as he had found it, using a shirt-tail to wipe off any potentially incriminating fingerprints, before ducking out and heading back to the tent he shared with Watson.

That worthy was still at the hospital; there were almost always a few minor cuts, blisters, and the like to tend each day. So Holmes opened his trunk, dug down, and triggered the hidden compartment in its base, putting the sketch-pad and the kerchief containing the rock sample inside. He closed it again and locked it, then sat down to think.

SHERLOCK HOLMES AND THE MUMMY'S CURSE

*****

"Holmes!" Watson exclaimed, as his friend entered the hospital tent. "Are you all right, old fellow? Have you been hurt?"

"No, no," a serious Holmes said, raising a calming hand. "I am fine, my dear Watson. But I need...a favour."

"Then name it."

"I need to talk to Leigh," Holmes declared. "In private."

*****

Behind the hospital tent, Holmes and Watson carried on an intense conversation.

"No, no, Watson, it isn't what you think," Holmes protested. "By all means, come along if you like. I've no objection. Leigh has...well, it could be the key to solving this mysterious dig find."

"What? What do you mean, Holmes?"

"Are you and she at a place where the rest of your staff may run matters for five or ten minutes?"

"Yes, I think so."

"Then go fetch her, and bring her back to our tent. I shall be waiting."

*****

When Watson arrived with Leighton on his arm, Holmes was sitting at the table, his eye to his microscope, looking at something. A crumpled handkerchief lay beside his left hand. He turned to meet them.

"Forgive me, Leigh," he murmured, rising and gesturing her to the other camp stool. "I know you are likely not comfortable with me as yet, but it cannot be helped. Do be seated, please."

"What is happening, Sherry?" she asked, green eyes displaying her confusion and uneasiness. "John told me I might do something important for the expedition?"

"It is possible," Holmes admitted, as Watson saw her seated on the stool, then perched himself nearby on the end of one of the cots. Holmes resumed his seat, but facing them. "Are you still wearing the necklace you made of the pebble from my shoe?"

"Yes, it is right here," she said, fishing the chain from beneath her dress collar and pulling the small pebble from its hiding place in her bosom.

"May I have it?"

"What on earth for?" Leighton wondered, as Watson gently unfastened the clasp on the chain and removed it, placing it in the palm of her outstretched hand.

"Because it may be the confirmation I need to identify the stone slab," Holmes answered, reaching for the pendant. Leighton laid it in his palm, but refused to let go of it.

"How will you do that?"

"Well, I will need to powder it and run some chemical analyses upon it."

"No! Sherry, no!" Leighton exclaimed, jerking it out of his grasp. "It's...it means so much to me! You mustn't destroy it!"

Holmes bit his lip, thinking quickly.

"At least let me look at it a moment, Leigh," he said. "If it is big enough..."

She opened her palm and let him look at it. It was of irregular shape, slightly ovoid, and fully an inch or better across its long axis; nearly as much in the others. He studied it for several moments, poking it with a fingertip while Leighton and Watson looked on, then his grey eyes lit up.

"Ah!" he exclaimed. "Leigh, would you object if the pebble were only a bit smaller? If we were to, say, have a small piece cut from the back of the stone, it would lie flat about your neck, instead of tumbling about..."

"Oh," Leighton said, suddenly understanding. "Well, that might work. But why do you need it?"

"Because I believe, if I compare it with..." Holmes turned and unfolded the handkerchief, "this sample I took this afternoon, it will help me to identify the type of stone inside the grotto."

Leighton and Watson both gasped. "You didn't!" Leighton exclaimed.

"Hush, Leigh," Holmes murmured. "Keep your voice down, please. It had to be done, and I made sure to choose a very unobtrusive spot. There were quite a few chips and dings along the base of the slab anyway; I checked it all out very carefully before I took the sample, and made sure to obtain it from a small protrusion along the base of the stone. It is unlikely to be noticed, especially given time for the rough edge to age somewhat. But now we have a sample to test."

"What shall we do?" Watson wondered.

"Watson, when we landed at the village just on the Nile, do you recall seeing the lapidarist along the quay, selling the jewellery he had made?"

"The one with all the scarab beetles of lapis lazuli, turquoise, and the like? I do. I thought he seemed rather skilled, actually."

"Indeed. That was my impression as well. Can you arrange to run down to the village on some errand, first thing in the morning, perhaps?"

"I could," Watson decided. "Aha. Let me guess. You want me to take Leigh's necklace to him, have him cut off a piece from the back, smooth up the remainder so it will not cut her skin, then bring the pendant back to Leigh and the fragment to you."

"Capital summation, my dear fellow. Can you do it, or do I need to devise some other means?"

"No, I think I can," Watson decided. "Perhaps with a bit of help from Leigh."

"How can I help, John?" Leighton wondered, puzzled.

"First, by compensating for me at the infirmary to-morrow morning, for it is doubtful I shall return before lunch," Watson explained. "Secondly, help me think: is there anything, any supplies or the like, which we might need that could be found in the village?"

"Hm," Leighton hummed, then fell silent, her blonde brows knitting as she considered his request. "Oh! Yes, there is, I think. You know we've had that rash of shoulder and wrist sprains..."

"Yes," Watson recalled. "I strongly suspect that new batch of spades is to blame. You remember, Leigh, I mentioned it just the other day. Something about the way the handles are set on, I think; it just isn't right, and the repeated force of wielding it ends up injuring the digger, rather than the spade."

"Well, you might go into the village to obtain some more cloth for slings," Leighton suggested. "In truth, we are running low."

"Really? Then by all means, yes, I shall," Watson decided.

"But could not one of your staff fetch it just as well?" Holmes wondered, concerned. "It must at least appear to be a legitimate errand, else the Professor may wonder..."

"No, Holmes, I should desire to do it myself in any event," Watson declared, "to ensure a strong, good quality linen is obtained, and it is legitimate. We must have enough slings to immobilise shoulders and wrists if need be."

"And we ARE running out," Leighton averred. "Why, we've had four or five such sprains in the last week. I was considering telling Da about your notion about the spades, like we talked about yesterday on our walk. Now, I think I shall. He needs to set aside those spades in favour of the older ones, even if the handles are weaker. They are better for the workers."

"Very well, then, it will do," Holmes decided. "Watson, do you have the lapidarist remove about a third of the stone, from the rear, and bring it all back to me. And," he extracted his pocket-book from his trousers, "here is the money to pay for it, and here is additional money to purchase one of those dainty little lapis scarab necklaces for Leigh, as a 'thank-you' and repayment."

"That isn't necessary, Sherry," Leighton said softly.

"Perhaps not, Leigh, but I am sorry to have to damage this one," Holmes pointed out. "However, I have a strong suspicion that it is very important."

"Consider it done, Holmes," Watson said, taking several Egyptian pound notes from Holmes and tucking them into his pocket. "With perhaps a pretty bauble or two purchased with my own funds, to go along with it." He gave Leighton a smile, and she returned it.

"Very good, then, my dear Watson, Leigh. Off to the infirmary with you!" Holmes said, rising.

He watched them leave, then moved to the door flap and watched until they entered the hospital tent across the way.

He turned and went back to the table. A few quick wrist flips wrapped the stone samples back up in his handkerchief. Then it, and his sketchbook, returned to their secretive hiding place in the bottom of his trunk.

*****

Professor Whitesell was informed of the rash of shoulder and wrist sprains that very night over dinner, and of Watson's suspicions as to their cause. Disturbed, the archaeologist promptly summoned Udail in the middle of the meal, to instruct him to reissue the old spades to the workers.

The next morning at the end of breakfast, Leighton sent Watson off to the village with a chaste little kiss to the cheek; behind them, Professor Whitesell beamed, Phillips glowered, Holmes raised an amused eyebrow, and Lord Trenthume looked on, bemused. Watson drove himself in the dog-cart, as the rash of injuries had left the dig a bit short-handed of workers. But this was as he and Holmes wanted it, for there would be no driver to see the business transacted.

Watson returned shortly before lunch; he went first to the infirmary to leave the bulk roll of unbleached linen for Wahbiyah and Alimah to cut and fold into ready slings, and to fetch Leighton. Then he brought her by the tent he shared with Holmes, where that worthy awaited.

Leighton glanced around, then went to the tent flap, pulled its tie and released it, letting it fall closed and wave gently in the breeze.

"Are you sure you want to risk being caught alone with two men in their tent?" Holmes murmured, raising an eyebrow.

"Da will know we were discussing something important," she replied, confident. "He trusts both of you implicitly. He knows you would never harm me. Uncle Parker knows, too. And Dr. Beaumont seems to like you both."

"Mr. Phillips is another matter," Holmes muttered under his breath.

"What?"

"Nothing, Leigh. Watson, were you successful?"

"I was," Watson said, opening his wallet. He fished out the chain of Leighton's necklace, the newly-modified pendant dangling from the end. "Here you are, my dear Leigh. Does it suit?"

"Yes, that's fine," a pleased Leighton agreed. "Very nice, actually. It tended to bobble around a bit anyway. And if it helps Da and Sherry, all well and good. Put it on, would you, John?"

"Certainly, dear." Watson moved behind her, unfastened the clasp, eased it over her head and refastened it. "There. And here," he reached into his wallet again, "is the other part of the stone, Holmes. I had the lapidarist catch the stone dust, too, in case it should be of use to you in your chemical analysis." He handed a thickly-folded paper to the sleuth as Leighton tucked the necklace into her collar.

"Capital, Watson, very well thought out. And the other acquisition?"

"The lapis scarab necklace is in here, too." And Watson extracted another paper parcel, tied in red string. "And a bit more beside. Here, Leigh." He handed the parcel to the girl, who promptly tugged at the bow in the string. Moments later the parcel was open in her hands, to disclose the scarab pendant Holmes had requested, along with a matching bracelet and earrings, all placed into delicate gold settings. She stifled a squeal of delight, for the workmanship was indeed masterful.

"Oh! It's beautiful! Thank you both, so much! John, please help me put them on!"

A smiling Watson obliged, fastening the new, shorter pendant over the older; it displayed nicely over the collar of her blouse. She tucked the hooks of the earrings into her ears, and Watson helped her fasten the clasp of the bracelet around her wrist.

"I think Watson and I do rather well, outfitting you for jewellery, don't you, Leigh?" Holmes said with a grin. "The lapis lazuli sets off your dress very nicely."

"Oh yes! Thank you, Sherry!" Leighton lunged forward and gave him an impulsive hug before turning and doing the same to Watson. A slightly diffident Holmes chuckled.

"I suppose this means you are over your discomfort, then?"

Leighton suddenly blushed, tucking her head shyly. "Yes, I...I suppose it does. I am sorry about...all of that."

"Let it go, Leigh," Holmes said gently. "I am pleased to see you and Watson happy together; we can all get along just fine, so." He ran a light fingertip over the scarab hanging from her throat. "And should anyone ask, this is...an apology, to which Watson decided to add, by way of..." he broke off, and glanced at Watson, "appreciation for your infirmary work?"

"Which is all entirely true," Watson declared staunchly, then added with a hint of mischief, "if not entirely inclusive," and Leighton laughed softly.

Just then, the luncheon gong rang.

"Ah. Do the two of you go on to luncheon," Holmes said, "and I will put this away, out of sight, and join you shortly."

"Very good, Holmes," Watson said, offering Leighton his arm. "Leigh, shall we go?"

"We shall," Leighton said with a smile.

*****

After lunch, most of the scientific team returned to the field. As afternoon surgery hours had not yet begun, Watson took Leighton for a walk, making sure he had his revolver, fully loaded, in his pocket, in the event of cobra encounters.

Holmes murmured something about translation duties as he left the luncheon table, and betook himself back to the tent. There, he fastened the tent flap securely from the inside, and extracted the rock samples and the little note-pad from the compartment beneath the false bottom of his trunk.

"First, the control sample," he murmured to himself, unwrapping the paper parcel to expose the fragment of Leighton's pendant, as well as a small brown paper packet of rock dust where the lapidarist had cut the pebble. This latter he laid aside for the moment; he picked up the fragment and examined it under his jeweller's loupe, then scratched it across the same unglazed ceramic tile he had used on the stone slab in the interior vault. He had carefully preserved the streak the slab had left, and now chose to parallel it with the tiny pebble piece. He raised an eyebrow, then brought the loupe to bear upon both marks. He nodded, and scribbled into the pad.

He pulled out his jack-knife, opening the blade, and stared at it in thought. *It took half the evening to re-sharpen this and buff out the scratch,* he remembered. *I do not want to repeat that process, merely for a test; I have more important things to be done.*

A sudden thought occurred to him, and he dug around in the wooden box containing all of his scientific equipment that either did not fit on the small camp table, or was small enough to be easily lost. He extracted a largish stainless steel spoon that he had sometimes been wont to use for measuring powdered chemicals; it had gotten bent in his travels, and would have to be replaced in any event. It was, he knew, also somewhat harder than the blade of his jack-knife, which had been intended to be kept sharp on a whetstone.

Catching up the fragment from Leigh's pendant, he scraped the cut edge across the outer bowl of the spoon; it left a significant laceration on the steel surface. Then he flipped open his handkerchief, exposing the sample from the slab. Taking it, he repeated the process, leaving a very similar, and quite as deep, blemish on the spoon as he had with the other stone. He sat it back down on the kerchief and considered the scratches for a bit, even examining them under his jeweller's loupe, before recording his observations.

The bit from Leighton's stone next went under his microscope, and again he jotted into the pad as he studied it. He removed it, setting it back on the unfolded paper, and picked up the chip from the interred block. This went under the microscope in its turn; he recorded his observations, then nudged the stone to one side of the instrument's field of view, placing the pebble shard hard against it, and bent back to the eyepiece.

"Amazing," he murmured. "It may just be...I had thought it a long shot, but..."

He set aside the large pieces, and turned back to the paper packet Watson had brought, opening the small pouch of rock dust that had come with it. This he emptied with due deliberation onto a clean sheet of paper torn from the note-book. Taking a small steel spatula from the rack containing his chemical equipment, he meticulously separated the pile of powder into several smaller piles, each of which he weighed on the minuscule balance scale he had packed with his equipment. Then he used the spatula to carefully spoon each pile into a separate test tube.

To the first, he added several drops of carbonic acid, attempting to replicate the same test he had made on the slab itself; as with that earlier test, nothing happened. He nodded to himself: he had not expected differently.

Then he performed several different tests in turn on each of the test tubes, vigilantly recording his findings after each test. The last two samples he went to some lengths to dissolve as completely as possible, then added additional reagents to each solution until he got precipitates settling into the bottom of the test tubes. Each of these precipitates was extracted, carefully dried, and placed on the tiny balance scale for weighing.

"Well, that is hardly surprising," he decided, as he commenced thoroughly cleaning the test tubes; he had only brought a few from Baker Street into the desert, for fear of breakage, and he did not have enough to run all of his tests in parallel. "It is a known petrology, after all. Now for the real test."

Holmes took the small bits, splinters, and dust he had collected from beneath when he had struck off his sample from the main slab, and dumped it all into a small, scrupulously clean mortar, the hardest in his collection, an expensive little utensil which had been fashioned out of one solid piece of milky-white quartz. He wielded the matching pestle for quite some time until he had a reasonably finely ground powder, though it was not as uniform as that which the lapidary saw had made. This likewise went onto its own fresh sheet torn from the note-book, and separated into as many piles by the other end of the delicately-wielded spatula. After weighing, each pile went into its own clean test tube, and he repeated the exact tests he had performed on the material of Leighton's pebble necklace.

Once those tests were complete, he sat down and began to scratch calculations into the note-book, based on the numbers obtained in the chemical investigations.

SHERLOCK HOLMES AND THE MUMMY'S CURSE
*****

At the end of his work, several hours after he had started, and having completely forgotten about tea, he sat back and studied his results, then shook his head.

"It should not be possible, but it is," he muttered in amazement. "Even to the percentages."

He cleaned his equipment and put it away, then tucked the two principal samples into his pocket; it would not be possible to mistake them, for one had the flat surface and slight cuts of the lapidary saw, whereas the other was more rough-hewn on the raw edge. He caught up his note-book and tucked it into a special, inside pocket of his waistcoat.

"Now I must confess to the deed, and convince Nichols-Woodall of my findings," he declared, and set off to find the geologist.

*****

"You DIDN'T!" Nichols-Woodall exclaimed, when once Holmes had managed to separate Landers Phillips from the geologist's coat-tails and convince Nichols-Woodall to return — alone — to the tent he shared with Watson.

"I did," Holmes admitted. "It had to be done, Doctor, no matter what the Professor may have wanted. You know it, and I know it. And while he refused you permission, he said nothing to me, after all. I have reason to think we may be able to get away with a mild subterfuge, if you are willing to work with me; surely you noticed the chips, dings, and whatnot along the bottom of the, mm, billet, if we may thus term so large a stone?"

"Yes, I did," Nichols-Woodall averred. "I tried to tell Will, for I see where you are going, and had thought to do so myself, but he would not hear of it. Undoubtedly the damage was produced in the moving of so large a rock, for it was all along the bottom, where we might expect contact to be made, with...with whatever they used to transport such a heavy weight."

"Precisely," Holmes agreed with a nod. "More than likely, the stone's own weight caused it to spall at the contact points, based on my observations. So that area, along the base, is where I took my sample. I estimate in a few days' time it will be indistinguishable from the rest. And it is, ah, rather carefully located in shadow right now, in any case."

"Well...good, then," Nichols-Woodall decided. "What Will doesn't know, in this case, won't hurt him. And you say you have identified it?"

"Positively," Holmes asserted. "To easily within the margin of error of the analyses."

"Show me."

"The various end-products themselves are preserved over here, on these papers," Holmes gestured to small mounds of material of various colours, ranged along the back of the table. "But here are my observations and calculations."

Holmes produced his note-pad, opened it to the first page containing his observations of the stone slab, and laid it on the table in front of the geologist, gesturing to him to take a seat and read, which he did. Holmes, meanwhile, took a more casual seat on the end of his cot, and watched Nichols-Woodall as he read through Holmes' work.

It took a while, but Holmes was a patient man. When Nichols-Woodall finally looked up, there was wonder in his hazel eyes.

"You have done it, Holmes. This is a masterful little piece of research, and done in a tent in the field, no less," Nichols-Woodall declared. "For there can be no mistake, though I have no more idea how it got here than how the others got to the Salisbury Plain, let alone their point of origin. No wonder I did not recognise it, for I was considering the wrong continent!"

"You agree, then?"

"Oh, yes. There can be no mistake," Nichols-Woodall proclaimed. "It is dolerite, from the exact same source as that which produced the bluestones of Stonehenge."

CHAPTER 9
REVELATIONS AND RAMIFICATIONS

It was nearly dinner, and they decided that Nichols-Woodall should tell Professor Whitesell about the identification in private at the earliest possible opportunity, but maintaining Holmes' participation as confidential, for so the sleuth wished.

"May I keep this to show him?" the geologist asked, holding up the remnant from Leighton's necklace. "If I am to abide by your desire to seem uninvolved, thereby preserving the both of us in his good graces, then I dare not reference your chemical analyses. It would make for an obvious identification if I can show him I have a comparison, and then he can see for himself the similarities."

Holmes hesitated. Nichols-Woodall saw, and suddenly understood.

"It came from young Leighton's necklace, didn't it?" he asked perceptively. "I see the cut surface, and it is of the right size. And it has been polished."

"Yes, it did," Holmes admitted.

"Do you have to give it back to her? Were you forced to destroy the rest in the analysis? Is this all that is left of the pendant?"

"No, and no," Holmes noted. "She is left with probably some two-thirds of the original, still around her neck, with the flat surface now enabling it to lie nicely. The lapidarist collected all of the rock dust from the cutting, and that dust is what I was able to analyse chemically."

"I see. So the hard-nosed, uncompromising detective does have a small sentimental streak, after all?"

"I...had thought to keep it, in memory of a day, it is true," Holmes disclosed a bit diffidently. "Several days, actually. Leigh was a dear little moppet, as a child."

"Holmes, I must say, there is far more to you than you ever let on. I think it a pity, given your intellect and your many talents, that you have chosen a life of celibacy. With the right spouse, you could pass on some amazing traits to future generations. And probably enjoy the raising of said generations, from what I have seen."

Holmes flushed, and his manner became austere.

"It is as I told Leigh, Doctor: men's lives not uncommonly hang in the balance of my successful conclusions. I cannot afford distractions."

"So you bury those sentiments, deep down. I understand," Nichols-Woodall said softly. "You are a strong, brave man, Holmes. I admire you for that, even young as you are. And I swear by my honour and our friendship, I shall return this to you," he waved the tiny slice of pebble, "as soon as I have convinced Will of the validity of our — of your — conclusions. Which hopefully will be in private, sometime after dinner."

"Very good, then," Holmes agreed.

*****

After dinner, Holmes watched as Dr. Nichols-Woodall drew Professor Whitesell away from the main group, murmuring something in his ear. Whitesell did something of a double-take, meeting Nichols-Woodall's gaze with a question in his own. Nichols-Woodall jerked his head in the general direction of the dig field.

"Very well; let us fetch lanterns and carbide lamps," the sleuth just heard the archaeologist say.

There were few left to see the geologist and the lead archaeologist depart on their enigmatic errand. Phillips had already tried to leave in a huff after a dinner spent watching Leighton flirt delicately with Watson; Beaumont had intercepted him and taken him off with a promise to discuss Central American ruins, presumably either to avoid another brawl or to protect any antiquities upon which Phillips might take out his wrath, Holmes was unsure which. Lord Trenthume had promptly retired to his tent as soon as the meal was complete; Holmes suspected that he kept a very high quality private stock of liquor hidden in his tent.

Which left Watson and Leighton, who were still sitting at the table, chatting quietly. Holmes laid light hands upon their shoulders, and they looked up. Wordless, he nodded at the departing backs of Whitesell and Nichols-Woodall.

"What is that about?" Watson wondered, keeping his voice low as the pair rose from the table.

"Dr. Nichols-Woodall confirmed my identification of the interred stone, shortly before dinner," Holmes murmured to the pair. "He is going to show the Professor."

"You did it?!" Leighton hissed in excitement.

"I did, Leigh. Thanks to your necklace."

She let out a soft squeal and gave him a brief hug. He chuckled, a bit self-conscious, and after a moment returned it gingerly, in remembrance of the child she had once been. When he released her, it was to be met with a firm, enthusiastic handshake from Watson.

"Capital job, old chap," the physician told him, adding a clap on the back into the bargain. "By way of celebration and a bit of relaxation, would you like to join us in a moonlit walk and a little chit-chat?"

"Would I not be, er, in the way?"

"Not at all, Sherry," Leighton vowed, taking his near arm and hugging it for a moment, before tucking her hand in his elbow. Watson moved near, and she tucked her other hand into that worthy's elbow. "I think it would be a splendid stroll, with two such intelligent men to talk to! My oldest friend and my beau; how wonderful is that? Do say you'll come? I promise I shan't do anything that will make you uncomfortable."

"Very well," Holmes decided. "It has been a very busy day, and I should not mind a chance to stretch my legs in company with friends."

They set off.

*****

"...You've identified it?" Whitesell said with excitement as the pair entered the vestibule of the crypt.

"Strictly speaking, a...colleague did," Nichols-Woodall corrected, the slight hesitation going unnoticed by Whitesell. "But I was certainly able to confirm it. Come, I'll show you."

They passed through into the inner chamber, standing alongside the large block of stone. The lanterns hanging from the sconces had been extinguished by workers at sundown to preserve lamp oil. Now Nichols-Woodall sat the lantern he carried on top of the big stone, reached into his pocket, and directed the carbide lamp from his helmet onto the object he withdrew.

The small fragment of polished pebble glimmered with a slightly waxy sheen in the light, a deep shade of slightly greenish blue, shot through with specks of cream and white. The geologist set it, flat side down, on the top of the slab.

It was a perfect match.

"Where did you get that?" Whitesell wondered. "And what is it?"

"Do you remember the story your daughter told, that first night after Watson and Holmes arrived, about the expedition to Stonehenge, and Holmes falling into the dig pit atop you?"

"Yes? Oh, surely you don't mean to say that is the pebble from Holmes' shoe? The one she had made into a necklace?"

"It is a fragment of it," Nichols-Woodall informed him. "The pebble was a tiny piece of a so-called 'Stonehenge bluestone.'"

"Which makes this..."

"From the same source," Nichols-Woodall declared.

"But...how on earth...all the way to Egypt?!" the flabbergasted archaeologist sputtered.

"That, I cannot explain, any more than I can explain how Stonehenge was built, or where the stones came from in the first place, Will."

"Good Lord," was all Professor Willingham could think of to say.

*****

Breakfast was a bit hectic the next morning; what appeared to be a small den of cobras had invaded the kitchen area overnight. Nichols-Woodall discovered much later that a small landslide on the other side of the ridge, possibly triggered by a slight earthquake too small for humans to feel, had disturbed the snakes and caused them to flee their lairs. But no formal meals could be served until the area was rid of the creatures: they had found the heat from the coal-fuelled stoves and ovens to their liking over the Egyptian winter, and were attempting to settle in for the duration.

Holmes and Watson extracted their weapons and joined Lord Trenthume as he assisted in clearing the kitchens...after Watson had sent urgent messages to his staff to attend the hospital at once and prepare for multiple cobra victims, just in case.

Professor Whitesell, meanwhile, went off with Nichols-Woodall and Udail — all of them properly-armed as well — to inspect the rest of the encampment, then check out the dig pits. Whitesell left Phillips and Beaumont behind with revolvers and strict instructions to ensure that his and his daughter's tents remained safe, with his daughter well-guarded inside, despite her protestations that she should be helping in the infirmary. Whitesell also left orders that, rather than resuming digging, the manual labourers should spend the morning cautiously checking the pits — and the crypt — for any more of the deadly reptiles; he did not desire any more snakebite victims than Watson and his staff had already treated.

By dint of sheer luck, none of the kitchen staff had been bitten in the discovery of the snakes' incursion, and in relatively short order the men had either killed or driven off the reptiles. But it took a while for the understandably jumpy cooks to calm down sufficient to work; several cookpots, kettles, and frying pans were dropped on the ground, accompanied by short screams, if the least little unexpected thing happened.

"I think," a morose Watson decided, watching, "that we will not be getting breakfast to-day."

"I believe I agree with you," Holmes said, amused. "We may be lucky to get luncheon, as well, but there should still be some cups and tea canisters on the sideboard in the 'mess tent,' as you call it. Perhaps even a few biscuits, though they are likely to be stale. And I can heat water over my Bunsen burner if I can lay hands on some alcohol to refill it. It will have to do, for now."

*****

Luncheon was a little addled, and the courses served were simpler than usual, but it was understandable in the circumstances, and no one complained. Professor Whitesell seemed excited, and the group found out why, just before the dessert course was served. He tapped his fork against his water goblet to get the attention of the others at the table; quite a lively little discussion about the cobra invasion had ensued, and it was necessary to interrupt it. The Professor stood, beaming.

"I have an announcement to make," he said with a broad smile, blue eyes sparkling. "I know to-day is proving uncommonly hot for the time of year in despite of our little reptile friends, and we are all a bit irritable, especially after being forced to skip breakfast, but I believe this news will decidedly improve morale! It seems our most excellent geologist, Dr. Parker Nichols-Woodall, with the assistance of his colleagues and, I have it to understand, my daughter's willingness to allow something of hers to be, ah, altered, well...Parker has managed to identify the stone inside the crypt!"

Applause went around the table, and Holmes and Nichols-Woodall studiously avoided meeting each other's gazes. An excited Leighton locked eyes with Watson, and the others watched Whitesell in expectation.

"And?" the Earl of Trenthume demanded. "Don't keep us in suspense, man! I've been racking my brains over this for days!"

"Stonehenge," Whitesell said, succinct. "The slab of rock in our Egyptian 'tomb' is nothing less than one of the missing bluestones of Stonehenge!"

Gasps went around the table, and several averted gazes shot to the elder archaeologist in shock and surprise.

"Now Will," Nichols-Woodall objected, "I never said it WAS one of the bluestones! I simply said it was a dolerite derived from the same source!"

"And where is that source, Parker?" a jovial Whitesell demanded to know, quite pleased with himself. "No one has ever found that source, so you cannot say it was NOT taken direct from Stonehenge! And there are certainly stones missing from that monument, as I myself ascertained!"

"Surely not," Beaumont started to protest, just as the Earl of Trenthume jumped to his feet.

"THAT'S IT!" he shouted in jubilation, punching a fist into the air. "THAT is where I've seen that kind of stone before! At Stonehenge! My father used to take me there as a boy! I was fascinated by it...but I have not been there in years! No wonder I forgot!"

"And no wonder it was so hard to identify," Phillips said. "Wrong bloody continent!"

"Precisely!" Whitesell crowed.

"But how on earth did it arrive HERE, *mon ami*?" Beaumont remonstrated. "Surely it cannot be one of the stones from the fabled Stonehenge, for the ancients could never have carried it so far!"

"There are no dolerites on the Salisbury Plain either," Whitesell pointed out. "So they had to be carried from elsewhere to begin with. If they can carry it a few hundred miles — for surely it would have had to be carried from a mountain region — then why not a few thousand? What difference can it make?"

"But Will, I already told you, I never said it was an actual piece out of Stonehenge," Nichols-Woodall dissented. "And nor can you say that. We have no proof, just the knowledge that it is likely a dolerite or diabase from the same geological dike that produced those particular *menhirs*[56]. I don't believe for one second it actually CAME from Stonehenge."

"It is as likely to have done, as to have come from this semi-mythical

---

56   Standing stone, from the French.

source of yours," Whitesell shot back. "And you know as well as I do that there are gaps in the ring of bluestones, places where the stones are missing."

"And the last I heard you mention it," Nichols-Woodall riposted, "you were of the highly logical opinion that they had been broken up to use in local constructions."

"That was before you identified this one, Parker."

"Da, Uncle Parker," Leighton spoke up, "how do you know it is the very same? Maybe it just looks very much like, but this one is from somewhere in Egypt."

Nichols-Woodall avoided glancing at Holmes, replying, "The colour, the distribution of crystals, the crystal sizes, Leigh. All are telling, to the trained eye. But of course," he hesitated just slightly, "we would need to perform chemical analyses upon this stone, and then again upon the ones at Stonehenge, to prove that they were...or were not...the same."

"But wouldn't it be possible to get a similar looking stone, crystals and all, if the formation processes were the same?" Phillips wondered. "I truly paid attention while we hiked about, Dr. Nichols-Woodall. It was fascinating. But if you had a similar melt, that cooled over a similar time, under similar conditions, wouldn't it produce a look-alike stone?"

"That is precisely my point, young man," the geologist confirmed. "Now, if your professor there would let me take some samples from the lower edge of the slab, where its own weight has caused spalling anyway, then we might get a bit farther along in this little mystery."

"It is indeed the mystery," Beaumont agreed. "Would not you say, Monsieur Holmes?"

"I would, indeed," a subdued Holmes replied.

*****

"Now we are going to start looking for any sort of connexions to Celtic Britain amongst the relics," Whitesell declared as he, his student, and his colleagues left the dinner tent for the dig field. Holmes threw a concerned glance at Watson, as the physician, with Leighton on his arm, headed for the infirmary — surgery hours had been expanded in light of the cobra incursion.

But offhand, nothing that had already come out of the dig, nor anything that was found that day, seemed to have anything to do with matters of the British Isles, Celtic or otherwise.

SHERLOCK HOLMES AND THE MUMMY'S CURSE
*****

A hungry, hot and tired Beaumont, who had been at the bottom of a pit all afternoon in an unsuccessful attempt to extract another amphora intact — it broke apart even as he was trying to strap it into the sling of the block and tackle crane — had left the dig field after collecting the various pieces and seeing them back to the artefact tent for reconstruction. Frustrated and irritable afterward, he had retired to his own tent, where he apparently cleaned up a bit and changed into fresh clothing before dinner, then arrived at the dinner tent early. There he tided himself over until dinner was served with some biscuits and tepid beverage left from tea, earlier in the afternoon. So he was seated at table already, having convinced Abraam to go ahead and pour the wine, by the time the others arrived. He even appeared to be on his second glass of the alcoholic libation.

That night at dinner, the mood was quiet and thoughtful, if somewhat listless; the unusually sultry weather which had moved in that morning with the snakes had sapped the strength of all. Little was said, for a wonder, even between Beaumont and Nichols-Woodall, and Phillips did not bother to attempt afflicting Watson with his glares, but merely stared at his food. Everyone was simply hot, out of sorts, weary, and above all, puzzled over the remarkable, enigmatic find in the vault in the mountainside.

"It is likely the earthquake," Nichols-Woodall remarked, offhand. "Some researchers are theorising that such seismic activity is connected to hot weather. It may even be triggered by it. We may have another, and larger, quake coming."

"I should be interested in seeing the coupling mechanism," Holmes noted. "I have heard of the hypothesis, but I have never seen the logic in it."

"It is an ancient notion, dating back to the Greeks around the time of Aristotle, at the least."

"That does not necessarily imply causality, in either direction," Holmes replied. "No more than the presence of a tidal whirl off the coast of Sicily in the Straits of Messina proves the existence of the sea monster Charybdis — or any monster, sea or otherwise, for that matter."

This triggered a sporadic discussion for a few moments, but not even that could raise the energies of the diners sufficient to maintain a conversation.

As the meal progressed, Professor Whitesell's mood, so ebullient at luncheon, seemed to deteriorate. Several times he passed his hand over his eyes, finally rubbing his forehead with his fingers.

"Is something wrong, Da?" Leighton wondered solicitously.

"Oh, no, my dear, I'm fine," the archaeologist blustered. "It was an unusually hot day to-day, and I probably just got a bit overheated. I was quite excited, you know."

"Perhaps you should go lie down, Professor," Watson suggested. "I can come by later with something, if you need it."

"That may be wise," Whitesell agreed. "I have a bit of dyspepsia in any event. I think I shall pass on dessert. Watson, young man, see my daughter back to her tent after, would you?"

"Certainly, sir."

Whitesell rose and left the table, but Holmes noticed he appeared a bit unsteady.

*****

Moments later, a very pale Beaumont rose from the table also.

"*Pardonnez-moi*,[57]" he murmured. "I am also unwell. I fear I may have overdone in the heat to-day."

"It WAS damnably hot — oh, forgive me, Leighton," Nichols-Woodall apologised. "It was very hot to-day, earthquake or no. Perhaps you should lie down too, Thomas?"

"I should, perhaps," Beaumont agreed. "I contracted malaria some years ago, and when I over-exert, it sometimes recurs upon me. It rendered me comatose initially, so I am told, and prolonged unconsciousness sometimes occurs with the relapses. I should not like that to happen in this desert region. Dr. Watson, perhaps you might be so kind as to come by my tent, when you have finished with the good Professor?"

"I will, Dr. Beaumont, and I'll get the quinine from the infirmary, just in case," Watson promised.

Beaumont left the dinner table as well.

*****

Having seen to both Whitesell and Beaumont, prescribing plenty of water for both and a dose of quinine for the latter, Watson returned to the tent he shared with Holmes. Over their tobacco pipes, Holmes and

---

57 "Pardon me," French.

Watson chatted softly about the matter, late into the night.

"So you have already done all of the necessary chemical analyses that the geologist mentioned?"

"I have, Watson. And though I understand Nichols-Woodall's reluctance to make such a bold statement, I must admit that the evidence indeed points to Professor Whitesell's assertion — that this is really a piece of Stonehenge, or a slab of rock taken from the exact same quarry, contiguous with the henge's stones — as true. The elemental percentages I was able to determine, both from the fragment of Leigh's necklace, and from the sample I took of the slab, are identical to well within the error bars of the measurements."

"But how?"

"That would seem to be the new mystery."

Just then a frantic Leighton Whitesell burst into their tent.

"Oh! John! Sherry! Come quick! I can't find Da!"

"What?" Both men jumped to their feet. Holmes extracted his pocket-watch. "It is a quarter-past ten," he noted. "Why cannot you find him, Leigh? Is he no longer in his tent?"

"No," she said, verging on tears. "He isn't there, and I can't find him. He was ill earlier...I heard him, ah, purging his stomach, oh, perhaps an hour after John left him...so I went in to see about him. He was not at all well — very pale, and his eyes so big — and I put him to bed and gave him some of the medicine you left for him, John. And then I went back to my own tent and lay down for a few minutes, for it WAS very hot in the surgery to-day, as you know, John, and I just felt drained. Anyway, I must have dozed off, and when I woke, I went to see about Da. His chair was upended, the blankets from the cot dragged into the floor. The table with his books and such was overturned, and the books scattered all across the floor, too! I can't think how I slept through it; it must have made a dreadful din! But Da was gone! Sherry, you're a detective! Oh, please, help me find him!"

Holmes grabbed for the lantern, and both men rushed out of the tent, following Leighton back to her father's tent.

*****

There, Holmes veritably turned into the bloodhound that Watson sometimes facetiously accused him of being. Keeping Watson and Leighton well away from the entrance, he looked over the interior of

Professor Whitesell's tent with a practised eye, then stepped to the door and scanned the sandy soil just outside.

"Ah," he said, bending over. "Here we are. I recognise the imprint of his hob-nailed boots quite readily over your daintier feet, Leigh. Mm..."

"What, Holmes?" Watson asked, keeping Leighton's hand tightly in the crook of his elbow, partly to reassure her and partly to keep her from rushing off.

"...He was indeed unwell, Watson. We may be glad of having you along."

"How do you know that?"

"His footsteps are very uneven. He is dragging his feet, and even staggering. Come; let us see where this leads, for at the end, we are certain to find him. Leigh, be prepared to run fetch Watson's hospital staff, for we may well need them. Heat stroke appears to be a distinct possibility."

Holding the lantern aloft, Holmes hurried on ahead of the pair, tracing the sandy indentations of Whitesell's footprints. The erratic prints led them out of the camp and across the periphery of the dig field, hard by the northern spur. Glancing up, Holmes saw a faint light shining from the opening of the grotto, and let out an exclamation: the lanterns within should have been extinguished at sundown.

They ran forward, Holmes in the lead.

*****

Holmes sprinted down the earthen ramp and through the outer door, holding up the lantern; Professor Whitesell was not there. The light he had seen from without, however, came from the interior chamber, and he hurried across to the inner door just as Leighton and Watson entered the outer door. Holmes abruptly blanched.

"Oh, dear God! Watson, grab Leigh, quickly! Keep her back there!" Holmes cried from his position just within the inner door, spinning and waving a hand in warning. Without question or pause, Watson swiftly caught the young woman as she sought to run past him, wrapping his arms firmly about her waist and holding her against him as she fought to get to her father's side.

"Ah! Let me go! John, it's Da! He's sick! He needs me!" Leighton cried, struggling against his gentle but firm hold. "Let me GO!"

"Hush, Leigh. Wait a moment. What's wrong, Holmes?" Watson

asked then. When Holmes finally responded, it was in a tone Watson had never before heard his friend use: low, hoarse, and horrified.

"No woman should have to see her father in this condition, Watson."

"What condition?! What's wrong with him, Sherry??" Leighton called. "Let me help!"

"Hush, Leigh," Watson murmured. "Let Holmes take care of him. If he needs help, I am far more able to provide medical assistance—"

"NO!" Leighton abruptly and unexpectedly twisted in Watson's arms, head-butting him in the face just hard enough to startle him and cause him to release her. As he briefly saw stars, she darted out of his reach, and leaped across the inner threshold.

*****

Holmes, who had already set down the lantern, lunged for her. But Leighton was just as nimble and swift as she had been as a child: she dodged Holmes' long arms, and only stopped when she caught sight of her father's body. Then she screamed.

For, illumined by the flickering light of a single torch — not a lantern — Professor Whitesell's body rested on the bluestone in perfectly arranged repose, save for the fact that his head had been removed from his neck; it sat next to his right shoulder, blank, empty gaze staring across his own chest. Two pools of slowly congealing blood collected below the head and the open neck wound, respectively; a single scarlet rivulet trickled over the edge of the stone slab and down its side, like some macabre offering to the gods — whether Egyptian, Celt, or other, Holmes could not say.

Hanging from the open mouth was a sprig of foliage that looked like some varietal of mistletoe; across his chest lay a small, dried oak branch. A sickly-sweet stench filled the air; its source apparently came from the puddle of regurgitated matter near the base of the stone. An archaic Egyptian sword, the bronze blade sickle-shaped, honed to a fine edge, and heavily inlaid with gleaming gold, stained and smeared with fresh blood, rested across the bluestone at his feet. The overall effect was of some strange ritual burial of the old North peoples, rendered all the more macabre by the ancient Egyptian chamber around them.

Just then, the rest of the scientific team and several husky workers, led by Phillips, thrust through the outer door of the antechamber.

"STOP RIGHT THERE!" Holmes shouted, and one and all stopped

dead at the command.

"I thought I heard Leigh scream," a truculent Phillips demanded, jaw thrust out. "What have you lot done? Have you dared to hurt her? What's going on?"

"It is murder," a stern Holmes declared, succinct, just before Leighton Whitesell fainted, collapsing into his arms.

*****

"Oh, for heaven's—" Holmes grumbled under his breath, then turned. "Watson, come here and get her! I haven't time for this! I must examine the scene and try to ascertain what happened!"

"I—" Phillips began, then subsided, as Watson carefully relieved Holmes of his feminine burden.

"You what?" Holmes barked then, out of patience as he spun on the younger man. The physician scooped up the young woman into his arms and bore her into the outer chamber, where he gently laid her on the floor in the corner, then reached for the carotid pulse.

"I...would have taken Leigh," Phillips finished his aborted sentence with a sigh, watching Watson tend her. "But.. she's probably happier where she is, I guess."

"Such are women, young Landers," a still-pale Beaumont remarked, dry wit verging on cool. He leaned up against the wall near the outer door, and shivered noticeably. "They can be cruelly fickle. You will learn, soon enough."

Holmes raised an eyebrow.

"Will someone tell me what the deuce is going on?" Lord Trenthume demanded. "You said it is murder, Holmes. Who is dead?"

"Look around you, Cortland. Who is missing?" Dr. Nichols-Woodall pointed out, sombre and a bit short with the Earl. "Will isn't here. And Leigh's passed out cold on the floor."

"Good Lord," Phillips expostulated fervently, horrified. "You cannot mean to say it is Professor Whitesell who is dead?!"

"He does, and it is," Holmes snapped from the other room. "Do you all please remain where you are, try not to move, be quiet, and whatever you do, do NOT touch ANYthing! I am attempting to investigate the matter."

*****

It only took a few minutes for Holmes to survey the crime scene with his characteristic thoroughness. Then he turned, removed the torch from its sconce, and went into the anteroom, closing the inner door behind him.

"He will rest there, well enough, until we are done with this," he declared in a milder tone. "The bluestone makes a decent enough bier, I should think. Where is Udail?"

"Here, Mr. Holmes," Udail said, sticking his head in through the entrance. "We heard the lady scream, and came running, thinking it was another cobra."

"Good. Pick three or four of your most trusted men. Station one of them just in here, and the rest right outside the main entrance, within easy conversing distance. Under no circumstances is anyone to go into the inner chamber, and absolutely no one is to be let into even the outer chamber except myself or Dr. Watson, here...on pain of death. Is that understood?" Holmes' grey, drawn visage was grim.

"Yes sir," Udail nodded, accepting the torch from Holmes. "Professor Whitesell was a kind man. But you say he is dead?"

"He is, I am very sorry to say," Holmes admitted, melancholy despite himself. "His body lies inside." He waved a hand at the inner door.

"Is it...was it...the mummy?" Udail whispered. "The curses you said were on the door...did the mummy of the old pharaoh come back for him?"

"Nonsense," Holmes responded, steadfast. "Even if it were a curse, there is no mummy here to begin with. There never was. Stay here, stand guard, and do not fear such superstition. Watson, fetch Leigh and let us go back to the tent. I have work to do. The rest of you...go back to your tents, and do not go far."

"What? Why not?" Trenthume blustered.

"He means that one of us did it," a pensive Nichols-Woodall explained, "and he wants us where he can reach us when he figures out who."

"Precisely," Holmes replied.

"Then he will have to find me in my bed," a blanched and haggard Beaumont declared, "for I am returning there at once. I do not feel at all well. I only roused from it when I heard the clamour, and feared something dreadful had happened...as it appears to have done."

"I will send Sati to see to you," Watson offered, watching the others go, and Holmes turned to him as Udail and his men took up stations around the vault to maintain their vigil.

"Come along, Watson. Get Leigh, and let us begone from this God-forsaken place."

*****

"Take Leigh to our tent, Watson, and stand guard over her until she awakens," Holmes ordered as they left the erstwhile tomb and climbed the earthworks incline. "Keep your revolver in your hand. I have somewhat to accomplish before I return thence. And it may be that whoever killed Professor Whitesell will not stop with Papa Whitesell. Or with us. So watch your back, old boy. And if you have a few moments, and can divide your attention between guardian, physician, and errand-boy for me, do you please set up the rest of my chemical apparatus on the camp table in the back of the tent. It is all in the mahogany trunk."

"What? Why?"

"I must go quickly and ascertain if the remains of the professor's dinner have yet been disposed-of," Holmes explained. "At the least, perhaps some residue of food or drink may tell me what we need, so desperately, to know."

"You think..." Watson stopped dead, the unconscious Leigh still in his arms, "you think Professor Whitesell was...poisoned?"

"Almost certainly."

"But why on earth would you think such a thing? He was beheaded!"

"Several reasons, Watson," Holmes responded, gesturing him to follow, as he urged them farther away from the underground crypt. "It is highly improbable that the decapitation was what killed him, for there was insufficient blood drained from the corpse for that, implying that he was already dead when beheaded. Had he been still alive, that chamber would have been a veritable charnel-house of gore. And if you will recall, he left the dinner table somewhat early, complaining of dyspepsy..."

"True..."

"Then there is the fact that his footprints, left in the sand leading up to the vault's entrance, showed most decided evidence of a severe lack of co-ordination and possibly blurred vision into the bargain, though the latter can be somewhat difficult to tell from the former..."

"You discerned his footprints in all that sand?"

"You did not? Tch, Watson," Holmes tsked, "you see, but you do not observe."

"Well, but what else?"

"The eyes were open; it was patently obvious that the pupils were severely dilated, and mildly uneven as well."

"Mm, yes. I recollect that."

"There is also the puddle of stomach contents which was beside the stone slab, where he vomited, as well as evidence that he then fell, alongside the slab; and...did you happen to get close enough to notice the smell, Watson?"

"Yes, but I took it to be the vom— ah. There was more, then? Soiled trousers, perhaps?"

"Rather. It appeared his bowels had released. All taken together, I think we may proceed on the likelihood that he was poisoned."

"Well, well. As a medical man, presented with those symptoms, I must agree."

"More: his footprints were not alone, at least not along the ramp into the crypt."

"They weren't?!"

"No; he was followed, without doubt. And whoever followed him was undoubtedly the murderer, for no one but the murderer could have known what was happening. Only after Whitesell had expired of the toxin was he lifted to the top of the slab, his head removed from his shoulders, and the, ah, vegetable 'adornments' added, in the form of the various sprigs of foliage. And perhaps you remember one of the curses I translated from the outer lintel?"

"I remember you did, and that they were horrid. I don't recall them precisely, no."

"Then think about this and consider Professor Whitesell's state, and who was first into both chambers," Holmes said, then quoted, "'...*First bit by the haje-snake, to whom was given your head after it had been cut off. Even so shall you be if you breach what lies within.*'"

"Damnation! It is the curse, fulfilled! Poison, then decapitation!"

"Precisely."

"But surely...I mean, the curse..."

"Was enacted by a very human agency, Watson. So it should be no surprise that said human agency took the curse as inspiration...and subterfuge. What we must now determine are how, and with what," Holmes explained. "Which will, in turn, lead us to who."

"I'll have everything ready when you return, then," Watson agreed. "Good hunting."

"Hurry back to the tent. Do not dawdle, and under no circumstances permit Leigh to leave. Stay safe."

And they parted ways.

*****

Holmes was in luck: As Professor Whitesell had been the first to leave the table, his dishes and utensils had been the first collected, therefore were on the very bottom of the stack to be cleaned. He appropriated a large wicker basket and loaded everything in it that he could ascertain had held Whitesell's food, including his wine goblet with a few dribbles of wine still in the bottom, and carted it all away.

*****

Watson had just set up the last of Holmes' chemical apparatus, and Leighton, lying on Watson's camp cot, was only beginning to stir, showing evidence of coming around at last, when Holmes fairly staggered into the tent with the huge basket laden with soiled eating utensils.

"For the first time," Holmes panted, setting the basket down on his own cot, "I believe I may regret the good Professor's preference for multi-course meals! I thought I should drop something before I got it here."

"Mmh. What's all that?" Leighton wondered, sitting up despite Watson's mild protestations.

"The...remains of your father's dinner, Leigh," Holmes admitted. "I am sorry, my dear. I had hoped you might still be...sleeping." The girl studied Holmes' face, seeing the paleness that still lingered, as well as the lines of strain and grief the detective was still exerting effort to control. Then she seemed to slump inward on herself.

"Oh," Leighton replied, very subdued; she sighed, a weary, disconsolate sound, and her eyes filled with tears. "I...hoped, for a moment...I thought it might...all have been a, a nightmare."

"I fear not, my dear," Watson said softly, placing a gentle, affectionate arm around her shoulders. "I only wish it were."

"B-but why," she stammered, confusion in the emerald gaze, watching Holmes, "why are you...why do you have his d-dishes from dinner?"

"To search for the poison," Holmes admitted frankly, extracting each plate and utensil in turn and arranging them on all the available horizontal surfaces, in some semblance of an order. Watson, watching silently, decided that it had something to do with the sequence in which Holmes adjudged the likelihood of poisoning, and in which he must intend to test them.

"Poison!" Leighton exclaimed in surprise. "But Da was— he was... his head, whoever it was...I mean...didn't he...?" She could not bring herself to say the words, but she gazed at Holmes in distress.

"Hush, Leigh," Watson murmured. "Let 'Sherry' work. He and I discussed it earlier, while you were unconscious. And as a physician, I am in full agreement: your father's actual death was surely caused by poisoning. And the only means of introducing it must have been in his food at dinner, for he showed no symptoms prior to that time, and grew ill quickly thereafter."

"Oh, thank God!" To both men's surprise, Leighton sighed in what sounded like immense relief. Holmes spun, abandoning his sorting task, and both men scrutinised the girl. She stared at them blankly, blinking a few times, then seemed to understand their scrutiny, for she offered, "Oh. No, I...I mean, well, it is simply good to know that...that whowhoever did...it," she paused, and apparently dredged up courage from a well deep within, "that Da was...already gone...when they c-cut off his..."

"Ah," Holmes said in understanding, nodding before he returned to his dish organisation. Watson, meanwhile, briefly pulled Leighton close, offering a consoling hug, before easing his hold.

"Yes, I think we can all agree to that," he concurred. "Now, do you try to relax while I help Holmes." Watson rose and moved to assist Holmes in extricating cups and forks from their wicker container, placing them where the detective pointed.

"All right," Leighton mumbled, and stood. Again, both men stopped what they were doing and turned.

"Leigh — where are you going?" Holmes asked, tone sharp.

"Back to my tent to rest, like John told me," Leighton said, headed for the tent flap.

"No, no, no," Holmes said firmly, moving to intercept her. "It will not do. You must stay here. We must be able to protect you."

"But..." Leighton paused, and gazed up into Holmes' grey eyes with an empty stare, "why?"

"Because we do not know the reason they killed your father," Holmes allowed, having gentled his tone as he took her elbow and guided her back to Watson's cot. "Until we do, we may all be in grave danger."

Leighton's knees gave way at that, and she sat on the cot with a plop.

CHAPTER 10
THE CURSE WALKS

Holmes bent over his chemical apparatus in his shirtsleeves, waistcoat unbuttoned and necktie having been discarded altogether, sleeves rolled up, hard at work isolating the poison he had established from Professor Whitesell's wineglass; the butt of his revolver protruded from the rear waistband of his trousers, right next his braces buttons. Behind him, a staunch Watson, indignant over the murder of Leighton's father, stood guard at the door-flap with his own revolver, a loaded shotgun lying close at hand. Leighton Whitesell sat on the end of a cot in a corner of the tent, huddled in frightened, grieving misery, and trying hard not to cry. Her gaze shot from Holmes to Watson and back.

"S-Sherry, listen: someone k-killed Da," she finally broke the silence. The statement caught the attention of both men; it was the first thing she had said in several hours. "Viciously, cruelly. Without mercy. I have to know. Tell me: who was it, and why?" Her tone was no longer soft, but demanding; her gaze was hard, despite being tear-filled. It did not take a detective of half Holmes' skill to realise she had processed the events of the evening and had passed from shock to anger.

"That is precisely what I am attempting to ascertain, Leigh," Holmes answered without looking up from his work. "I do not yet know, nor yet have I determined the specific means, nor the poison used. But until we know the who, and the why, and the how, we must keep you where we can protect you. It is very late — or early, rather; I have no doubt you would prefer to release your grief, anger, and fear alone in your tent. I am sorry for the inconvenience."

"NO!" Leighton exclaimed. "No, Sherry, I. .I am very glad to be under your — and John's — protection."

"We are very glad to do it," Watson offered over his shoulder, gruff. "Now, that's my cot you're perched on, Leigh, and I'll not be needing it for quite some few hours. I must guard Holmes' back, while he works — and yours too, while I'm about it. It's getting quite late—"

"Yes, it is well past midnight now, fast approaching one in the morning," Holmes interjected.

"—Why don't you lie back there and try to get some rest?" Watson shoved his revolver into his own trousers and turned toward the girl. "Here, let me get a blanket for you. It won't do for you to catch a chill from the desert night air — it will be very cool soon, even within the tent."

"Yes, this tent catches the breeze coming down off the mountain, here, I'm afraid," Holmes agreed, still focused on his analysis. "In the day, it is rather pleasant. At night, it can be very chilly."

"Though it is useful, to disperse the tobacco smoke," Watson offered the bleak attempt at humour, and the girl gave him a wan smile as reward. A snort came from Holmes' general vicinity, and that, on top of Watson's wry observation, elicited a weak giggle from the girl. With that, Leighton settled into the army cot and allowed herself to be covered by Watson's blanket, gently spread by his own hand.

"Thank you," she murmured, gazing up at him, vulnerable.

"You are quite welcome, my dear," Watson replied in a soft tone. "You just stay right there and sleep. I swear to you upon my honour, you are safe."

Holmes smiled fondly to himself, an absent expression, and continued work.

*****

It was well into the wee sma's, nearing dawn, when Holmes finally finished his chemical analysis. He sighed, then sat back and stretched. Without turning from his guard position, Watson said, "Well?"

"Hush, my dear chap. Keep your voice down. Leigh is still asleep."

"Oh, sorry. Didn't think."

Holmes tiptoed to Watson's side, the better to murmur into his ear without being overheard.

"Yes, I have it, Watson. It took a bit of doing, especially out here in the desert, but I would have it at last. There was extract of *Viscum album* — European mistletoe or devil's fuge — in his drink last night at dinner. From what I can tell, it was almost certainly from the same source as the twig found in his mouth, though the latter was placed there post-mortem. The preliminary analysis, upon one or two leaves I found fallen by the Professor's shoulder, confirmed the same chemicals in both, in the same quantity...though I probably should do a more rigorous analysis with a bigger sample. Likely the extract was made from the original, and larger, sprig, and the remainder used to put into the corpse's mouth. Note, Watson, that it was the EUROPEAN species, not the African, *Viscum cruciatum*. Telling, that."

"Yes, it is. For an Egyptian would have used the local herb, surely. It would have been far easier to obtain than the European variety."

"Precisely. Well done, Watson; you are learning my methods. It eliminates the notion of superstitious obstruction by one or more of the diggers, and narrows our suspects to the leaders of the dig."

"Good Lord, Holmes. So they truly did kill him several times over."

"Whoever it was, yes," Holmes agreed, nodding. "Just as we first postulated. Poison, then beheading, then poison again — which is a kind of murder in triplicate. Very Celtic, that. It was, for want of a better term, a ritualistic killing. And undoubtedly he was laid out as a warning to someone. The mistletoe in his mouth, the oak branch on his chest, the antique blade, which bears such a resemblance to the golden sickle of the Druids, all were placed there as a message to someone. Someone who would recognise that message. Who that someone is, remains in question."

"Might they also be after Leigh, do you think?"

"I do not yet know, Watson. The data are insufficient, you understand. I shouldn't think so, but it is possible. Some cultures visit ritualistic killings upon the family, as well as the intended victim. Consider *La Cosa Nostra*,[58] the Sicilian Mafia; they have been known to use such a ritualistic *modus operandi*[59] as we now postulate. Until we can ascertain the purpose of the murder, we simply cannot say for certain."

Watson shot a quick glance at the sleeping form in the cot before muttering, "Damnation."

"Exactly." Holmes shifted his pistol from his back to his side, and extracted his pipe from his waistcoat pocket. "It is good, at least, to ascertain that the killer was not after one or both of us, on account of Leigh's affections, and only got the dear old professor by mistake."

"That was an option?"

"It was," Holmes averred. "It had occurred to me...I suppose you noticed young Phillips' extreme jealousy whenever one or the other of us was with the girl?"

---

58   lit., "Our Thing." Italian.
59   "Mode of operation," Latin.

"Well, I did — it was hard to ignore, actually — but really, I thought little of the matter, Holmes. I presumed him to be enough of a gentleman to at least allow a young woman to make her own choice." Watson paused. "At least after his multiple dressings-down for taking you on."

"A fair and just consideration, Watson, and one which proves you to be a gentleman yourself, but the heart has been known to rule the head in crimes of passion, on many more than one occasion," Holmes pointed out. "What was it that Pascal said? 'Le cœur a ses raisons que la raison ne connaît point.'[60] And I can tell you that, although the Professor gave him strictest instructions to apologise to me over that little affair, Phillips never did do so. And, judging by a few remarks the Professor let slip, possibly then lied to him about it." Holmes shook his head, then sighed despite himself. "Go on to bed, old chap. You have been on alert for quite some few hours now, and I suspect I have a several-pipe problem before me. Take my bed, and get some rest. I expect Leigh will not object if you were to remove your waistcoat and shirt for the sake of comfort. And I will be here to observe the proprieties."

"Thank you, Holmes. But...are you certain? We can talk, if need be. I heard your sigh just now."

"Quite certain, John, my dear friend."

*****

Watson tucked his head slightly, deeply moved by Holmes' use of his Christian name. It was the first time since they had met that the detective had been so familiar, or so affectionate, toward his friend.

"It was grief, then...Sherlock?"

"Yes, old fellow, I fear so. Yes, it was grief. I..." The detective sighed again, a world of pain in the sound. "I was fond of the old man, as much so as if he had been a cherished uncle. He was one of my favourite instructors when I was at Oxbridge. I shall miss him deeply. But that is neither here nor there right now; you need rest, John, and I need to think. Give me but a moment to light my pipe, and then you may put your revolver within easy reach, and retire." Holmes waved a dismissive hand, and commenced packing and lighting his pipe while Watson was still available to provide defensive assistance should the need arise. Then he took the folding stool, placed it just outside the door flap, and settled in for what was left of the night.

---

60   "The heart has its reasons, which reason knows not." French; Blaise Pascal.

Within a few moments, the familiar sound of Watson's soft snore emanated from the tent at his back.

*****

After an uncomfortably silent breakfast the next morning, of which few actually partook, the digging did not resume. Holmes, Watson, and Leighton did not eat at all, and only drank water which Holmes himself fetched, fresh from the water butt, and then tested for poison and infection to ensure it was safe.

Out of respect for the dead archaeologist, the workers remained in their tents, except for a small cadre led by Udail; these worked with the quartermaster to have a coffin brought up from Luxor via boat. When it arrived just before luncheon, this same cadre loaded it upon a shoulder-borne catafalque and carried it up by hand from the small village on the Nile, across the camp, and into the vault where Professor Whitesell's body lay, still under honour guard by the workers. Behind this procession, a trained undertaker followed, prepared to take care of the body.

*****

About the same time, Dr. Nichols-Woodall showed up at the tent which Holmes and Watson shared, with Phillips in tow. Watson emerged, Leighton peeping out over his shoulder from her position on a stool; Holmes sat at the table, still studying the results of his chemical analysis, in a valiant attempt to glean even more information from it.

"May I help you?" Watson asked, concerned. "Is someone injured or ill?"

Phillips grew red-faced and opened his mouth to speak, but Nichols-Woodall cut him off.

"Be silent, Landers. Nothing is wrong, Doctor. We simply came by because young Phillips here was worried as to what had become of the Professor's daughter."

"I'm right here," Leighton said, coming to the tent flap, but remaining half a pace behind Watson. "I'm fine."

"You've not been back to your tent since your father was found, Leigh," a scandalised Phillips pointed out. "Where have you been?"

"She has been here, where we could keep watch over her and protect her," Holmes' voice floated out of the tent. Moments later his dark head appeared in the peak of the tent flap, peering out over the top of Leighton's golden chignon.

"Again you besmirch her honour!" Phillips growled. "To spend all this time in the company of two unmarried—"

As the younger man spoke, the geologist watched as black brows and light brown drew together in extreme annoyance, and a pale feminine face flushed in anger.

"Phillips, did I not tell you to be silent?" Nichols-Woodall cut him off once more. "There is a murderer running loose in the camp, you young fool. What else did you expect them to do, but to protect the daughter of the murdered man with their very lives, until Holmes can ascertain who did the contemptible deed? Surely you did not think they would let her go back, alone, to her tent, with her father gone and unable to protect her himself?"

"I am just on the other side of the Professor's tent," Phillips protested.

"And you have already attempted to assault Sherry!" Leighton exclaimed hotly. "And do not think I have not seen the nasty looks you give to John, as well! If Sherry hadn't given you a proper dressing-down with his fists, and if you didn't know John had been in the Army, you'd probably try to 'teach him a lesson,' too! How do I know YOU didn't do it, Landers? Tell me that!"

"Wh-what?" Phillips mumbled, stunned, taking a step back as he paled. "Surely you don't think...but, but Leigh, I loved your father! You know that! He took me out of, of a less than optimal situation, and opened up the very world to me!"

"And what if it wasn't the Professor you were after?" Watson demanded. "What if it was me, or Holmes, that you desired out of the way, to see your way clear to Leigh, and you killed the Professor by mistake? Or what if you only wanted your way clear to the Professor's inheritance? Killing him, and marrying Leigh, would be a fine way to become rich and respected, wouldn't it?"

"You are, after all, attempting to climb out of a...'less than optimal situation,' shall we say?" Holmes pointed out.

"Oh, dear God! Is...is that what you think of me?!" Phillips whispered in horror, backing up. "You, Leigh...a-all of you?"

"No," Holmes spoke succinctly for all of them. "But until we do know who killed Professor Whitesell, everyone is a suspect. Including the both of you." He met Nichols-Woodall's gaze. "I am sorry, sir. But I do know of the... disagreement... you had with the Professor, earlier in the year."

"No, Holmes, don't be sorry," the geologist replied, sincere. "You are being cautious and thorough. And that is the kind of good investigative work that produces results — whether in a scientific investigation, or in solving a crime. The innocent will never have anything to fear from you, for you will find out the truth. I am not worried in the least." He took Phillips firmly by the shoulder and his voice grew grim. "Now, young man, you have seen her, and you can see she is safe. More, she is well-protected, by two very honourable men. Back to your tent with you, and if I catch you out wandering again — for ANY reason — until Holmes here gives the word, I will personally tie you to the tent pole. And rest assured, I am NOT in jest."

The pair left, with a stern Nichols-Woodall steering, and Holmes, Watson, and Leighton returned to their seats within the tent.

*****

Shortly after the end of the luncheon hour, Udail came to Holmes to ask for instruction on whether or not the body might be made ready and placed within the casket.

Holmes sighed, and turned to Watson and Leighton, a question in his grey eyes. Leighton's eyes filled with tears, and she dropped her head. Watson responded.

"Is there any further data you need from him, old chap?"

"No, Watson. I made a sufficient study last night, when we found him. I even managed a small blood sample, which I had forgotten about until a little while ago; I tested it while the two of you slept, and verified the same substance in his blood as I found in his wineglass, as well as possibly a few metabolites thereof."

"So there was quite a bit of it, then."

"I suspect it was concentrated, in some fashion," Holmes offered. Leighton sniffled, and she extracted a little lace-edged handkerchief, dabbing her eyes. "Come, my dear. Watson and I will escort you to see your father properly...seen to."

*****

The casket was rather attractive, Watson thought. It was resting on the floor of the outer chamber, made of the local sycamore wood, engraved with crosses and inlaid with colourful ceramic tiles. Its highly-polished surface gleamed softly in the lantern light, occasionally twinkling where a tile caught a glint. The lid was open, and it was lined within with red silk and velvet. The coffin was not perfectly rectangular, nor was it an oblong hexagon, but rather was gently curved to the shape of a human form, not unlike the sarcophagi of ancient Egypt.

"Will it do, sirs, madam?" Udail asked softly. "We had Abraam's help in acquiring it; you see, it was made by a Coptic carpenter, as we knew that the dear Professor is Christian. We...wished only to honour him. He was ever kind to us, and he shall always be considered friend. As," he added, looking at Leighton, "shall his daughter."

"It-it's l-lovely," Leighton murmured, tears overflowing. She turned and buried her face in Watson's arm.

"It is...most excellent," Holmes offered then, voice hoarse. "Entirely appropriate. Was it made especially for the Professor in so short a time?"

"Not entirely," Udail admitted. "We chose one which seemed..." The foreman's voice wobbled and he broke off, himself grieving for an old friend, and finally managed to choke out, "We chose one which the craftsman had already created and which was shaped as if for a pharaoh, then had the decorations added, per Abraam's instructions. It went faster, so." He turned to Leighton. "Mistress, I will sorely miss your father. I worked with him for many years."

"I know, Udail," came from Watson's shirt sleeve. It was a low wail of grief.

"Does the undertaker know what to expect?" Holmes asked Udail.

"Yes. I told him the condition of the...of the body."

"Then let me remove the, er, embellishments," Holmes said, gesturing to Udail to open the inner door. "I should like to take them with me and run a few additional tests, in any event. I ought to have got them long since, but I knew I would have all of the tableware when I left here, and I did not wish to leave Leigh or Watson along too long..."

Within moments, and upon the detective's instruction, one of the workers had brought the large basket that had held the Professor's dinner dishes from the tent. Into this Holmes now placed the dried mistletoe, oak branch, and sword; the others opened the inner door, and the undertaker began work.

"Sir," Holmes murmured to the undertaker, as Watson kept Leighton occupied in the outer chamber, "I think he would have liked it, if..." He leaned over and breathed something into the embalmer's ear. "Is it possible?"

"Ah, I see," the mortician noted with a slight smile. "Yes, I like that idea. And it will help with… the other situation. I will see what I can do. If you could have Udail step in…"

"Certainly." Holmes bowed, lifted his basket, and exited the inner sanctum, in search of the foreman.

*****

On Udail's orders, various workers came and went with embalming supplies and other materials, and after a couple of hours, the mortician signalled them to bring in the coffin. With the help of several workers, Professor Whitesell's body was gently lifted and deposited into the coffin, and the lower part of the lid closed.

"Mr. Holmes?" the undertaker called softly to the group who still awaited in the antechamber.

Holmes entered the inner room and looked around.

The blood and other matter had been carefully and reverently sponged away from the bluestone slab and floor, and the coffin containing Whitesell placed atop it for the time. Holmes stepped up and peered into the casket, then smiled and moved to the door between the rooms.

"Leigh, come here, dear," he said, voice gentle.

"I…I don't want to, Sherry." She tucked her head; her eyes were swollen and her cheeks stained from crying.

"Watson, bring her. Leigh, you need to see this now, my dear."

Watson urged her gently, and eventually the pair stood beside Holmes, gazing into the coffin. Leighton gasped, then broke into a strangled mixture of laughing and sobbing.

Professor Willingham Adelbert Whitesell, lately the Quatermain Chair of Archaeology of the University of Oxbridge, lay quietly within his sycamore sarcophagus, his head once more sitting on his shoulders, held there by the tightly-wrapped linen bandages of an Egyptian pharaoh's mummy. Only his face was visible through the wrappings, his eyes and mouth now closed; a peaceful expression rested on the lifeless face, and Holmes was more than a little reminded of the death masks which some of the pharaohs had been wont to use.

Protruding through the bandages over the crossed arms were a whisk and a brush, and a small pack spade, the tools of an archaeologist instead of the shepherd's crook and flail of Egyptian royalty, placed into the dead man's hands and held in position by the linen wraps. A necklace of scarab beetles and crosses carved in various semi-precious stones, and by the workmanship from the same lapidarist Watson had patronised, rested around his throat. A sweet, aromatic smell wafted to their nostrils, testament to the spices and resins with which the body had been treated, and Holmes knew that the undertaker had managed a lovely facsimile of an ancient Egyptian entombment.

They were silent for a long moment. Finally Watson offered, "Well, it looks as if this crypt finally has a mummy of sorts, after all."

"Indeed," Holmes replied, sombre. "But it would appear that the curse rebounded upon our own pharaoh, to do so." He turned to Leighton. "Do you like it?"

"It's perfect," Leighton choked out between laughing and weeping. She put out a hand and lightly fingered the whisk broom. "And he would love it. Was this your idea, Sherry?"

"A bit," Holmes admitted. "Udail and his friends had the initial idea of a sarcophagus-like casket; I merely asked the embalmer if he could wrap the Professor appropriately."

"So that's what all the workers have been coming and going about," Watson realised.

"Precisely. They were bringing in the linens, spices and ambers and aloes, the scarabs, and the like, so as to make it just right. And now, if Leigh is quite ready, let us return to the tent so I may see what additional clews may be found from this." Holmes pointed to the basket, then added, "Udail, perhaps you will see to having the Professor brought back to his tent?"

"Of course, Mr. Holmes," Udail replied, bowing, and Holmes, wagging the large basket, escorted his best friend and the daughter of the dead man back to his tent.

*****

There was little more to be gleaned from the items Holmes had brought back with him, or so he initially thought. The mistletoe that had been in Whitesell's dead mouth was indeed of the European variety; a few quick tests indicated it possessed a chemistry similar enough to make a reasonable assumption that part of it had gone into making the toxin from Whitesell's wineglass. The sword's grip was of leather and held no prints; Holmes had already looked for prints of any sort in the dead man's blood anywhere in the chamber, within moments of the discovery of the murder, and come up empty. He handed the weapon to Watson.

"Would you be so kind as to clean the blade, Watson? I think...this shall return to Baker Street with us. It would look well over the mantle in the sitting-room, do you think?"

"After...what happened, Holmes? Are you sure?"

"Yes, in remembrance, old fellow, for on the first Egyptian expedition in which I accompanied him, we found several of these."

"Does it not belong in a museum?"

"No, for it is not a particularly uncommon relic. But judging by its condition and evidence of maintenance, I should say it belonged to the killer, probably obtained for the express purpose," Holmes declared. "And I have no intention of returning it to him, when once I find him. Except, just possibly, in his entrails." He threw a quick glance at Leighton, who sat in the folding camp chair, silent, listening to this exchange. Then he returned his attention to the objects on the table, while Watson began gingerly, if expertly, cleaning the sharp blade of the ancient weapon.

The oak branch proved more interesting. Holmes had, at first glance after the gruesome discovery, taken it for a holm or holly oak, *Quercus ilex*, but as he studied it in the light of day and a more composed mind, he realised this was not so. *No,* he thought, considering, *this is a variety of what is called* Quercus virginiana. *That...is most interesting.*

"Aha," he said, looking up. "The game is afoot. Now we must—"

"Doctor Watson!" came Sati's cry from without. "Come quick! You are needed!"

"What's wrong?!" Watson said, starting up, as he discarded the sword on Holmes' bed.

"It is Dr. Beaumont, sir! He has got worse, much worse! He is unconscious! Alimah says it is a malaria paroxysm! Hurry, or I fear we shall lose him, too!"

*****

Upon arriving at the hospital tent, Watson found Beaumont prostrated in one of the cots, shivering violently and quite feverish. He was conscious again and able to answer questions with some difficulty, however, and soon Watson obtained additional details from the man himself that he had indeed contracted malaria in the swamps of the Amazon jungle basin some ten years earlier, of a particularly dangerous form known as cerebral malaria, and had had periodic recrudescences ever since.

"Fetch the quinine, Alimah. Hurry," Watson ordered. The Muslim woman smiled beatifically.

"I have it right here, Dr. Watson."

"Good. Let's give him a higher dose than before, and see what happens. I don't much care for the slight yellowish tint to his sclera. And set up a schedule of doses sufficient to put him right on the edge of chinchonism[61] without throwing him over. If this really is cerebral malaria, he will need high doses for it to reach the brain."

"Right away."

*****

"How is poor Dr. Beaumont?" Leighton asked when Watson returned to the tent. Holmes perched on his stool in the corner, puffing his pipe in silence and thoughtfulness, and looking like nothing so much as a giant bird of prey waiting patiently for its quarry.

"He could be better," Watson said wryly, taking a seat on the edge of his cot. "He is beginning to jaundice. The whites of his eyes were already turning yellow. I hope I got enough quinine into him, soon enough."

Holmes looked up.

"He is quite indisposed, then?"

"I should say so," Watson assented. "He was shivering so badly I thought he would fall out of the cot, and his gaze was not well focussed at all. He is also going in and out of fever delusions."

"Is he being tended? Is someone with him?"

"Alimah volunteered to stay the night in the hospital. He will be well cared-for."

"Good, then you are free. Come, both of you. The game is afoot," Holmes declared, setting his spent pipe aside and rising.

*****

They stopped at Phillips' tent, and Holmes went inside, emerging moments later with the professor's student assistant.

"This way," Holmes said.

"What's this all about, Holmes?" a mildly peevish Phillips wanted to

---

61   The syndrome of side effects produced by high doses of quinine.

know, tagging along reluctantly. "I was just about to retire for the day."

"That can wait, Phillips. I have a far more important task for you," Holmes replied. They paused in front of Dr. Nichols-Woodall's tent.

"Doctor?" Holmes called softly. "Dr. Nichols-Woodall? Are you up?"

"I am," came the geologist's voice, and the man himself appeared in the opening seconds later.

"Would you be so kind as to get your revolver and keep it at the ready? Phillips, you have yours, as I instructed?"

"I do, though I don't understand why. We've seen no more snakes in camp."

"It depends upon the kind of snake," Holmes said, cryptic. "Watson and I need to look into something. Leighton, do you stay here; you will be safe with them."

"But I want to come with you, Sherry," she protested.

"No, Leigh, this is serious work for a detective, and I cannot guarantee that there will be no danger. You are the Professor's sole heiress, and you must remain safe. Stay here, and Watson and I will come back as soon as may be."

"Then you have a theory, Holmes?" Watson asked.

"I do, though perhaps it is better termed a hypothesis, in the circumstances. You and I are going to find out if it is correct."

"And so you trust us now?" Nichols-Woodall wondered.

"I do."

"Then you know who did it," Phillips declared, certain.

"Sherry! TELL ME!" a determined, furious Leighton cried, lunging at him, catching him by the shoulders. "Tell me who did it!"

"No, Leigh. I cannot be positive of that, as yet, though yes, I have my suspicions. Say rather that I now know of a certainty who it is not," Holmes corrected, gently removing Leighton's clinging hands. "I should know more in a few hours, if Watson and I are successful. Leigh, go inside with your Uncle Parker and your friend Phillips; the three of you stay here until I tell you otherwise. Guard her well, gentlemen. You shall answer to me most severely if anything ill befalls her." They nodded solemnly, and he turned. "Come, Watson, let us go see what may be seen."

*****

SHERLOCK HOLMES AND THE MUMMY'S CURSE

Holmes made a bee-line for the crypt, taking Watson all the way in to the interior room with the bluestone, and using the waterproof container of matches he carried to light all of the lamps there.

"What are we doing in the crypt, Holmes?" Watson wondered, as Holmes began exploring every inch of the room.

"There is more here than meets the eye, Watson," Holmes tossed over his shoulder without looking up. "Somewhere in this room, there must be a hidden chamber containing something significant. As important a find as it is, this slab alone cannot be worth killing a man over. Not without some sort of additional explanation. And it MUST be here."

"Then how do we find it?"

"I have an idea," Holmes admitted, then pointed to a particular inscription on the wall, tracing it out with his index finger. "Do you see this hieroglyph right here, Watson? It looks something like the end of a steamer trunk, with its handle, and a bird sitting atop it."

"Yes, I see it in several places on the walls."

"That is the name of Ka-Sekhen," Holmes explained. "The box around it sets off his name, and is called a serekh; later versions of hieroglyphics used an oval around the name, and called it a cartouche. The bird is the falcon of Horus, meaning that this is a royal name."

"All right. So...?"

"I have a notion about it, and I strongly suspect that we will find a variant on Ka-Sekhen's royal serekh, somewhere in this room," Holmes said, still examining the walls.

"What kind of variant?" Watson asked, beginning to study the inscriptions himself.

"I have no idea; it could be anything. Look for one that is not identical to the others."

They were quiet for a long time, running hands lightly over the walls, looking for the serekh of Ka-Sekhen, and finding only duplicates. Finally Watson tapped the wall thoughtfully in a particular spot on the inscription.

"Holmes, come here," he said. "I think I may have something. Look here. What is this?"

Holmes came to his side and studied the markings Watson indicated. "Oh, very good eye, Watson," he said. "I think you may have found it."

"What does it say?"

"Mm, this shape is 'house,' and these two symbols could mean 'desert' and 'sun,' in which case this structure we are in is, 'Ka-Sekhen's house of the desert sun,' which is not quite right, as we are in the mountains; or it could mean...oh, now this is interesting...'house of the light of the foreign nation'..." Holmes shook his head. "Why, this elucidates a good deal, Watson."

"So it does, Mr. Holmes, so it does."

Holmes and Watson spun.

Dr. Thomas Brockingthorpe Beaumont stood there in the doorway, pale and sweating profusely, glaring at them with baleful saffron-tinted eyes, his cocked revolver trained upon them.

CHAPTER 11
A ROYAL ALLIANCE

"So I was right," Holmes declared. "It was you."

"Ah, no, no, young Monsieur Holmes," Beaumont replied with a foreboding smile, tipping back his helmet to wipe his perspiring forehead with the back of his hand; the carbide lamp strapped to its front momentarily spotlighted a patch on the ceiling, sending golden inlays glittering. "Strictly speaking, no, it was not I. It was the Alliance. I was merely its hand."

"Hand, foot, eye or brain, it was you who administered the poison in Professor Whitesell's wine that night," Holmes accused, one arm herding Watson slightly behind him, as Beaumont advanced into the room, and the investigative pair retreated toward the bluestone slab. "And it was your hand that wielded the khopesh which beheaded him."

"Well, it is no matter if I admit to it now, for you will not tell anyone, *mes amis*. Now, I see the revolvers in the waistbands of your trousers. *Non, non*, get your hand away from it, Monsieur Holmes, or I shall shoot! Now, please remove them very slowly, and lay them on the bluestone slab where I can see them. If you so much as wave the barrel in my direction, I will kill you both."

"But WHY?! Why did you do it?" Watson exclaimed, doing as Beaumont ordered; beside him, Holmes followed suit. "What could be so important as to be worth a man's life? A colleague, dare I even say friend?"

"Whitesell was no friend," Beaumont spat venomously. "He was a fool. He was given every warning, and he ignored them all. Und die beiden von ihnen,[62]" he added, beginning to mix languages freely as his face flushed with fever, "are too stubborn for your own good. You should have remained in London, or turned back at once, and never come here."

"Then it was YOU!" Watson cried. "It was you who kept trying to

---

62   "And the two of you," German.

divert us!"

"Sim, é claro, doutor, esta certo,[63]" Beaumont replied. "But you, Monsieur Holmes, are too smart for your own good — or for those around you. And yet, not quite smart enough." He laughed.

"So you already have what was hidden here," Holmes said.

"*Non, non*, I do not have that, not yet," Beaumont's malevolent smile returned, "but thanks to you, I know where it is now."

"Damnation, we led him right to it," Watson muttered in disgust, and Beaumont laughed. It was an evil, scornful sound, with an edge of hysteria, or maybe madness, to it, sufficient to make the skin crawl.

Then the archaeologist moved to the unusual serekh which Watson had spotted and Holmes had predicted, keeping his weapon trained upon them. He spared a moment to glance over it, then with his free hand pressed each symbol of the serekh in a sequence. Some half-a-dozen soft clicks echoed in the chamber, their direction impossible to determine; then the rectangle of the serekh opened into a small door with a shadowy recess behind it. Beaumont pulled it open as wide as it would go, then crouched low, so that the carbide lamp on his helmet would shine into the small safe and reveal its contents: a single leather cylinder, some eight inches long and three in diameter, closed on each end, tooled and dyed in a design which appeared to resemble the serekh. Beaumont laughed and pulled out the tube, briefly removing the cap, exposing one end of a scroll within, before sealing the cylinder once more.

"So it is as I thought, another scroll was hidden with it," he murmured. "A scroll and a bluestone, a scroll and a bluestone. Even then, the Alliance kept *los excelentes registros*.[64]"

"What is this Alliance of which you speak, and what record is that?" Holmes asked, gesturing at the tube.

"Oh, this is not the first such scroll I have found, *zanmi mwen yo*,[65]" Beaumont murmured. "Nor yet the first bluestone from Stonehenge. No, I found another, some ten or twelve years ago, in a ruin hidden in the depths of the Amazonian jungle, where I first contracted the malaria. It is a treaty of my ancestors, you see! Did you not know? Could you not tell?" Beaumont drew himself upright and gazed haughtily at them. "I am descended of the very Atlantean royal family itself, *mes amis*. The

---

63   "Why yes, Doctor, you are correct," Portuguese.
64   "...the excellent records," Spanish.
65   "My friends," Haitian Creole.

Aletean kings! The very house which negotiated this! The Atlantean Alliance!" He shook the cylinder in the air. "For my ancestors came to me, as I was recovering from the malaria, and told me of my true nature! I am the very incarnation of Thoth himself! I am the hereditary King of Atlantis! Bow before me, commoners!"

Holmes blinked in some surprise, both at the nature of Beaumont's frenzied command, and at his vehemence. Watson placed a firm hand between the detective's shoulder blades and pushed down as he bent himself. From their bowed position, the physician murmured, "See his flush? The wild eyes? The malaria parasite is in his brain. He is delirious. This is fever-talk. Do as he says, use all your wiles, and we may yet walk away from this." Holmes gave a slight nod of acknowledgement.

"And now you will obey your sovereign," Beaumont was continuing, as he backed toward the doorway, keeping the revolver aimed at them. "You will remain here and guard the bluestone. Under no account must Stonehenge ever be rebuilt, you see. It is far too dangerous." He smiled again, a chilling expression, as he reached the door. "And so your king commands you to stay here forever and guard it! I shall bring down the side of the mountain with the dynamite I have concealed around the door, and you will remain, telling no one what you know, while your spirits will drive off any future misguided attempts to rebuild the engine." He stepped across the threshold to the outer room.

"NO!" Watson cried, lunging forward.

"Watson, STOP!" Holmes shouted, tackling his friend and bringing him to the ground...

...Just as the floor of the antechamber opened up underneath Beaumont. He flung up his hands in desperation, the revolver discharging into the roof of the room with a loud boom, then with a shriek, he vanished into the pitch-black abyss.

*****

Holmes clambered to his feet, offering Watson a hand up. Then he went over to the bluestone and retrieved their revolvers, tucking his own into his trousers waistband once more, before handing back Watson's service revolver. Together they walked to the doorway and surveyed the scene.

The entire floor of the outer chamber appeared to have opened up as if on giant hinges, yawning into a black pit. From somewhere in its depths came a soft skittering sound. Holding carefully to one side of the door frame lest he fall, Holmes peered over, into the cavity.

"Look!" he exclaimed. "Watson, LOOK!"

Watson mimicked his stance and grip on the other jamb, and looked down.

*****

Beaumont's helmet had come off in the fall, and now lay on its side, some three or four feet away from the archaeologist's prostrate body, and illuminating it. Beaumont lay sprawled on the stone below, arms and legs randomly akimbo, unmoving and apparently unconscious. His revolver was not in sight.

But what brought a chill to Watson's heart lay just along the periphery of the beam of light.

Cobras.

Hundreds of cobras.

All crawling toward the unconscious man's body.

Within moments, they were swarming over Beaumont, striking this intruder to their lair hard and repeatedly. The doomed man's form jerked reflexively with the force of the bites. Suddenly Beaumont rolled over, having regained consciousness — and screamed in agony, just as the largest cobra struck him full in the face.

But, with his helmet turned on its side, the water no longer dropped onto the calcium carbide fuel to produce acetylene. The carbide lamp flickered...and went out.

Beaumont kept screaming horribly for several more minutes, over the sounds of hissing and slithering, and the loud thumps that Watson knew were made by the reptiles' strikes. After several moments, the screams grew progressively weaker. Finally, with a gurgle, Beaumont's voice faded into silence.

*****

Torches flamed in the distance, outside the tomb entrance — for so it certainly was, now — and suddenly Udail appeared in the doorway, flanked by at least a dozen men.

"STOP WHERE YOU ARE!" Holmes shouted. "DON'T COME FORWARD! IT IS DEATH!"

The men froze.

"What is wrong, Mr. Holmes?" Udail shouted back.

"Hold a torch through the doorway and look down, Udail," Holmes called. "But hold on tight to the door frame."

The foreman did so, and he and all that were with him gasped in horror.

"The floor opened up?!" Udail exclaimed.

"It did," Holmes replied. "Dr. Beaumont is at the bottom."

"Then we must get ropes and rescue him!"

"There is no rescuing him," Watson declared, sombre. "There is a cobra temple at the bottom. They...resented his sudden intrusion."

"He… is dead?"

"He is," Watson averred.

"Which is justice most poetic," Holmes declared, "for he was the murderer of Professor Whitesell. He poisoned him."

"No!"

"Indeed."

"Udail, what of my nurse Alimah?" Watson asked then, concerned. "She was tending Beaumont in the hospital tent..."

"I am sorry to say, she is dead also, Doctor," Udail replied morosely. "We found a knife in her chest, where she lay on the surgery floor. Dr. Beaumont must have killed her in order to try to capture you. Her death cry was the first inkling we had that something was wrong."

"Damnation," Watson cursed bitterly. "I had great respect and liking for her. She was an excellent nurse and an exceptional woman."

The men on both sides of the chasm were silent for long moments, out of respect to the dead nurse. Finally Udail turned to the others.

"We must get them out. Fetch the longest ladder we have," he ordered.

*****

It was not a particularly pleasant experience, especially having seen the fate that awaited them should they slip, but once Udail and his comrades succeeded in finding a ladder long enough to anchor across the opening, first Watson, and then Holmes, managed to crawl across the chasm and exit the crypt. Holmes promptly ordered the outer door closed and latched, and the sticks of dynamite carefully removed.

"For it would not do for someone to accidentally fall in," he said. "There is no return from that pit, as Watson and I have seen. Nor is blowing up the mountainside a wise plan, in my opinion. For if one man falling into the cobra temple angered them, what might that do?!"

Then they made their slow, weary way to the tent of the geologist, where the remaining scientists of the expedition team — and the expedition leader's daughter — awaited news.

*****

Nichols-Woodall took one look at the two ashen-faced men and opened his tantalus, pouring them both stiff shots of brandy. Without hesitation, they both knocked the drinks back, then took the extra camp chairs that the geologist hurried to bring from Professor Whitesell's tent nearby. The others sat quietly, watching, until Holmes and Watson could regain a measure of composure. Finally Leighton leaned forward and laid a hand firmly upon Holmes', squeezing gently.

"Who killed my father?" she demanded.

"Beaumont," Holmes replied, succinct. "He is dead."

"What?!" Phillips gasped.

"It is true," Watson vouched.

"Tell us everything," Nichols-Woodall said.

*****

It took the rest of what was left of the night. Watson noted that Holmes omitted most of the details about the supposed scroll and Atlantis, merely alluding to Beaumont's wild hallucinations, fever dreams, and nonsensical babblings about ancient civilisations. Then he urged Watson to explain the malarial infection of Beaumont's brain. Finally, as the sun was rising over the Nile in the distance, Holmes told of Udail's improvised scaffolding which had enabled their escape from what had earlier promised to be their tomb. Leighton paled and gasped.

"He nearly took the both of you with Da," she whispered. "How... horrible!"

"But he did not, Leigh," Watson soothed. "We are here, and we are safe, and the man who killed your father over some crackpot notion is the one who died a horrible death, in the end."

"And now, if you do not mind," Holmes murmured, "I think Watson and I have rather earned a rest."

"I should say so, old boy," Nichols-Woodall agreed, rising and offering Holmes a strong hand to stand. "More than, I'd think. I'll lay odds you've hardly slept since you found the Professor."

"And you would be correct," Watson averred. "I slept for a couple of hours… was it yesterday in the wee sma's? And I don't think Holmes has slept at all."

"Then by all means, rest now," Nichols-Woodall recommended.

"Absolutely," Phillips concurred. "Leigh is safe here with us, I swear. Why don't the two of you go back to your tent and get some sleep? We'll have someone bring you a tray of food in a bit; the breakfast gong should ring any minute now. You can eat, then collapse."

"A capital plan," Holmes said, rising. "Come, Watson."

They went.

*****

After a largish breakfast, which Nichols-Woodall sent to their tent on a tray, the pair retired to their camp cots and slept the deep sleep of the just. They missed luncheon entirely, but Watson woke from a nightmare, in which cobras featured heavily, shortly before tea-time.

Leaving Holmes sleeping soundly, Watson freshened up and dressed properly, then slipped out of the tent and made for the mess tent, having decided that his belly could stand a bit more in it. Leighton was sitting at the table, a teacup in hand, a tea tray at her elbow, and a plate of dainties before her. On either side sat Phillips and Nichols-Woodall, still dutifully watching over her, vigilant body-guards. At a meaningful glance from her, they rose, nodding affably to Watson, then stepped just outside the awning. Leighton patted the seat that Nichols-Woodall had just vacated, and he sat down. Immediately she began preparing him a cup of tea, as he took a plate and started helping himself to the fruit, tea sandwiches, and biscuits.

When his hunger had been sated, he smiled at his companion.

"Thank you, Leigh," he said. "I was surprisingly hungry when I awoke, given how much food you sent over to our tent this morning."

"I knew you would be," she said, sanguine, nodding. "Stressful events tend to increase the appetite, Da…used to say."

They paused. Watson studied Leighton's face, deciding it looked pinched and pale. She cast him a sorrowful glance, and he averted his gaze, not knowing what to say.

Finally she continued, "Did you sleep well, John?"

"Reasonably so," he admitted, rueful, "if dreams full of cobras can be said to permit sound sleep."

"Ew," she murmured, wincing. "Yes. It was dreadful, wasn't it?"

"I have seen worse, I suppose. But...yes, it was dreadful." He reached out and took her hand in his. To his surprise, she withdrew it gently.

"Leigh?"

"John, we...need to talk," she confessed.

"What is wrong?"

"This has been...all too much," she said, shaking her head with a weary, disconsolate sigh. "First Da, then Dr. Beaumont — though he received his comeuppance, I must say — and...John, he killed...Alimah is dead. Dear, sweet Alimah. Did you know?"

"Yes," Watson said, deeply regretful. "Udail told me, last night, when I asked after her. I was afraid, when Beaumont turned up in the vault, that, well, you know..." he broke off, then finally added, "...and it seems that fear was justified."

"I cannot...it is all too much," Leighton reiterated, visage forlorn. "I cannot face it, dear, dear John. Not yet." She paused, drew a deep breath. "Nor can I face you, nor Sherry. I...am sorry; in time, my feelings may change. I sincerely hope they do, for you are both dear to me. But for now, you both cause me to...to recall too much. Sometimes I think I shall never be able to erase the memory of Da's body lying there, with his head...dear Lord forgive me, his head...with his eyes staring so blankly..." She rose abruptly and took several deliberate steps away, then turned, face paler than ever. "I must leave here, John. I must get away. I must go home, where I can...begin to forget...all I have seen. And I must ask you not to come to visit me for some time to come. You...I love you both deeply, you and Sherry, but it will be many months, possibly years, before I can see either of you and not immediately think of, of what we...of finding Da, in the, the tomb..."

"I...see," Watson murmured, dismayed. "What will you do?"

"I talked it all over last night with Uncle Parker and Landers — mostly Uncle Parker, because he wouldn't let Landers say much," Leighton revealed. "While you and Sherry were...nearly getting killed, I suppose. I am so very glad you are both safe! But, but, they have offered to escort me back to London, and I have accepted. We will depart as soon as we can get all of Da's things packed. If Udail is willing to send Da's stuff on, we may depart even sooner. Under the circumstances, I should like to be home in time for the holidays. If I could leave this very instant, I would."

"What of Holmes? Do you need me to convey this message to him?"

"No, no, I...I will tell him later, when he is up and about," Leighton said, straightening with determination, then she gave a wry chuckle. "Somehow, I suspect he may actually be glad to see the back of me."

"I think you might be surprised, Leigh," Watson said, swallowing his hurt and disappointment. "But… do try to stay in touch, won't you? At the least, drop a letter in the post from time to time. And if you should ever need — or want — me back in your life..."

"I will, John," Leighton murmured. "But...too much has happened. I hope you understand."

"I do," Watson conceded with a doleful sigh. "I could easily wish I did not. I had hoped for more out of our relationship, Leigh."

"I know, John. I did, too. But I fear it was not to be."

She left the tent, where Phillips and Nichols-Woodall fell into step on either side of her, dutiful guardians, and Watson was left staring into the bottom of his empty teacup.

*****

Late that evening, before sunset, Watson saw Leighton approach Holmes as he left the mess tent, and say something to the detective. Holmes nodded, and followed her away from the camp, chatting with her.

Some half an hour later they returned. There were tear stains on Leighton's face, and Holmes' expression was closed, giving nothing away. But by now Watson knew his friend well enough to see the pain hidden deep in the grey eyes, and he nodded to himself.

"There's an end of it, then," he murmured, and joined Holmes as Leighton departed.

*****

Two days later, Leighton Whitesell left the expedition camp in company of Landers Phillips and Dr. Parker Nichols-Woodall. Michael McMillan Cortland, Earl of Trenthume, chose to accompany them, as well.

Holmes decided to stay for a few more days, issuing final orders and seeing to the equipment and payrolls. Then he and Watson packed their things as the campsite was dismantled around them. Udail helped them load their trunks, and he personally drove the baggage cart, while

SHERLOCK HOLMES AND THE MUMMY'S CURSE

Holmes drove the dog-cart down to the village, where they hired a steam launch to carry them down the Nile to Cairo.

CHAPTER FINAL
CONFEDERATIONS AND COUNCILS

"Well, that is that, Watson," Holmes sighed. It was a melancholy sound.

The pair sat in a small, cool upper room in the *Zhalam Al-Qamar*[66] Inn in Cairo; the screened windows were open to the refreshing evening breeze off the Nile, gauze curtains billowing gently. They had gone across the street to a food stall earlier, for a delicious, exotic, and filling meal of *koshary*[67], and now relaxed with their pipes.

"I am sorry, Holmes."

"So am I. I shall miss Professor Whitesell, but there it is. And in the end, he failed in his quest to find the first Pharaoh. That, in itself...pains me."

"Will Miss Leighton...Whites-..." Watson broke off, tried again, "will Leigh be all right, do you suppose?"

"I've no doubt. The Professor left everything to her, you know, and it has been a prosperous family for generations, so she is quite well off now. That young lady has the wit of her father and the passion of her mother. In all likelihood Phillips will find himself with a handful for a wife, I should think. In about a year's time, look for wedding invitations in the post, I expect."

"But Holmes! He is beneath her," Watson protested. "His behaviour leaves considerable to be desired!"

"Oh, Leigh will take care of that in a very short time, I am sure. The lady is EXTREMELY determined, as you may have noticed."

It was Watson's turn to sigh. Holmes cast him a sympathetic glance.

"Watson, as much as I care for Leigh, I think you likely got the better end of that deal," he offered. "She was a veritable ball of fire as a child, and is just as headstrong as an adult. I cannot think that she would

---

66   Dark of the Moon, Arabic.
67   A traditional Egyptian dish of rice, macaroni, and lentils with a tomato-vinegar sauce.

have been happy to have a husband with the freedom to which YOU are accustomed."

"You are probably right, Holmes. But I should have liked more of an opportunity to find out for myself."

"No doubt, old chap. I am sorry — on many levels."

"So am I."

They sat for a time in silence, puffing upon their pipes, thoughtful. At last Holmes laid his spent pipe aside and stood, hefting his satchel from the floor and placing it upon his bed.

"Now, pack the rest of your things, my dear fellow. The boat train to Alexandria leaves early on the morrow. Thankfully, our trunks are already upon it, with no misdirection, and I shall be glad to see Baker Street once more."

*****

The trip home proved far less eventful than the trip out had been. There were no cases of tainted food, no misrouted baggage, no problems with ticketing. In good time, they found their carriage pulling up in Baker Street, and Mrs. Hudson emerged to welcome them home to a holiday-festive flat, as the driver unloaded their trunks, enlisting the boots to help him carry them upstairs.

*****

After Watson went to bed, Holmes extracted the leather cylinder containing the strange parchment from the secret compartment of his trunk and examined it carefully.

"Interesting," he murmured to himself, gingerly turning it over in his hands, lest he damage it. "Archaic cuneiform, but it is on parchment, not clay. Yet pulled from its hiding place in the depths of an ancient Egyptian construct… containing a bluestone from Celtic lands. And according to its possessor, a virtual duplicate to some which were found in the jungles of South America. How very…unique. This will take some time to translate…"

Removing several large reference tomes from a lower shelf, he spread the parchment out on his desk, laid the books beside it, and began work.

*****

The next day, Billy came into the sitting-room while Watson was at his club.

"Mister Holmes, suh, it's Wiggins, suh. He's downstairs, waitin'. He has that information you wanted afore ye left."

"Ah yes, excellent. I'd almost forgotten. Send him up, please; there's a good lad."

Billy scampered down to the front door, and moments later another pair of small feet, clad in tatty, oversized leather shoes patched with pasteboard — Holmes decided by the sound — came pounding up. Wiggins entered and saluted.

"'Ere, Mistuh Holmes, suh!" he exclaimed, handing over a sheaf of papers and telegraph flimsies. "Oy gots ever'thin' yer asked for roygt 'ere, an' 'en some." He puffed up his chest. "Oy writ it all out me own self, Oy did, from t' boys' an' girls' reports."

"Very good, Wiggins! You took my advice and you've been going to the school, I gather?"

"Yas suh! Oy kin bof read an' write now, suh!"

"Capital! I'm very pleased. You will find that a proper education will only help you get ahead, lad. You might pass along the advice to the other Irregulars; it is likely to help me, as well. Now, let me see this." Holmes accepted the rag-tag collection of scraps of paper and flipped through it, murmuring to himself. "Mm. A professor, eh? Of mathematics, no less. I suppose it makes for a good cover, though... indeed? He is quite serious about it, then. I shall have to keep my eye on him in future. This bodes...hm. Well, at least I now know whom I might consult on the other matter. Very good, Wiggins. The Irregulars have done an outstanding job this time. Payment at the usual scale, with a guinea bonus all 'round. How many Irregulars were on the trail?"

"A round dozen, suh."

"Very good then," Holmes said, rising. "Let me fetch my pocketbook."

*****

The day after, while Watson was looking into the possibility of setting up a small practice in Baker Street, Holmes unpacked a few more things from his trunks. This included the khopesh, which he had had mounted on a plaque in Cairo, and which he now hung on the wall of his bedroom, opposite the bed.

Then he wandered into the sitting-room and over to his desk. There, he picked up the latest edition of the Times and studied its headlines, growing melancholy as he spotted a particular article. Reaching into his pocket, he extracted his pocket-book, opened it, and fished out a wrapped paper. Undoing it, he produced a little greenish-blue pebble with creamy markings, flat on one side. He let it lie in the palm of his hand, studying it for long moments, thoughtful.

Finally he opened the top drawer of his desk and tucked the little stone into the corner, where he could see it each time he obtained writing implements.

Thereupon he closed the drawer, walked over to the book-case, and took down his violin.

*****

"Listen to this, Watson," Holmes said a few days later, turning from his desk in their flat in Baker Street, where he still reviewed the strange scroll.

"I am all ears, Holmes. What is it?"

"It is the scroll that Beaumont wanted from the room containing the bluestone."

"Great Scot! You have it? I thought it went down into the snake-pit with him!"

"No, no, he dropped it as he fell. 'Flung' is, perhaps, a more accurate term. I picked it up and put it in my pocket before we made our way out. I have been translating it; it is written in Sumerian cuneiform."

"Sumerian! In Egypt?! Well, I suppose it is no less likely than a rock from Stonehenge being found in an Egyptian tomb. What does it say, then?"

"It appears to be possibly the original document from which Plato excerpted in his *Timaeus*. It is in a truly ancient and archaic form of Sumerian; I have put forth my utmost in its translation, and I think I may well have surpassed myself. I am rather pleased with my efforts. Hark:

> "'Many great and wonderful deeds are recorded in our histories. But one of them exceeds all the rest in greatness and valour. For these histories tell of a mighty power which, unprovoked, undertook such as would be against the whole of Europa and Asia and the lands beyond, and to which the Peoples of the Great Sea-Centre

> *put an end. This power came forth out of the north of the Great Ocean, for there were islands there, many and habited, and one principal island situated in front of the straits which are by you called the Pillars of Heracles; the island group was larger than Libu'*

"— that is Libya of our day, though by the context, they may mean all of North Africa," Holmes interjected —

> *"'and lesser Asia put together, and was the way to other islands, and from these one might pass to the whole of the opposite continent which surrounded the true ocean; for this sea which is within the Straits of Heracles is only a harbour, having a narrow entrance, but that other is a true Sea, and the surrounding land may be most truly called a boundless Continent.'*

"They could only be speaking here of North and South America, Watson, for they are in reality but one land mass, though that will change if France has her way with the canal across the Isthmus of Panama. It goes on:

> *"'Now in this island of the Great Sea-Centre there was a high and wonderful confederation of kings, Aleteans which had rule over the whole island and many others, and furthermore, the men of the Great Sea-Centre had allied the parts of Libu within the columns of Heracles as far as Egypt, and of Europa north of Libu, and more beside, including the peoples and coalitions of that boundless continent across the Great Ocean. This vast power, gathered into one, endeavoured to subdue at a blow the whole of the region of Albion, which sued for peace. But afterwards there occurred violent earthquakes and floods, when a bolt fell from heaven; and in a single day and night of evil misfortune, the island of the Peoples of the Great Sea-Centre sank into the earth and disappeared in the depths of the sea.'"*

Watson had pulled down his Jowett's translation of Plato and followed a passage as Holmes read his translation. When Holmes finished, Watson looked up.

"It is indeed wondrous like, Holmes. Perhaps you have it. Or perhaps when Beaumont composed that before he hid it," he gestured at the parchment in the sleuth's hands, "he copied from Plato."

"Possibly. But Watson...I had opportunity to decipher a few of the old...for want of a better term, 'pre-proto-hieroglyphics'...in the chamber where we found the stone slab. I said nothing at the time, because it was...unexpected. More...it told that anyone who found the copy of the treaty itself could never leave the crypt alive."

"What? So you knew..."

Holmes nodded.

"As soon as Beaumont opened that small compartment where the scroll was hidden, he triggered the booby-traps that were built into the place. Did you not hear the additional clicks? Those denoted the arming of the traps. As soon as anyone's body weight rested upon the floor of the outer room, it would open up and let him down. That is why I let Beaumont leave, when I had him covered from the beginning with the derringer in my pocket; it was far better that he trigger the traps and end the matter, than that we should." He paused. "More, I went back late the next day, only to discover that the floor had re-set."

"But the wall inscription?"

"Yes. As I said, unexpected. For it read, in part, '*Herein lies the token of that treaty of peace between the Confederation of the Peoples of the Great Sea-Centre and that rebellious land of the islands to the north.*' It was even the same phrasing...as one might expect of an international treaty which had been translated into the native language of one of the signatories. And Beaumont could not possibly have created those. Even his forged Middle Kingdom hieroglyphs were awkward, at best, and likely pulled from a lexicon of such; I doubt he could even read them — which is confirmed by his being unaware of the traps."

"But...surely you jest."

"Not in the least. Moreover, I have found a...a positive correlation, shall we say...between a particular Egyptian name and a certain Sumerian name in this scroll."

"Tell on, then."

"There is some confusion in archaeological circles," Holmes explained, "over the name of the first Pharaoh. Based on different depictions of the hieroglyphs, some claim it as Ka; others make it Sekhen —a variant of Ka — and some hyphenate permutations on those, as I have mentioned before."

"Yes, I recollect it."

"A literal translation accepted by most has the name rendered into English as, variously, King Arms, King of Arms, or Arms King, similar to one or more of his successors, who appears to have been dubbed 'King Scorpion,' or the like," Holmes continued. "At any rate, I found the name, or title, as it sounds to me to be rendered, inscribed in the antechamber of the crypt where we found the large bluestone slab. Now, the hieroglyphs reference arms as the limbs of a human body. Yet the Sumerian proto-cuneiform, which is even older, makes reference to a King of All Armaments."

"What?!"

"I now believe, based on these various documents I have translated, that Pharaoh Ka-Sekhen is so much fiction, and the serekh, a play on words," Holmes declared. "I believe the term refers to a THING, not a person."

Watson blinked, and stared at a solemn Holmes for a long moment.

"So...you are saying that...it really..."

"Indeed." Holmes nodded confirmation. "And the record of the chamber confirms it. No, Watson, this scroll is no forgery; it has lain there with the bluestone slab, concealed in the chamber within the Cobra Mountain for untold aeons, protected both by the cobra temple beneath, and the wile of a forgotten people. According to the document which was briefly in Beaumont's possession, which I hold here and in which I have expended much effort in translation, and which may have had a twin that previously also had fallen into Beaumont's hands, the nation we now know as Britain has been in existence in some form for far longer than anyone realised," Holmes began, fingering the ancient parchment as Watson settled back with his pipe. "Known once as Albion, it, along with many other ancient peoples, comprised members of an alliance headed by no less than the actual, lost kingdom of Atlantis."

"Atlantis?!" Watson exclaimed. "But that is only a myth!"

"Is it?" Holmes asked, sceptical. "I wonder. In any event, apparently Albion and her rulers grew...mm, cocksure, is perhaps a good way of putting it. Under the rule of one Goëmagot, whose title it seems was Gaawr Maddoc, 'the Great Good,' as I make it, the Albions constructed a device — a weapon — which frightened their allies and outright terrified their enemies. Insofar as I can tell, it was this device, and not a man, to which was given the title, 'King of All Armaments.' I gather it was not so much the capability of the actual device built that alarmed, as that was in nature by way of what engineers term a 'prototype,' but rather the potential of the overall concept which was dangerous. Were it to be brought to culmination, it seems Albion would have had the capacity to destroy Atlantis itself, in its entirety. Given that the entire nation of Atlantis seems to have consisted of a main island — named 'Ætalente' as nearly as I can make it — somewhat smaller than the main island of Britain, and a few accessory islands similar to the Hebrides, this might not have been as difficult as it at first appears. Though the archipelago would have been rather more spread out if the group were really the size of northern Africa. In any event, apparently Atlantis, in its technological dominance — at least, until this Albion weapon — was responsible for keeping the world peace. There were, apparently, numerous civilisations of that ancient day, both in the Old World and the New, of some considerable sophistication, and not all of them were of a peaceable nature. Some were, apparently, altogether vicious. So there existed a kind of 'Pax Atlantea' one might say, as once there was the Pax Romana, as now we have the Pax Britannica. Loss of the nation at the head of the coalition would have allowed Atlantis' enemies — not all of whom were ALBION'S enemies, mind — to run rampant, descending the entire world into war, chaos and ruin such as has never been seen. A world war, Watson. Just imagine it. And so the coalition decided it must take action. It gathered a fleet and blockaded Albion."

"What?! They started a war?"

"Not quite. They threatened it. With such a military force as would have ravaged the British Isles and laid waste." He tapped the parchment in his hand. "From the tiny islands in the North Sea to the chalk cliffs overlooking the Channel, the land would have been left so desolate that nothing could have lived upon it."

"But...but how? Nothing can do that!"

Holmes shook his head.

"I cannot tell, Watson. There are references to weaponry, to colossal war machines of land, sea, AND air, that I cannot translate, because they have no correspondence to our modern weapons." He waved the parchment for antecedent. "There are gleaming silver airships, fleeter than the wind; swift naval vessels powered by something far stronger than coal; cannon the like of which we cannot imagine; something I can only describe as 'death rays'...and explosives, Watson, explosives which bring down the lightning when they detonate, which wipe out entire cities in a single blast, which raise titanic clouds of, of, poisonous...dust, to settle on the surrounds in a black rain of death." An appalled Holmes shook his head in perplexity, waving his hands in the air. "I am only able to derive this much from the descriptions in the parchment. I cannot begin to tell you how they function."

"But that's simply not possible, Holmes! It makes no sense," Watson reasoned. "How can an ancient culture have weapons more powerful than our modern ones? Weapons not even we understand? Surely your translation is in error." An earnest Watson leaned forward; his long-forgotten pipe extinguished itself, the thin trail of smoke drifting away and dissipating as it ceased altogether.

"I can assure you, it is not. And I shall get to the 'how' in a moment, Watson. Obviously, since we do not live upon a bleak, lifeless, Godforsaken rock, war did not ensue. This was because evidently Premier Goëmagot and his staff came to their senses when they looked out and saw the vast armada, and promptly sued for peace. A treaty was drawn up, and pursuant to that treaty, Goëmagot was deposed and later executed. The weapon at the centre of the structure we now know as Stonehenge was in essence destroyed: it was removed, completely disassembled, and sent to the Atlantean capital. Then Stonehenge as it existed at that point in time — merely the outermost resonance, support and aligning structure, for that was all which remained when once the weapon itself was removed — was partly dismantled, with a slab of that most peculiar blue diabase or dolerite stone being sent to every nation of the coalition as affirmation of the pact. Yes, yes, I know — we do not know how they moved such huge stones to begin with, let alone sending them to every continent of the known world. But however it was done, Stonehenge was left in large part even as we see it to-day, and never rebuilt."

"Why have we not heard of this before now, then?"

"Because it would appear that there may be more than merely Beaumont still guarding the secret. And, like Beaumont, it seems the... cabal...is willing to do whatever it takes to guard their ancient enigma. There may even be a chief, someone at the head of the conspiracy, pulling the threads; I find there is something vaguely familiar about their *modus operandi*. So I contacted...a high member of the government's accounting office, shall we say for now...to see if he had any information on the matter."

"And did he?"

"He did. It took him a bit of doing; the matter is evidently quite effectively hidden even at his level, but he was able to confirm that, to date, there have been some dozen other slabs of bluestone found...elsewhere in the world; the majority being found by various archaeological groups on different continents, though several of the most recent finds were by, er, especially-formulated… mm, teams, we shall term them… dispatched by Her Majesty's government. A total of five such teams were sent out. Three of the teams sent back word of their finds...but did not themselves return alive. Two more were never heard from again. Which is telling." Holmes drew a deep, thoughtful breath. "And do you remember Professor Whitesell remarking on the death of Professor Gärtner, of Heidelberg University?"

"Yes. Tunnel collapsed on him, didn't it?"

"Indeed. While he was attempting to excavate a Viking funeral boat. And do you know what was in that boat?"

"Probably some dead Viking king, I suppose." Watson shrugged indifferently.

"No, Watson. It was another slab of bluestone dolerite. Likely from Stonehenge. Does that suggest anything to you?"

"Good Lord, Holmes! He was killed for the sake of this bloody secret, as well?"

"That is how I read it." He tapped the scroll. "At any rate, in the end the peace treaty did little good, either to Albion, Atlantis, or much of anyone else. Only five years later a substantial meteor, of a size which a," Holmes' expression grew grim, his lips twisting in patent distaste, "an expert I consulted asserted to be an asteroid, struck Atlantis nearly perfectly centrally — 'a bolt from heaven,' one might say. The island was obliterated by the impact, leaving, presumably, a gigantic Barringer-style crater in the ocean bed for scientists of some future time to find. The monstrous tidal wave that resulted, combined with mammoth earthquakes, devastated not only Albion, but much of the then-civilised world. Beaumont's document, here, indicates worldwide devastation, chaos, a collapse of civilisation as they knew it, and finally a subsidence into their own dark ages. Whether this was the source of the Biblical great Flood of Noah, I cannot say. But the catastrophe was certainly nearly of a proportion to it, so it may well be. Ironically," he added, "it may also be that the Albion weapon might have provided an adequate defence against the asteroid, had it been allowed to continue."

"So...that is how their inventions would have been lost to us. They — all of it, of them — were wiped out in some horrible, world-wide cataclysm."

"That is how I make it, yes. For there is an appendix on the parchment, written much, much later, if the cuneiform style is to be adjudged, that purports to fill in a few subsequent details. The beings of Irish myth, the Tuatha de Danann — which have direct parallels in the legends of all of the ancient peoples of the British Isles AND the Celts of the Continent, so we may readily assume them all to be the same — seem to have been in truth Atlantean refugees, by some miracle escaping that disaster which destroyed their homeland, cast up on the shores of these islands. They were likely charged with the task of maintaining the treaty — their much-vaunted treasures, and the 'clouds' on which they arrived, probably some sort of airship fleet, were likely the last functioning advanced devices of Atlantis...which were, like their homeland, lost to time as whatever provided their power gradually exhausted itself. Later, as the tribe of Danae intermarried with the remnants of the Albions, and their Atlantean blood — and allegiance to that shattered land — waned, the Milesian Spanish invasion served a similar purpose, for evidently their leader, Amergin the 'Druid,' was in fact of pure-blooded Atlantean descent, likely made possible by his being from a larger outpost of that race, possibly an original colony that survived the cataclysm. In the end, whatever the reason, Stonehenge was never rebuilt. Which may be as well."

Holmes paused in thought, staring at the record in his hands.

"Perhaps Stonehenge really was some fantastical, powerful weapon, and perhaps it was not. But in the end, it was the 'weapon' that preserved an island nation — the nation we call home, the nation in which we dwell: Great Britain."

There was a long silence. Finally Watson spoke.

"Now what?"

"Hm?"

"What do we do now, Holmes?"

Holmes gazed pensively at his friend. "Nothing."

"Nothing?!"

"Indeed. In fact, I left orders with Udail to have the slab and its crypt reburied, and the location hidden as well and as deeply as our current science permits. And I must swear you to absolute secrecy on the matter, my dear Watson. This is one adventure that must never be published."

"But Holmes—!" Watson half-stood from his chair in shock and dismay. "The truth! Surely we must tell the world the truth!"

"In the end, some truths are too dangerous to be known, old chap. Consider, Watson," the detective explained patiently. "We know that this is indeed a part of Stonehenge, not merely a piece of the same bluestone, whatever its source and origins — the chemical analysis proved as much. Beaumont claimed he had seen a scroll and a bluestone as well, from some lost ruin buried deep in the South American jungles, with a seemingly outlandish tale about ancient war machines from Atlantis and the slabs of dolerite that were removed from 'Albion' — England. We know that we found precisely such a slab...in an ancient Egyptian archaeological site. We have the scroll of the treaty which was hidden there… which was written in Sumerian proto-cuneiform. We know that other blocks, other copies of the treaty, have been found around the world. We know that this man Beaumont believed it sufficient to kill. Maybe it was; maybe it was not. We do know that several other expeditions sent deliberately in search of these bluestones have been wiped out, to a man. At least two teams were never seen nor heard from again, their fates completely unknown.

"So, was Beaumont simply a malaria-ridden madman, or...something more? Perhaps one day mankind will be sufficiently advanced to determine if his claim to be Atlantean was true; the chances are vastly against it being his personal history, of course, let alone of the royal family, as he claimed at the end. But...what if it WERE true? In all, or even in part? What if Atlantean blood did run in his veins, however diluted? And what if there are others like him? For it is almost certain that the message conveyed by the Professor's highly ritualistic killing was directed at them, so that they might be confident that the matter was dispensed-with in this instance and the discovery lost; Beaumont could not know that it was I who identified the stone for Whitesell...and I have sent word to Nichols-Woodall to be silent, and burn all records he has of the matter, as his life depends upon it. I have his assurances he has done so, and that he is strongly advising young Phillips, and Leighton, of discretion on the matter into the bargain. The Earl of Trenthume, I gather, has all but forgotten the matter, and moved on to another archaeological dig, so we need not to be concerned on that account.

"But, Watson, what if these secretive enforcers are in positions of power, for good, or for evil? By the evidence we have uncovered, there can be no doubt but that the modern Aletean confederation is as worldwide as the antediluvian one claimed to be. What dangers do we open to Mother England, by revealing this to the world? What advantages do we accrue in the reveal, and can they possibly outweigh the dangers? I see many dangers, and few — if any — advantages. No, Watson. I am afraid I must ask you to bury any notes you have made for this case, deep, deep, in that bank vault of yours, and never let them come to light.

A deal is a deal. No matter how ancient."

"But...what about...about the Professor? How are we to explain his death? You saw the newspapermen waiting on the quay. If you hadn't slipped us off the ship, incognito, by the cargo gangplank, we would have been swarmed."

"I...have taken care of the matter," Holmes responded obliquely, avoiding Watson's worried gaze.

"But...how?"

Holmes raked a hand through his hair, then confessed, "I dropped a little flea in your agent's ear."

"Doyle? What on earth did you tell him?"

"Do you remember the faked stone tablet?"

"The one with the supposed curse that caused us so much trouble with the workers? I should think I do."

"I quoted it, so: '*Death shall come on swift wings to him who disturbs the peace of the Pharaoh.*' And implied that Professor Whitesell had brought it all down upon himself by disturbing Ka-Sekhen. And then Beaumont followed suit."

"Oh," Watson said, somewhat blankly, as he settled back into his armchair. "Did he buy it, as the Americans say?"

"Have a look at to-day's newspaper." Holmes tossed it across. Watson picked it up and read the headline, *Archaeologists Killed by Mummy's Curse?* He snorted.

"Well, I suppose it is as good as anything," he decided.

"Indeed. More, it sends a message to any who may consider themselves guardians, as Beaumont did."

"And what does our message say?"

"That we agree with them. The secret remains safe...as will Albion. For now, at any rate."

Holmes carefully rolled up the venerable old scroll, slipped its fragile leather thong tie about it, and eased it into its protective cylinder. Then he opened his strong box, placing the cylinder safely in the rear of the interior, shutting it away from the light once more. He spun the dial on the lock and slid the portrait of General Gordon back over the safe. Then he turned as young Billy entered.

"Telegram from Scotland Yard, suh," he murmured, offering the flimsy paper to Holmes on a tray. "I expect as Inspect'r Lestrade is wantin' ye again. He was right put out at your not bein' available whiles you were gone. Kept coming by, wanting to know when you was gonna get back, most once or twice a week! An' 'cordin' to th' papers, I don't think one single case got solved while you were away. Mrs. Hudson an' I kept a running tally on her slate in the kitchen."

"Thank you, Billy," Holmes said with a slight smile, taking the telegram and glancing over it. "Mm. Yes, lad, you may go. Watson?"

"Yes?"

"Are you available, old chap?"

"Is the game afoot?"

"It is, indeed."

Watson shook his head. "And us scarcely complete with the last one."

"So it goes, my dear Watson. Neither time, nor the forces of evil, wait for mere mortals such as ourselves. Now, into your coat and come! A case awaits!"

The pair threw on their greatcoats and cravats, caught up canes and silk hats, and ran for the stairs.

AUTHOR'S NOTES

As usual, there are numerous people I need to thank for this work in your hands. First and foremost is publisher Tommy Hancock, who likes and reads my other books, most notably the *Displaced Detective* series with Lida Quillen's Twilight Times Books, and so asked me in the first place, for what we are now calling the *Gentleman Aegis* series. This new series will chronicle the adventures of Continuum 114's version of Sherlock Holmes and John Watson, beginning with the pair as young men, just establishing themselves as gentlemen businessmen in London, with all the excitement, problems, personal foibles and more, that that entails.

There's also my husband Darrell to thank, who brainstorms with me when I get stuck and is VERY supportive and encouraging, as are my parents, Steve and Colene Gannaway. Without these four — five, counting Lida Quillen — this book would never exist to begin with.

Historical assistance came from numerous sources, including Bob Buelow, Cie McCullough, Karen Ramsey McGinn, Christopher McArthur, Paul Dion, Deb Fuller, Wesley Thomas, and the other members of Lady Osborn's Pub fan group on Facebook.

Research into certain medical matters was verified by my uncle, Dr. Robert R. Murphy, M.D.

Fellow author and native Portuguese, Sarah A. Hoyt, helped me verify Dr. Beaumont's Portuguese remarks. This was a HUGE help, as it is a language that "skews" just a bit for me, relative to the Spanish and Latin I've studied. My very great thanks to her for taking time to help, in the middle of moving her domicile, no less.

I'd also like to thank beta readers Dr. James K. Woosley and Evelyn Hively for their invaluable comments.

The style of this book, and subsequent books in the series, may seem unusual to you. However, there is a reason for that: I chose to use a more Victorian English writing style than my usual. So, as nearly as I can make it, the spelling is British, and phrasing, expressions, and euphemisms are based on those of Victorian England, including the more frequent use of adverbs, which is currently out of fashion but was very much the style in the late 1800s. Also for those of you who know me as a writer of hard SF/mystery, I am using, for the most part, the science of the day, and so the SF is correct per the period — though it may have been disproven later. This can result in some interesting juxtapositions, and I have a lot of fun with them. I hope you, the reader, do too.

~Stephanie Osborn
Huntsville, AL
May 2015

ABOUT THE AUTHOR

Few can claim the varied background of Stephanie Osborn, the Interstellar Woman of Mystery.

Veteran of more than 20 years in the civilian space program, as well as various military space defense programs, she worked on numerous space shuttle flights and the International Space Station, and counts the training of astronauts on her resumé. Her space experience also includes Spacelab and ISS operations, variable star astrophysics, Martian aeolian geophysics, radiation physics, and nuclear, biological, and chemical weapons effects.

Stephanie holds graduate and undergraduate degrees in four sciences: astronomy, physics, chemistry and mathematics, and she is "fluent" in several more, including geology and anatomy.

In addition she possesses a license of ministry, has been a duly sworn, certified police officer, and is a National Weather Service certified storm spotter.

Her travels have taken her to the top of Pikes Peak, across the world's highest suspension bridge, down gold mines, in the footsteps of dinosaurs, through groves of giant Sequoias, and even to the volcanoes of the Cascade Range in the Pacific Northwest, where she was present for several phreatic eruptions of Mount St. Helens.

Now retired from space work, Stephanie has trained her sights on writing. She has authored, co-authored, or contributed to nearly 25 books, including the celebrated science-fiction mystery, *Burnout: The mystery of Space Shuttle STS-281*. She is the co-author of the Cresperian Saga book series, and currently writes the critically acclaimed Displaced Detective Series, described as "Sherlock Holmes meets The X-Files." She released the paranormal/horror novella *El Vengador*, based on a true story, in 2013 as an ebook.

In addition to her writing work, the Interstellar Woman of Mystery now happily "pays it forward," teaching math and science through numerous media including radio, podcasting and public speaking, as well as working with SIGMA, the science-fiction think tank.

The Mystery continues.

FROM AIRSHIP 27 PRODUCTIONS- THE GREAT DETECTIVE:

PULP FICTION FOR A NEW GENERATION

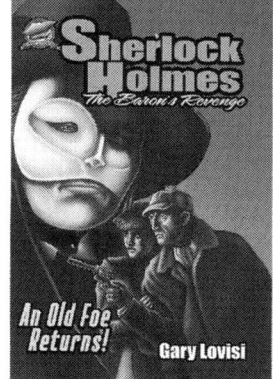 

FOR AVAILABILITY OF THESE AND OTHER FINE PUBLICATIONS CHECK THE WEBSITE: AIRSHIP27HANGAR.COM

Printed in Great Britain
by Amazon.co.uk, Ltd.,
Marston Gate.